STAR TREK®

STARGAZER

BOOK ONE

GAUNTLET

Michael Jan Friedman

Based upon STAR TREK: THE NEXT GENERATION®
created by Gene Roddenberry

POCKET BOOKS
New York London Toronto Sydney Singapore

This book is a work of fiction. Names, characters, places and incidents are products of the author's imagination or are used fictitiously. Any resemblance to actual events or locales or persons, living or dead, is entirely coincidental.

An *Original* Publication of POCKET BOOKS

POCKET BOOKS, a division of Simon & Schuster, Inc.
1230 Avenue of the Americas, New York, NY 10020

Copyright © 2002 by Paramount Pictures. All Rights Reserved.

STAR TREK is a Registered Trademark of Paramount Pictures.

A VIACOM COMPANY

This book is published by Pocket Books, a division of Simon & Schuster, Inc., under exclusive license from Paramount Pictures.

ISBN: 0-7434-2792-0

First Pocket Books printing May 2002

10 9 8 7 6 5 4 3 2 1

POCKET and colophon are registered trademarks of Simon & Schuster, Inc.

For information regarding special discounts for bulk purchases, please contact Simon & Schuster Special Sales at 1-800-456-6798 or business@simonandschuster.com

Printed in the U.S.A.

Acknowledgments

This, the first in an ongoing series of *Stargazer* books, owes its existence to a number of people beyond its humble and shiftless author. John Ordover, Pocket Books editor, was the one who first encouraged me to take a stab at an ongoing series along the lines of the one pioneered by my friend Peter David. Scott Shannon, Pocket publisher, approved the darn thing for reasons I still can't fathom. And Paula Block, who heads up Paramount's licensed publishing program, didn't scream too loudly about it when it crossed her desk.

I would like to recognize the efforts of all those who helped me work out the science behind the character Jiterica and the Lazarus star system, which plays a key role in this book. The guilty parties include Allyn, Michael, Todd Kogutt, Deborah and Baerbell from the PsiPhi bulletin board run by Dave Henderson, as well as physicist Dave Domelen.

I would also like to express gratitude to David Stern, my first Star Trek editor, for giving me the chance to introduce the *Stargazer* crew in the first place; Larry Forrester and Herb Wright, who gave the *Stargazer* its place in Star Trek continuity with the TNG episode "The Battle"; and all the other TV and novel writers who provided me with walls to bounce off as I boldly go where few thought it prudent to go before.

Chapter One

Captain's personal log, supplemental.

We have arrived at Starbase 32, where Commander Gilaad Ben Zoma and I are to attend a convocation of starship captains and their executive officers. While such gatherings have rarely taken place before, our newly minted Admiral McAteer seems intent on closely coordinating the activities of all ships in his sector.

Ben Zoma thinks the entire meeting will be a waste of time—particularly the cocktail party the admiral is hosting this evening. I, on the other hand, am looking forward to the opportunity to rub elbows with my fellow captains.

No doubt there is a great deal I can learn from

them . . . considering I have officially been on the job less than a week now.

JEAN-LUC PICARD, captain of the Federation starship *Stargazer,* surveyed the imposing dome-shaped room that opened before him. It was filled with a sea of crimson uniforms and gold-barred sleeves, along with several matching crimson-draped tables bearing pale bowls of Andorian punch and piles of dark brown finger sandwiches.

Glancing at his first officer, Picard said, "I don't think I've ever seen so many command officers in one place."

Ben Zoma, a man with dark good looks and a mischievous glint in his eye, smiled at the remark. "One well-placed photon torpedo and you'd wipe out half the fleet."

"Perhaps not *half,* Number One."

"Close enough," Ben Zoma insisted.

"Think of it as a unique opportunity," Picard told him. He regarded a knot of a half-dozen men and women gathered around the nearest punch bowl. "A chance to pick the brains of those more experienced at this than you or I."

Ben Zoma, like Picard, had been promoted only recently. Before being named first officer of the *Stargazer,* he had served as the vessel's chief of security.

"Follow me," the captain said, meaning to take his own advice.

Joining the group by the punch bowl, he smiled at the glances that came his way. Then, as he helped himself to some punch, he listened in on the conversation.

"Of course," said a man with red hair that had begun graying at the temples, "I had never done anything like that before. But the circumstances seemed to call for it."

A large-boned woman with dark features nodded. "I've been in that situation myself."

A second woman grunted. She didn't look like the type who smiled much, despite the youthful scattering of freckles on her face. "I think we all have," she said soberly.

"I hate to interrupt," Picard chimed in, "but what are we talking about exactly? An encounter with a hostile force? A brush with some undiscovered phenomenon?"

He sounded more gung ho than he had intended. But then, he was *feeling* rather gung ho.

That is, until the others looked at him as if he had placed his hindquarters in the punch bowl. There was an awkward silence for what seemed a long time. Then one of the officers, the man with the red hair, offered a response.

"I was talking," he said, "about putting my dog to sleep."

Picard felt his cheeks grow hot. "Yes. Yes, of course you were. How silly of me to assume otherwise."

No one replied. They just stood there, looking at him. Finally, he took the hint.

"If you'll excuse me . . ." he said rather lamely.

When no one objected to his doing so, Picard separated himself from the group and strolled to the other side of the room. Ben Zoma walked beside him, a look of bemusement on his face.

"Gilaad," Picard said to his first officer, "is it my imagination or was I just snubbed?"

Ben Zoma looked back at the group they had just left. "I'd like to tell you that it's your imagination, Jean-Luc, but I don't think I can do that."

"What I said was admittedly a bit inappropriate, given the tenor of the conversation. But it wasn't deserving of that kind of response. Someone else might even have laughed at it."

Ben Zoma nodded. "True enough."

"Then why did they react that way?" Picard asked. He looked down at his newly replicated dress uniform. "Did I put my trousers on backward this evening?"

"Your trousers are fine," his friend said. "I have a feeling it has more to do with the age of the person inside them. You *are* the greenest apple ever to take command of a Starfleet vessel."

Picard couldn't argue the point. "So I am."

At the tender age of twenty-eight, he was the youngest captain yet in the history of the fleet. Even younger than the legendary James T. Kirk, and that was saying something.

"And it's not just your age," Ben Zoma said, ticking off the strikes against the captain on his fingers. "You've never had the experience of serving as first officer. You would never have gotten your commission so quickly if Captain Ruhalter hadn't been killed in the course of a battle with hostile aliens. And—because an inexperienced whippersnapper like you couldn't *possibly* have gotten a captaincy on merit—it was probably a political appointment."

Picard grunted. "Thank you, Number One. I was beginning to actually feel capable of commanding a starship for a moment there, but you have managed to completely disabuse me of that notion."

"My pleasure," his friend told him archly. "What's a

first officer for if not to deflate his captain's ego from time to time?"

"Indeed," Picard said thinly, sharing in the joke at his own expense.

He looked around the domed room again and noticed a few sidelong glances being cast in his direction. They didn't exactly look like expressions of admiration.

Perhaps Ben Zoma was right, the captain reflected. Perhaps his colleagues were looking at him differently because of his age and relative inexperience.

But if the looks on their faces were any indication, he wasn't just an object of curiosity. He was an object of disdain.

It hurt Picard to think so—even more than he would have guessed. After all, they had no firsthand observations to go on. They could only know what they had heard.

Yet these were starship captains and first officers—men and women who represented the finest the Federation had to offer. Picard would have expected them to be more welcoming of a fledgling colleague, more sensitive to his situation.

Apparently, he would have been wrong in that regard.

As was often the case, Ben Zoma seemed to read his thoughts. "All in all, not the friendliest-looking group I've ever seen."

"Nor I," Picard said. "I get the feeling I'm running a gauntlet."

"If you are, it's undeserved. You've earned your command, Jean-Luc." He jerked his head to include the other captains in the room. "Maybe more so than *they* have."

Picard didn't want to appear to feel sorry for himself, even if it was just in front of Ben Zoma. However, his colleagues' doubts weren't all that was bothering him. If they were, he could have taken the situation in stride.

Unfortunately, the glances they sent his way underlined a much more troublesome and insidious fact: the captain harbored some doubts *himself.*

Weeks earlier, when Admiral Mehdi called him into his office, he had expected the admiral to lay into him—to chew him out for the chances he had taken against the Nuyyad. Instead, Mehdi had ordained him Captain Ruhalter's successor.

Picard had been too stunned at the time to question the admiral's judgment. He had been too excited by the challenge to consider the wisdom of such a move.

But was he *qualified* to be a captain?

He had seized the reins in an emergency and brought his crew out of it alive, no question about it. But did he have the ability to command a starship over the long haul? Was he a long-distance runner . . . or just a sprinter?

"You're not saying anything," Ben Zoma pointed out. "Should I send for a doctor?"

The captain chuckled. "No, I don't think that will be necessary." He caught sight of a waiter with a tray of food. "Perhaps an hors d'oeuvre will brighten up the evening for me. I've always been partial to pigs in blankets."

His first officer looked skeptical. "Really?"

Picard smiled at him. "No. But they'll do in a pinch."

He had already embarked on an intercept course with the waiter when he felt a hand on his arm. Turning, he saw a tall fellow with a seamed face and a crew cut the color of sand.

Like Picard, he wore a captain's uniform. "Pardon

me," the fellow said. "You're Jean-Luc Picard, aren't you?"

Picard nodded. "I am."

The man extended his hand. "My name's Greenbriar. Denton Greenbriar."

Picard recognized the name. Anyone would have. "The captain of the *Cochise*, isn't it?"

Greenbriar grinned, deepening the lines in his face. "I see my reputation's preceded me."

In fact, it had. Denton Greenbriar was perhaps the most decorated commanding officer in Starfleet.

Picard pulled Ben Zoma over. "Captain Greenbriar, Gilaad Ben Zoma—my executive officer."

The two shook hands. "A pleasure to meet you," Greenbriar said. He turned back to Picard. "And a pleasure to meet *you*, sir. I've heard good things about you."

"You have?" Picard responded, unable to keep from sounding surprised. Embarrassed, he smiled. "Sorry, Captain. It's just that I feel like a bit of an oddity here."

"Why's that?" asked Greenbriar. "Just because you're the youngest man ever to command a starship?"

"Well," said Picard, "yes."

"People are often not what they seem, Jean-Luc." Greenbriar took in the other men and women in the room with a glance. "Looks to me like our colleagues here have forgotten that."

"I appreciate the vote of confidence," Picard told him.

Greenbriar shrugged his broad shoulders. "Admiral Mehdi is a sharp cookie. Always has been. If he has confidence in you, I'm certain it's well deserved."

"It is," Ben Zoma agreed.

Picard felt his cheeks turn hot. He cleared his throat

and said, "I'm not sure what I find more uncomfortable—the cold shoulder or the company of flatterers."

Greenbriar laughed. "That's the last bit of flattery you'll get from *me,* Captain. I promise."

And with that, he left to refill his glass.

Ben Zoma turned to Picard. "That was refreshing."

"Unfortunately," the captain replied, "it's not likely to happen again this evening."

"What do you say we find something else to do?"

Picard frowned. It was a tempting suggestion. He said as much. "Nonetheless," he continued, "I feel obliged to stick it out here a while longer."

"Your duty as a captain?" Ben Zoma asked.

Picard nodded. "Something like that, yes."

So they stayed. But, as he had predicted, no one else came near them the rest of the evening.

Not even Admiral McAteer. In fact, Picard couldn't find the man the entire evening.

Chapter Two

CARTER GREYHORSE, CHIEF MEDICAL OFFICER on the *Stargazer*, watched Gerda Asmund advance on him in her tight-fitting black garb. The navigation officer's left hand extended toward him while her right remained close to her chest, her slender fingers curled into nasty-looking claws.

"Kave'ragh!" she snarled suddenly, and her beautiful features contorted into a mask of primal aggression.

Then her right hand lashed out like an angry viper, her knuckles a blur as they headed for the center of his face. Greyhorse flinched, certain that Gerda had finally miscalculated and was about to deal him a devastating, perhaps even lethal blow. But as always, her attack fell short of its target by an inch.

Looking past Gerda's knuckles into her merciless, ice-blue eyes, Greyhorse swallowed. He didn't want to contemplate the force with which she would have driven her flattened fist into his mouth. Enough, surely, to cave in his front teeth. Enough to make him choke and sputter on his own blood.

But she had exercised restraint and pulled her punch. After all, it wasn't a battle in which they were engaged, or even a sparring session. It was just a lesson.

"Kave'ragh?" he repeated, doing his best not to completely mangle the Klingon pronunciation.

"Kave'ragh," Gerda repeated, having no trouble with the pronunciation. But then, she had been speaking the Klingon tongue from a rather early age.

The navigator stayed where she was for a moment, allowing Greyhorse to study her posture. Then she took a slow step back and retracted her fist, as if reloading a medieval crossbow.

"Now you," Gerda told him.

Greyhorse bent his knees and drew his hands into the proper position. Then he curled his fingers under at the first knuckle, exactly as she had taught him.

Gerda's eyes narrowed, but she didn't criticize him. It was a good sign. During their first few lessons, she had done nothing *but* criticize him—his balance, his coordination, even his desire to improve.

To be sure, Greyhorse wasn't the most athletic individual and never had been. When the other kids had chosen sides to play parisses squares, he had invariably been the last to be picked.

But he was big. And strong. Gerda seemed to know how to tap the power he possessed but had never made use of.

"Kave'ragh!" he bellowed, trying his best to duplicate his teacher's effort.

She spoiled his attack with an open-handed blow to the side of his wrist. It sent his fist wide of her face, where it couldn't do any harm. But at least he didn't stumble, as he had in their first few sessions. Maintaining his balance, he pulled back and reloaded.

"*Kave'ragh!*" he snapped again, determined to get past Gerda's defenses.

This time she hit the inside of his wrist and redirected the force of his attack upward, leaving the right side of his body woefully unguarded. Before he could move to cover the deficiency, Gerda drove her knuckles into his ribs.

Hard.

The pain made him recoil and cry out. Seeing this, Gerda shot him a look of disdain.

"Next time," she told him, "you'll do better."

He would too. And not because she had nearly cracked a rib with her counterattack. He would do better because he bitterly hated the idea of disappointing her.

The first time they had fought, in one of the *Stargazer*'s corridors, he had surprised her by getting in a lucky punch, and she had gazed at him with admiration in her eyes. It was to resurrect that moment that he endured this kind of punishment.

He didn't do it in order to become an expert in Klingon martial arts—he had no aspirations in that regard. He came to the gym three times a week and suffered contusions and bone bruises for one reason only: to force Gerda to see him as an equal. To see him as a warrior.

And eventually, if he was very diligent and very fortunate, to see him as a lover.

With this in mind, Greyhorse again assumed the basic position. Knees bent, he reminded himself. One hand forward, one hand back. Knuckles extended, so.

More important, he focused his mind. He saw himself driving his fist into his opponent's face, once, twice, and again, so quickly that his blows couldn't be parried. And he ignored the fact that it was Gerda's face he was pounding.

"Kave'*ragh!*" growled the doctor, a man who had never growled at anything in his life.

This time Greyhorse's attack was more effective. Gerda was unable to knock it off-line. In fact, it was only by moving her head at the last moment that she avoided injury.

He was grateful that she had. He didn't want to hurt her. He only wanted to prove to her that he could.

It was an irony he found difficult to accept—that he could only hope to win Gerda's love by demonstrating an ability to maim her. But then, the woman had been raised in a culture that made aggression a virtue. She had, to say the least, an *unusual* point of view.

Again, Greyhorse roared, "*Kave'ragh!*" and moved to strike her. Again, Gerda was unable to deflect his blow. And again, she managed to dodge anyway.

Getting closer, he told himself. She knew it, too. He could see it in her gaze, hard and implacable, demanding everything of him and giving away nothing.

Not even hope.

Yet Gerda knew how much he wanted her. She *had* to. He had blurted it out that day in the corridor.

She hadn't acknowledged it since, of course, and Greyhorse hadn't brought it up again. All they did was show up at their appointed time in the gym, teacher and pupil, master and enslaved.

"Kave'ragh!" he cried out.

Then he put everything into one last punch—too much, as it turned out, because he leaned too far forward and Gerda took painful advantage of the fact.

She didn't just elude Greyhorse's attack. She side-kicked him in the belly, knocking the wind out of him and doubling him over. Then she hit him in the back of his head with the point of her elbow, driving him to his knees.

Stunned, gasping for breath and dripping sweat, he remained on all fours for what seemed like a long time. Finally, he found the strength to drag himself to his feet.

Gerda was waiting for him with her arms folded across her chest, a lock of yellow hair dangling and a thin sheen of perspiration on her face. He had expected to find disapproval in her expression, maybe even disgust at the clumsiness he had exhibited.

But what he saw was a hint of the look she had given him in the corridor. A hint of *admiration.*

It made Greyhorse forget how Gerda had bludgeoned him, though his throat still burned and his ribs still throbbed and there was a distinctly metallic taste of blood in his mouth. In fact, it made him eager for more.

"Tomorrow?" she asked.

He nodded, inviting waves of vertigo even with that modest gesture. "I'll be here."

Gerda tilted her head slightly, as if to appraise him better. She remained that way for a moment, piercing his soul with her eyes. Then she turned her back on him, pulled a towel off the rack on the wall, and left the gym.

Greyhorse watched her go. She moved with animal

grace, each muscle working in perfect harmony with all the others. When the doors hissed closed behind her, he felt as if he had lost a part of himself.

How he loved her.

Chief Weapons Officer Vigo looked at his friend Charlie Kochman, contemplating the experience they had just shared. Then he broke out in a broad, toothy grin.

"You like it?" Kochman asked.

"I like it a great deal," Vigo told him.

"Thought you would."

Vigo considered the wooden sharash'di game board that sat between them, with its skillfully carved terrain and its clever simulations of various natural features. It was really quite a work of art—the kind the ship's lounge seldom saw.

But the game itself . . . it was like nothing he had ever played before, either on his homeworld of Pandril or anywhere else. And he couldn't wait to play it again.

"And you say you picked this up on Beta Nopterix?" he asked.

"Uh-huh. From an Yridian. He wanted to sell me the game, so he taught me how to play. Interesting, eh?"

Vigo nodded. "Quite interesting."

Kochman, who was one of the ship's navigators, smiled back at him. "And guess what, buddy? It's yours."

Vigo didn't understand. "Mine?"

"That's right. It's a birthday gift."

The weapons officer held up his large blue hands. "I can't accept it. We don't celebrate our birth anniversaries on Pandril."

"But we celebrate them on Earth," Kochman reminded him. "And as my friend, I can't imagine that you'd deprive me of the opportunity to celebrate *yours.*"

When he put it that way, it was hard for Vigo to turn him down. "I don't know what to say," he said.

"Say thank you," his friend advised.

Vigo looked down at the board, then flashed another expression of delight. "Thank you, Charlie. Thank you very much."

Idun Asmund, the *Stargazer*'s primary helm officer, was almost finished with her dinner when she saw Pug Joseph approaching her with a tray of food.

As Joseph got closer, steam from his meal wafting in front of him, he seemed to notice that Idun's plate was already empty. "Aw, geez," the baby-faced, sandy-haired security officer said, making no effort to conceal his disappointment.

She looked up at him. "Lieutenant?"

"It's all right," he told her stoically. "I guess we can talk some other time."

There wasn't anything that demanded Idun's attention at the moment. "What was it you wished to talk about?"

Joseph set his tray down and pulled out a chair opposite the helm officer's. Then he looked around to make sure no one in the mess hall was listening too closely.

"Actually," he said, leaning forward, "I wanted to talk to you about your voice."

Idun wasn't sure what she had expected the security officer to ask, but that wasn't it. "My voice?"

Joseph nodded enthusiastically. "You've got a way of making people listen when you speak. Your sister has it too. I want them to listen to *me* that way."

"In my experience," Idun said, "people *do* listen when you speak. You're widely liked, Mr. Joseph."

"Liked," he conceded. "But not respected. And a security chief has to be respected."

Security *chief?* Now Idun was *really* confused.

She knew that Lieutenant Ang was leaving the *Stargazer* to accept a second officer's post on the *Sutherland*. However, she hadn't heard that Joseph would be succeeding him as security chief.

And now that she knew, she thought it a rash choice. Although Joseph was one of the more senior officers in the security section, he had never exhibited any particular affinity for command.

What's more, he seemed to be aware of his deficit—but to be fair, he was trying to address it, if in an unusual way.

"So you've been named our new security chief," she concluded.

Joseph blushed and shook his head. "Not permanently, mind you. It's only a temporary assignment until the captain can find a replacement for Lieutenant Ang."

Idun felt better about that. It wasn't that she didn't like Joseph or trust him implicitly, or that she would have hesitated for a moment to give him her back in a firefight.

It was only his ability to lead that the helm officer questioned. Nothing else.

"I see," she said.

"Anyway," he plunged on, "about your voice . . . do you have any tricks you might be able to share with me? Or . . . I don't know, suggestions?"

Idun thought about it. "I don't think so," she said at last. "I don't use any tricks. I just *speak.*"

Again, Joseph seemed disappointed. "Right. I just thought you might . . ." He shrugged. "Never mind. Thanks anyway."

"You're welcome," she said. But she wished that she could have been of more help.

Phigus Simenon was a Gnalish, a lizardlike being from a world called Gnala, who stood as high as the shoulders of most human males. He was also the *Stargazer*'s chief engineering officer.

Usually, Simenon could be found in the engineering section, scrabbling over the controls of a sleek, dark console. At the moment, however, he was in his quarters, studying the image of an old friend and former colleague on his computer monitor.

"Hans Werber," he observed with his customary sibilance.

The man who had been the *Stargazer*'s weapons chief nodded. "Good to see you again, Phigus."

"Where are you?" Simenon asked.

Werber smiled beneath his walrus mustache, his blue eyes dancing. "New Zealand. Not a bad place, actually. If you've got to be in a penal colony, you might as well be in *this* one."

"And they give you the run of the place?"

Werber shrugged. "I'm wearing an electronic anklet. It's not as if I can go very far."

"I see," said Simenon.

"How's Picard?"

"Well enough. He's at a meeting at the moment. Captains and second officers from all over the sector."

"Really. That's unusual."

Simenon nodded. "Very."

Werber swatted suddenly at his balding head, then inspected his palm and brushed his hands together. "Damned insects. You forget how annoying they can be when you're on a starship."

"I'll take your word for it."

"You know," said Werber, "I was wrong about Picard. I had him pegged as the vindictive type. But you know what he did?"

"What?" Simenon asked.

"He came to my cell at Starfleet Command and told me he'd put in a word on my behalf with the judge advocate general. He said that I put our differences aside and helped him."

"You mean *after* you entered his room in the dead of night and tried to stun him with a phaser beam."

Werber chuckled at the irony, his eyes crinkling at the corners. "Yeah. *After.* But the thing is Picard forgave me. He let bygones be bygones. Which, I'll bet, is why I'm doing short time here in New Zealand instead of life on some high-security asteroid."

"You're probably right," Simenon told him.

"Anyway," Werber said, "I thought I'd let you know where I am. You know, so we can talk from time to time. No friend like an old friend, I always say."

"I'd be happy to correspond with you," the Gnalish replied. "More than happy. That is, if I still considered myself your friend."

The man's brows met over the bridge of his nose. "What?"

"When you betrayed Picard, you betrayed me too," Simenon said. "I went charging into his office, accusing

18

him of incarcerating you for no good reason. Then he told me about your little mutiny."

"But Picard's *forgiven* me for that," Werber reminded him.

"*He* may have," Simenon snapped, "but *I* haven't. Good-bye, Hans. Enjoy New Zealand."

And with that, he cut the comm link.

Old friend indeed, the Gnalish thought feeling a single deep pang of remorse. Then, glad that it was almost time for his shift, he made his way to engineering.

Chapter Three

As JEAN-LUC PICARD WALKED into the dimly lit briefing room, he had an entirely different attitude than the one with which he had gone to bed the night before.

Having slept on the problem, he had woken up certain that there was only one course of action open to him. Despite the disdain he saw in the faces of his fellow captains, despite their obvious disapproval, he would do his best to earn their respect.

He would comport himself with dignity. He would do what was asked of him quickly and efficiently, deploying every resource at his disposal. In short, he would be the best captain he could be.

But if he came up short in that regard, he wouldn't fret over the outcome or let it distract him. He would simply accept the situation and move on.

He had a job to do, and a rather important job at that.

If it bothered people that he had been chosen to do it, it was *their* problem—not *his*.

Scanning the room, Picard found himself searching the shadows for a friendly face. Captain Greenbriar's was the only one that might have fit that description, but Greenbriar didn't seem to have arrived yet.

Looks like I'm on my own, Picard thought.

He didn't even have Ben Zoma for company. His friend had transported down to the base forty-five minutes earlier for a separate first officers' briefing.

Picking out the nearest unoccupied chair, Picard deposited himself in it. He found himself shoulder to shoulder with a rail-thin Vulcan, who turned to glance at him with narrowed eyes.

Picard smiled as cordially as he could. "Good morning."

The Vulcan didn't say anything in reply. He just inclined his head in the smallest gesture possible, then returned his attention to the unmanned podium at the front of the room.

Somehow, Picard reflected, being snubbed by a Vulcan didn't seem as objectionable as being snubbed by someone else. Maybe it was because they were so reserved to begin with.

Someday, he told himself, *I would like to get to know a Vulcan better. Get inside his head, as it were.*

Putting the thought aside, he looked around some more. The stream of captains passing through the open doorway was rapidly increasing in volume. No doubt, they were nearing the time when the briefing was scheduled to begin.

Greenbriar was among the last to walk in. He took a

seat on the other side of the room, between an Andorian and a heavy-tusked Vobilite.

A moment later, a stocky man in an admiral's uniform blew into the room, stopped behind the podium, and turned on a light that illuminated his face. He had lively eyes, a ruddy complexion, and a receding shock of pale-yellow hair.

"Good to see you all," he said in a deep, resonant voice that required no microphone. "For those of you who haven't run into me yet, I'm Admiral McAteer. I considered attending the cocktail party last night, but I decided you'd have a better time without the boss looking over your shoulders."

A ripple of laughter made its way through the gathering.

Picard thought it strange that McAteer hadn't attended his own event. On the other hand, he was relieved to know he wasn't the only one who had been unable to find the man.

McAteer appeared to sober a bit. "I know you're not used to meeting this way. Until now, you've all been pretty much on your own, operating independently except in the rare instance where two or three of you might need to coordinate your efforts."

The rare instance indeed, Picard mused.

"I'm afraid," said the admiral, "that such an approach is no longer viable. The galaxy is too big and our responsibilities too great for any of you to continue operating in a vacuum—no pun intended."

Again, there was a ripple of laughter.

"From now on," McAteer told them, "we're going to get together like this periodically. That way, we can approach our workload in an organized and logical manner."

Picard sampled his colleagues' reactions. The Vulcan beside him was nodding his head in quiet agreement, but many of the other captains seemed less than enthusiastic.

Ruhalter, Picard's predecessor, would have come down firmly in the latter group. Picard had no doubt of that. Ruhalter was a man who had preferred to respond instinctively, avoiding meetings and planning sessions as much as possible.

If the same topic was being discussed in the first officers' briefing, Ben Zoma would be resisting it as well. Picard had no doubt of that either.

Nor could he help agreeing with his predecessor and his exec.

Captains had always been chosen for their ability to act on their own. It was the strength of the fleet, indeed one of the principles on which it had been built, and it didn't seem wise to inhibit it.

On the other hand, McAteer was the man Starfleet had put in charge of this sector. If he thought it was time for something new, Picard would at least try to keep an open mind about it.

The admiral looked out over his audience. "I've made up a list of missions that we need to tackle. The first one—and the most critical—is the capture of the pirate known as the White Wolf."

McAteer's announcement fell like a stone into the midst of the assembled captains. In the ripples of silence that followed, Picard saw his colleagues exchanging glances.

He had no trouble understanding why.

"For the last two years," McAteer said, "the White

Wolf and his crew have raided Federation cargo ships left and right. And every time we've sent a Starfleet vessel after him, he's managed to elude us by hiding in one of the odd features of Beta Barritus—which, as you'll note, is rather a unique system by anyone's reckoning."

As he finished his sentence, he manipulated the controls before him and created a hologram to one side of the podium. It was a computerized representation of the Beta Barritus system—a sun surrounded by a thick layer of gases and who knew what else.

But then, Beta Barritus was a Lazarus star—one that had burned out and somehow resurrected itself. It couldn't help but present an unusual set of problems to anyone seeking to plumb its depths.

Which was why the White Wolf, a man reputedly named for the color of his hair as well as his resourcefulness, had picked Beta Barritus as his favorite hiding place.

"Until this point in time," the admiral told the assembled captains, "the apprehension of the White Wolf has been a low priority for us. That changes as of this moment."

Picard wondered why that might be. McAteer didn't take long to satisfy his curiosity.

"His latest attack on a defenseless transport vessel took place less than a week ago. It netted him a cargo of exotic flora from Elekiwi Prime." The admiral scowled. "I think you all know how difficult it is to extract anything from that world—and how valuable such cargo can be to our research people at Starfleet Medical."

Picard nodded. Elekiwi Prime was a dying world, increasingly beleaguered by volcanic eruptions and resulting clouds of carbon dioxide. A team of scientists had risked their lives to obtain the flora samples in question, knowing that plant life wouldn't survive conditions on the planet much longer.

"Someone has to go after the White Wolf and attempt to recover the cargo," McAteer said, his voice steely with resolve. "But even if recovery is no longer possible, I want to end the menace of this pirate once and for all."

He had barely finished his sentence when half a dozen hands went up. *Volunteers,* Picard thought. No doubt they included the captains who had been thwarted by the White Wolf in the past. If he were one of them, he too would have wished to settle the score.

Picard studied the hologram of the White Wolf's hiding place. Beta Barritus appeared to be a complex system indeed. It presented the kind of obstacles Picard had heard about, even read about, but had never personally encountered.

If the captains who had hunted the White Wolf were any judges, the man was impossible to find, much less apprehend. And if his colleagues wanted the assignment that badly, he would do his best not to stand in their way.

"I appreciate your eagerness," McAteer told them. "I understand how important it is to you to bring the White Wolf to justice. But I think we need a new approach to the problem."

A new approach? Picard repeated inwardly. He wondered what the admiral had in mind.

He was still wondering when McAteer turned to him and smiled like a fox noticing an unguarded henhouse. "Captain Picard," he said, "I'm giving *you* this job."

Picard turned red in the face. *Me?* he thought.

Apparently, he wasn't the only one inclined to question McAteer's choice, if the stares and the muttered comments that followed were any indication. Obviously, his fellow captains were wondering why McAteer might tap a man who had been a mere second officer a month earlier over a wide assortment of seasoned veterans.

The White Wolf had beaten the best the fleet had to offer. How was a green apple going to do what those other captains couldn't?

Picard would have liked to hear what the admiral had to say in that regard. But McAteer wasn't offering any explanations at the moment. He was just standing there, staring at his youngest captain as if awaiting the man's response.

Picard gave the only one he could. "I hope to prove myself worthy of your confidence."

The admiral nodded. "I've no doubt of it."

Then he went on to dole out the other assignments. In each case, he discussed the difficulties of the mission and what Starfleet stood to gain by it. But Picard barely heard him. He was still trying to figure out what he had done to deserve the White Wolf.

Mollie Katz had served as a Starfleet transporter operator for more than thirty years, first on a series of space-spanning starships named *Phoenix* and *Exeter* and *Yorktown,* and now here at Starbase 32. In the course of her long career, she had met with more than her share of unusual transports.

But never anything like this.

The customized gray-and-white containment suit and matching helmet had been Katz's first clue. The second had been the ghostly visage visible through the helmet's transparent faceplate.

But even as the figure stepped up onto the transporter platform, Katz hadn't imagined the challenges with which she would be presented—challenges she was even now trying to meet as she made careful adjustments to her control settings.

Three humans stood to one side of the transporter operator, all of them Starfleet personnel, alternately watching Katz work at her console and gazing at the figure on the platform. They seemed curious, no more than that.

But it had to be a lonely thing for the being inside the containment suit. It had to be hard to endure the scrutiny of others when you were so different from them, so different from anyone within a radius of several light-years.

At last Katz felt certain that her settings were what they should be. Programming in the requisite destination coordinates, she obtained a lock on the place. Then she activated the targeting scanners and verified range and relative motion, which, fortunately for her subject, were both minimal.

Checking the diagnostics monitor in the upper left quadrant of her panel, she saw that the system was functioning well within acceptable parameters. *So far so good,* the operator told herself.

Normally this would have been the point at which the transporter's molecular imaging scanners came on-line. However, Katz had already been using the scanners for the last several minutes to get an idea of what she was dealing with.

She directed the primary energizing coils to generate an annular confinement beam, which would be used in a little while. Then, with painstaking care, she encouraged the phase transition coils to convert the subject into a subatomically debonded matter stream.

This was the tricky part, the part she would at other times have left to the computer but felt compelled in this instance to carry out on her own. It wasn't that she thought she could be more exact than an electronic device. It was that if something went wrong, she had more faith in her own ability to correct it.

Come on, she thought, watching the debonded matter migrate to the system's pattern buffer. *Get in there, and I mean now.*

Up on the platform, the subject would be vanishing in a sparkling column of light—containment suit and all. But the transporter operator didn't have the luxury of watching the spectacle. She was too intent on her instruments, too busy with the minutiae of the matter storage process to allow herself even the slightest distraction.

Almost done, she thought. *Almost there.* Seventy-five percent, to be more precise. Eighty. Eighty-five . . .

A bead of perspiration trickled down her forehead, but she ignored it and continued to monitor the matter stream, hands on her controls in case she had to abort the process or take some other emergency measure.

Finally, after what seemed like an eternity, Katz saw the blinking green stud that verified the subject's safe arrival in the system's pattern buffer. Taking a deep breath, she let it out and gave herself permission to relax for a moment.

But only for a moment.

Then she bent to her task again and projected the annular confinement beam from the starbase's emitter array to the target coordinates. It was within the dimensions of this beam that the subject's debonded matter would travel.

Next, the operator transmitted the matter from the buffer to the emitter. Once there, it was ready to make the journey across the void of empty space.

Here goes, she thought.

And she sent the accumulated matter streaming along the confinement beam to its destination.

Katz was certain that she had done everything right. Still, she found herself staring at her instrument panel, willing it to tell her that the process would end as it was supposed to—with the subject's safe arrival and rematerialization.

Because under the most perfect conditions, one never knew—and these conditions were far from perfect.

The seconds ticked by, more of them than Katz had expected. Her teeth had begun to grind together by the time she saw the words she was hoping for: *transport successful.*

In the privacy of her mind, the operator patted herself on the back. That hadn't been easy. In fact, she wouldn't complain if that was the last such transport she was called on to make.

At last, she wiped the perspiration from her brow with the back of her hand and reset her instruments to more conventional levels. Then, turning to the trio standing next to her, she said, "Next."

As they stepped up onto the platform, Katz wished the being in the containment suit good luck. She would need it.

* * *

It wasn't until after McAteer had turned up the lights and adjourned the meeting that Picard had a chance to buttonhole him. It wasn't difficult to do so. In fact, the admiral seemed to have been expecting the captain's approach.

"You're wondering why I asked you to go after our friend the White Wolf," McAteer concluded.

"I am," Picard confirmed.

"I don't blame you," the admiral said. "In your position, I'd be wondering the same thing."

He took the captain's arm and guided him to an observation port at the far end of the room. Apparently, he wanted to conduct their conversation where others wouldn't overhear it.

"I picked you for the mission," McAteer told him, "because conventional methods haven't worked with the White Wolf. Your predecessor, Captain Ruhalter, was known for his resourcefulness, his ability to think on his feet. I'm betting that those qualities rubbed off on you."

In fact, Picard didn't think of himself as particularly resourceful. However, he refrained from saying so.

"I'll try not to let you down," he said.

The admiral chuckled. "Modesty. I like that. Then it'll look even better when you nail the bastard."

It wasn't modesty that had compelled the captain to frame his response that way. It was a sense of proportion. But he didn't tell McAteer that either.

"If you say so," he told the admiral.

Chapter Four

As PICARD MATERIALIZED on the *Stargazer*'s transporter platform alongside his first officer, he noted that it was Lieutenant Refsland manning the facility's transporter console.

Refsland was his section chief, the most experienced of his several transporter operators. Picard always felt a little more secure in Refsland's hands.

Normally the man greeted him with a smile and a single word of greeting: "Captain." But not this time, Picard noticed. *This* time, Refsland appeared to have something on his mind.

"Something wrong?" the captain asked.

"I'm not sure, sir," Refsland told him.

"Not sure?" Picard echoed.

Refsland shrugged. "About half an hour ago, we received the new crewmen, sir. Seven of them, to be exact."

The captain found himself making a face. *New crewmen? What new crewmen?* "I haven't authorized any additions to the crew," he informed the transporter chief.

Refsland sighed. "I was afraid you were going to say that."

Picard glanced at Ben Zoma. "Gilaad?"

"Don't look at me," his friend said. "I didn't authorize any new additions either."

Certainly, Picard thought, there were berths to be filled after the casualties inflicted on them by the Nuyyad, and replacements to be arranged for officers who had subsequently left the ship. He and Ben Zoma had even considered some candidates, though they hadn't made any final decisions yet.

"Actually, sir," said an uncomfortable-looking Refsland, "the orders came from Admiral McAteer. He said you wouldn't object."

Picard scowled. *"McAteer said that?"*

"Aye, sir. He said you wouldn't want to be bothered. Otherwise, we would have contacted you immediately."

The captain had no doubt of it. The officers he had left in charge were both loyal and efficient. They wouldn't have accepted the transport if it hadn't come from a higher authority.

Placing his hand on his first officer's shoulder, Picard said, "You take care of our new crewmen. I think I need to have a word with our friend the admiral."

Then, doing his best to contain his anger, he made his way to his ready room.

Lieutenant Kochman stared at his friend Vigo across the sharash'di board. *"Another one?"*

Vigo reset the board, as oblivious to the look of discomfort on his friend's face as he was to everything else in the ship's lounge. "You go first and fourth this time."

Kochman sighed. "That's very nice of you, but . . ."

Vigo looked up. "Yes?"

The navigator held his hands up in an appeal for reason. "We've been playing for four hours straight, pal. I need a break."

Vigo blinked. "Three and a half, actually."

Kochman shot him a look.

"But," Vigo added, "that's very *nearly* four."

"I go on duty in an hour," Kochman continued. "I need to eat, wash up, grab a clean uniform . . ."

"As you should," Vigo said reasonably. "And now that you mention it, I have things to do as well. The last thing I want is to spend all my time playing a game."

But his expression said otherwise.

Kochman frowned. Little had he known what a monster he was creating when he gave his pal the sharash'di board for his birthday. *Or for that matter,* he added silently, *what a genius.*

Vigo had the same kind of knack for sharash'di that he did for weapons technology. He didn't just grasp the subject, he bonded with it—brain and muscle and bone. He *lived* it.

"You know," Kochman said, "you don't have to stop on my account. If you want, you can go on playing."

The weapons officer seemed to understand his friend's meaning. "You're suggesting I play with someone else?"

Kochman shrugged. "Well, yeah."

Vigo took in the room at a glance. "I suppose I could," he said after a while. "I would just have to teach them the game." He smiled, enthused again. "But if I could learn it, they can too."

Kochman doubted that anyone would embrace sharash'di as much as the weapons officer had. However, someone might at least give him a run for his money.

"This is what I'm saying," he told Vigo.

The Pandrilite nodded. "I think I'll follow your advice."

"Good," said Kochman, feeling a wave of relief wash over him. "Let me know how it goes, okay?"

And with that, he made good his escape.

Picard took several deep breaths before he was calm enough to proceed. Then, opting not to get his communications officer involved, he established a comm link with McAteer's office. After a second or two, the admiral's assistant appeared on the screen.

"I'd like to speak with Admiral McAteer," the captain said.

The assistant, a young man with a blond crew cut and a ruddy complexion, promised to tell McAteer that there was a call for him. Seeing the Starfleet logo come up on his screen, Picard had no choice but to wait.

As it turned out, he didn't have to wait long. But McAteer looked vaguely annoyed as he appeared on the screen, as if Picard had interrupted something important.

"Is there something I can do for you, Captain?"

Indeed there is, Picard thought. "You can help me understand something, Admiral. I've just been informed that several new crewmen have beamed aboard the *Stargazer.*"

McAteer shrugged. "As I understood it, you had several openings, owing to casualties in the course of your last mission."

It was true. Seven crewmen, including Captain Ruhalter, had died in their clash with the Nuyyad.

Also, they had lost their weapons officer, who had led a mutiny against then–Acting Captain Picard and been incarcerated as a result. And just before the *Stargazer* reached Starbase 32, Sciences Chief Angela Cariello had decided to leave the fleet to join her husband at an agricultural colony, and Security Chief Ang had accepted a position on the *Sutherland*.

"Nonetheless," Picard said, "it is highly irregular for a captain to have crewmen handed to him by a superior officer. As you know, sir, the normal procedure is for a commanding officer to review applications at his leisure before making any personnel decisions."

The admiral frowned at the remark. "I'm well aware of Starfleet procedures, Captain."

"Then you won't be surprised to learn that Commander Ben Zoma and I are already focusing on at least one candidate—a fellow who comes from a long-standing Starfleet tradition. His grandfather was an admiral, his aunt is on her way to becoming one, and his elder brother is currently serving with distinction on the *Exeter.*"

McAteer looked as if he was going to cut Picard's comments short. However, the captain didn't give him the opportunity.

"He has also posted dazzling grades at the Academy, been described by his professors as driven, bright, and capable, and served as captain of the parisses squares team that beat a squad of Academy alumni just prior to graduation."

The admiral knew who he was, of course. Picard could tell by the look in his eyes.

"Frankly, sir," he continued, "I cannot imagine anyone more qualified to join the crew of the *Stargazer.*"

McAteer's eyes narrowed. "Sign him on, then, Captain. Sign on anyone you want. Get rid of anyone you *don't* want. But do it *after* you catch the White Wolf. For the time being, I'd say you need all the help you can get—and that includes those seven new crewmen who have beamed aboard your starship."

"But, sir—"

"That's an order," McAteer told him.

Picard didn't like the idea, but the admiral wasn't giving him any choice in the matter. "As you say, sir."

McAteer nodded. "Again, good luck to you. McAteer out."

A moment later, his image winked off the viewscreen and was replaced by the Starfleet logo. The captain glared at it, then tapped the combadge on his chest.

"Navigation, this is Command—" He stopped abruptly, deeply embarrassed by the slip. "This is *Captain* Picard. Set a course for the Beta Barritus system."

"Aye, sir," came Gerda Asmund's reply.

"Helm," he went on, "take us out of here. Half impulse until we clear the base."

"Aye, sir," said Idun.

Through his ready room's lone observation port, Picard could see the hourglass shape of Starbase 32 receding in the distance, shrinking rapidly against the star-pricked darkness. In a matter of moments, it disappeared altogether.

Taking Admiral McAteer with it. *And none too soon,* the captain reflected angrily.

He sat in his chair a moment longer, trying to deal with his resentment. Only when he felt he had it under control did he get up and leave his ready room.

Picard reminded himself that there were seven new crewmen aboard the *Stargazer.* It wasn't *their* fault they had been foisted on an unwilling captain.

Chapter Five

ENSIGN ANDREAS NIKOLAS PRESSED the padd in the bulkhead next to his quarters, watched the duranium doors
slide apart, and went inside to examine his home away
from home.

Nikolas had served on other starships of this class, so
he had a pretty good idea of what awaited him. He
wasn't disappointed. Two beds, a couple of computer terminals, two chairs, two tiny closets, one bathroom door.

And one roommate.

In this case, the last item was of the tall, broad-shoul-
dered, and clean-cut variety. He was in the latter stages
of making his bed when Nikolas walked in on him.

The guy straightened, smiled, and held out his hand.
"Guess we're going to be roommates," he said, his blue
eyes twinkling beneath dark, close-cropped hair.

"Guess so," Nikolas returned. He shook the fellow's

hand. "Andreas Nikolas—but my friends call me Nik. And you?"

"Joe Caber." The grin behind the words was as white and perfect as they came.

Caber, Caber . . . It sounded familiar. "Where have I heard that name before?" Nikolas wondered.

The other man looked a little uncomfortable. "My father's Neil Caber. You know, the admiral?"

Nikolas snapped his fingers. "I knew I'd heard it somewhere." He considered Caber in the light of this new information. "So you're on a fast track."

His roommate shrugged. He looked a little embarrassed. "I sure as heck hope so. I'd like to be a captain someday."

You and every crewman from here to the Neutral Zone, Nikolas thought. "And how're you doing so far?"

Caber didn't seem eager to talk about himself. Still, he answered Nikolas's question. "From what I can tell, just fine. I was second in my graduating class at the Academy. And my stint on the *Mediterranean* couldn't have worked out any better."

Obviously, Caber was a shoo-in. He'd be sitting in a center seat by his thirty-fifth birthday.

Nikolas turned his attention to his unmade bed, so the other man wouldn't see the look of bitterness on his face. "They thought *I'd* be captain material too, once upon a time."

Caber smiled, but it was the kind of smile that tried to mask pity. "And you're not anymore?"

"I got in some trouble," Nikolas told him. Of course, that was a bit of an understatement.

"Everyone gets in trouble *sometime*," Caber said.

"I got in trouble a *lot,*" Nikolas expanded. "At the Academy they said I was reckless and headstrong. And I had a . . ." He dredged up the words they had used in his personnel file. ". . . a penchant for unbridled honesty, which was their polite way of saying I couldn't keep my damned mouth shut."

"That's not necessarily a bad thing," the other man allowed.

Nikolas chuckled. "Tell the folks at the Academy. They decided I'd be lucky not to get my butt kicked off the first ship whose captain was dumb enough to take me."

"Prove them wrong," Caber advised. No doubt, that's what *he* would have done.

The problem, Nikolas reflected, was that the Academy people were right. He was everything they said he was—stubborn, impulsive, ill-equipped to work within a command structure.

He wished he could be more of a Caber type. He wished he could be confident and cooperative, following a clear-cut path to a captain's chair.

But that wasn't the hand he had been dealt. He was who he was. And if he couldn't be a starship captain, he would be whatever fate had in store for him.

"Hey," Nikolas said, "you hungry?"

His roommate smiled that perfect smile. "I'm *always* hungry."

"Then what do you say we head down to the mess hall and see what's on the menu?"

"I say let's go," Caber told him.

"I'm already there," Nikolas said. Leaving his bed unmade, he led the way to the mess hall.

* * *

Dikembe Ulelo walked along the corridor next to his superior, Communications Chief Martin Paxton.

Paxton, a man with curly brown hair, was giving Ulelo a tour of the *Stargazer.* "You'll like it here," he said. "Captain Picard's as sharp as they come. And he treats his people well."

"That's good to hear," Ulelo responded.

But his attention was focused on the power-supply junction just ahead of them, its location easily identifiable by the little door set flush with the bulkhead. It was the second such junction they had passed since leaving the turbolift.

Ulelo's previous assignment had been on the *Copernicus,* an *Oberth*-class vessel. The *Copernicus* had had twelve power-supply junctions on each deck.

"You'll work the graveyard shift, of course." Paxton smiled sympathetically at him. "Just as I did when I was low man on the totem pole. But just for a few weeks. Then we'll all take turns."

"Of course," said Ulelo.

"So what do you like?"

Ulelo looked at him. "Like?"

"You know," said Paxton. "Food, hobbies, interests . . . ?"

"Ah." Ulelo thought for a moment, but nothing came to mind. "I don't have any real preferences."

Paxton seemed surprised. "Really?"

"Yes. Why do you ask?"

"Most people have pretty distinct likes and dislikes. Me, for instance, I'm a coffee man. Can't wake up without it. And when it comes to hobbies, I'm a medieval history buff."

"I like to try *new* things," Ulelo said, hoping that would assuage his superior's curiosity.

Paxton nodded. "Then you're going to like it here even more. We've got some really exotic tastes on board. Take Vigo, for instance—our weapons officer. He eats this Pandrilite stuff that looks like beach sand mixed with ground glass. Swears by it. Personally, I have trouble even *looking* at it."

He laughed. Ulelo took that as his cue to laugh too.

They came to a place where the corridor crossed another corridor. Paxton turned right. So did Ulelo—at which point he saw the set of double doors at the end of the corridor.

Paxton pointed to them. "Next stop, engineering."

Ulelo nodded. There would be many things to see in engineering. Many things to learn.

"I can't wait," he said.

Carter Greyhorse was sitting at his computer terminal, going over his list of scheduled medical examinations, when his first patient of the day walked in.

She was wearing a complete Starfleet-issue containment suit, domed helmet and all. That alone set her apart from anyone else who had ever visited Greyhorse's sickbay.

But even stranger-looking was her face—if indeed it could even be *called* a face. It seemed vague, insubstantial as he viewed it through the helmet's curved, transparent faceplate, and there was only a suggestion in it of humanoid features.

She looked around for a moment, her movements stiff and awkward in the suit. Finally, she spotted Greyhorse and crossed sickbay to get to him.

As the doctor got up and came out of his office enclosure, he forced himself not to stare. But it was difficult not to. He had been looking forward to this moment from the time the newcomers beamed aboard—one of them with more trouble than the rest.

"You're Ensign Jiterica, I take it?"

"Yes," came the reply—not an actual voice but a mechanical simulation, generated by a vocalizer in the containment suit. It sounded flat, tinny, and oddly paced. "I'm here for—"

"Your exam," he said, "yes. This way, please."

Greyhorse indicated the nearest biobed, which was just outside his enclosure. He had just recalibrated it the day before.

"Have a seat," he told Jiterica.

The doctor waited for her to reach the biobed and sit down—a clumsy affair at best, given the bulk of the containment suit. Then he activated the bed's biofunction monitors, ran a routine diagnostic, and examined the monitors in front of him.

Normally they would have shown Greyhorse the status of his patient's vital functions, each of them represented by a vertical white bar against a dark blue field. In this case, the bars refused to appear. In their place, a message came up: *Reset parameters*.

Clearly the bed was baffled—and that wouldn't change even if the doctor spent his whole day resetting parameters. The device was simply incapable of tracking Jiterica's life signs.

Nor was Greyhorse surprised.

After all, his patient wasn't a creature of flesh and blood like everyone else serving on the *Stargazer*. Jiterica was an anomaly in the annals of Starfleet personnel—a being made up of nothing more than positive ions and electrons.

Her species, the Nizhrak'a, was native to Nizhara, a gas giant in the Sonada Sin system. They were low-density, plasmalike life-forms held together by powerful psychokinetic forces, nature's response to the crush of gravity and atmospheric pressure—not to mention the vicious and volatile radiation fields—that prevailed on the ensign's planet.

The Nizhrak'a were also immense—in some cases, almost as big as the *Stargazer* herself. But they could condense themselves when necessary. The ensign, for example, could pour herself into a containment suit and move through what must have seemed to her a warren of tiny spaces.

According to Jiterica's medical file, she possessed all of the biological systems—nervous, digestive, ambulatory, circulatory, sensory, and so on—found in any humanoid life-form. However, the configurations of charged particles that comprised these systems were so spread out and seemingly unrelated as to render them unrecognizable to the sensors in the biobed.

The only part of Jiterica that approached the description of a solid was the particle membrane that served as her outer skin. It gave her body shape and definition, and kept it from being ripped apart by her world's arsenal of savage, high-velocity winds.

Like every other part of her anatomy, she could psychokinetically control this membrane down to the sub-atomic level. That was what allowed Jiterica to assume a more or less human form and facial features, which she had been advised would minimize the differences between herself and the rest of the crew.

So why did she need a Starfleet containment suit? For several reasons, Greyhorse had learned.

First, Jiterica couldn't maintain her condensed form for long. The suit, which was specially equipped with an electromagnetic reinforcement field, enabled her to remain in a tightly packed state indefinitely without placing undue strain on her resources.

Second, the ensign's physiology was designed for maneuvering in the roiling, nightmarish atmosphere of a gas giant, not the relatively narrow corridors of a Federation starship. The suit enabled her to move as her fellow crewmen moved—on foot, in a predictable direction, and at a reasonable rate of speed—thanks to a sensor-motor technology developed specifically with the Nizhrak'a in mind. All Jiterica had to do was generate an electrical shock in a particular part of the suit's sensor net, and its motor grid would do the rest.

The containment suit's third virtue was that it maintained a felicitous environment for its wearer, simulating the kind of gravity, air pressure, and atmosphere one was likely to encounter on her world. Jiterica could have survived without these benefits, especially for a short period of time, but over the long haul it made her existence on the *Stargazer* much easier to bear.

Last, the suit enabled Jiterica to communicate. By stimulating her vocalizer with a variety of electrical shocks—much as she did to achieve locomotion—the ensign could make use of a limited vocabulary. If the doctor recalled correctly, she had more than two hundred Federation-standard words and phrases at her disposal.

Likewise, a device under her helmet received the spoken word and translated it into electrical signals. That way, Jiterica could "hear" information as well as convey it.

Of course, she could have achieved neither speech nor movement without hours of rigorous training at Starfleet headquarters in San Francisco. Greyhorse could only imagine how difficult those hours must have been. How exhausting.

How utterly frustrating.

He asked himself if he could have learned to live among Jiterica's people, amid the hellish, howling tumult of a gas giant. *Not even for a moment,* he decided.

So why had Jiterica put herself to all this trouble, exposed herself to all this pain? What did she hope to gain?

The answer, like many answers, lay in the always arcane realm of interstellar politics.

As Greyhorse understood it, Nizhara wasn't a Federation member world. However, the Federation was courting it for its strategic location near Cardassian space.

Jiterica's presence in Starfleet was therefore something of a trial run—an attempt to see if Nizhrak'a and humanoids could establish a mutually beneficial relationship. To this point, the experiment hadn't gone very well.

The ensign's previous commanding officer, Captain Cepeda of the *Manitou,* had observed that the ensign was unhappy under his command. Worse, he projected for the record that she would be unhappy on *any* ship in the fleet. He said that Jiterica hadn't sought a discharge for one simple reason—her enduring belief that her people would benefit from Federation membership.

Apparently she was willing to suffer a great deal of hardship to see that happen.

For the time being, Greyhorse decided to dispense with the idea of identifying Jiterica's vital signs. That was a problem he would have to work on when time allowed.

"You may sit up," he said.

The ensign swung her legs around—another awkward motion, thanks to her containment suit—and did as the doctor suggested. Then she fixed her ghostly gaze on him and waited.

"I've familiarized myself with your personnel file," Greyhorse told her, producing a handheld padd from the pocket of his lab coat. "Unfortunately, it doesn't tell me everything I need to know—for instance, what diseases your species is prone to, and how your body is equipped to fight them."

"I understand," she said in the same tinny voice.

Jiterica went on to inform him about the parasites of her world, which came in two basic varieties. Greyhorse likened them to the bacteria and viruses that plagued solid life-forms.

According to the ensign, her species' defense against these parasites was to create a tiny gas bubble around the offending organism, effectively isolating it from the rest of their systems. Deprived of nourishment, the parasite eventually withered and died.

"Interesting," said the doctor, making a note of the information in his padd. "And what about other forms of injury? Say, from an impact? Or exposure to radiation?"

"Only my skin can sustain injury," Jiterica told him. "When it is compromised, I reform it."

"Consciously?" he asked.

Her features fuzzed over as she concentrated on the doctor's query. "If the injury is bad enough, I do it consciously. Otherwise, my body repairs itself in due time."

He asked her several other questions in the next few minutes, and she was able to answer all of them to his satisfaction. But it wasn't just the substance of her responses that enlightened him.

The more she was compelled to speak, the shorter and blunter her sentences became. What's more, her facial features fuzzed out for longer and longer periods of time.

Apparently, the effort required to converse with Greyhorse was taking its toll on her. Not wishing to cause her any more discomfort than necessary, he said, "We'll continue this another time. For now, you can return to your duties."

Jiterica looked at him, her features still in the process of reforming behind her transparent faceplate. To his mind, they didn't create an impression of contentment. Her expression looked strained, as if she were carrying a burden much too heavy for her.

Of course, Jiterica wasn't humanoid, so her expression wasn't necessarily a window on her feelings. It might simply have represented her best attempt to look like someone else—Greyhorse himself, perhaps, or one of her trainers at Starfleet headquarters.

"Thank you," she told him.

He nodded. "You're welcome."

Then he watched as the ensign slid off the biobed and walked away. Her movements were stiff, mechanical, almost painful to watch. But Greyhorse watched anyway.

He couldn't help admiring Jiterica. As difficult as it was for her to exist under these circumstances, she never made the slightest complaint. That took courage . . .

If not a great deal of common sense, he added inwardly.

Frowning deeply, Greyhorse returned to his enclosure and prepared for his next examination. But every now and then, he thought he saw a poorly defined face in the depths of his computer screen returning his gaze with a stubborn stoicism.

And his heart went out to it.

Cortin Zweller had red hair, boyish good looks, and a spray of freckles across the bridge of his nose. Just the sight of him on the monitor in Picard's quarters—courtesy of an unexpected subspace message—brought a smile to the captain's face.

At Starfleet Academy, Zweller and Picard had been the closest of friends, guarding each other's backs in one bit of ill-considered, late-night mischief after another. It was during one of their more raucous ventures that Picard had been stabbed through the heart by an angry Nausicaan.

Of course, both men had changed since then, gradually taking on the more sober mien expected of Starfleet officers. But of the two of them, Zweller had changed a good deal less than Picard had. He still played the occasional prank—though never on a superior officer.

"In case you were wondering," the redhead said, "I like the *Ajax* just fine. I like being second officer. I even like the new dom-jot table they installed in the rec room."

Dom-jot was the game of skill at which Zweller had excelled as a cadet. However, the captain noted inwardly, his friend had never been as good as he *believed* he was.

Picard was still chuckling at the thought when he saw Zweller's demeanor change. The smile drained from the man's face, and he leaned closer to the screen.

"The only part I don't like," Zweller said, "is hearing an old buddy is sailing into a trap."

Picard frowned. His pursuit of the White Wolf appeared to have become common knowledge.

"I know what you're thinking," Zweller said. "That I'm talking about the White Wolf. But I'm not. *I'm talking about McAteer.*"

It took Picard a moment to realize that his mouth was hanging open. He closed it. *McAteer?* What the devil was his friend talking about?

Zweller was already providing an explanation. "Turns out he was against Mehdi's decision to make you captain of the *Stargazer.* In fact, he's been against a great many of Mehdi's decisions over the years. That's why McAteer's sending you on this mission, Jean-Luc—a mission he thinks you can't possibly pull off. It's to make you look bad, so he can make your benefactor Mehdi look bad as well."

Picard leaned back in his chair. He had heard that such political games were played in the upper echelons of Starfleet, but he had never experienced any of them firsthand.

Welcome to starship command, he mused.

His friend went on. "If there's any way out of the mission, grab it and hold on tight. That's what I would do." He quirked a smile, though it didn't have its usual enthusiasm behind it. "Good luck, pal. You're going to need it."

As the Starfleet logo came up, replacing Zweller's

face, the captain touched a square on his keypad and erased the message. After all that his Academy chum had risked on his behalf, it wouldn't do for Picard to leave the evidence intact.

Folding his arms across his chest, he leaned back in his chair. Obviously, it was too late for him to even think about backing out of the mission. If it was true that McAteer had set a trap for him, he was firmly and inextricably caught in it.

But what if he could prove them all wrong—the admiral and anyone else who thought the White Wolf was uncatchable? What if he could do what no one expected him to do, his friend Corey Zweller included?

Picard resolved to find out.

Chapter Six

PETER "PUG" JOSEPH FELT A PIT OPEN in his stomach as he stood in the *Stargazer*'s security section and considered his newest officer.

"Is something wrong, sir?" Obal, a Binderian, looked down at his uniform and ran his hands over it, apparently thinking there might be something amiss in that department.

There was something amiss, all right. But it had nothing to do with the Binderian's clothes.

Caught off-balance, the acting security chief shook his head. "No. Nothing at all. Carry on."

Obal inclined his head slightly. "Thank you, sir."

As Joseph watched his new officer waddle away, he shook his head ruefully. There weren't any other Binderians in Starfleet, so he had never seen one before Obal arrived. Now that he had, he was appalled.

Obal resembled nothing so much as a plucked chicken. A beakless chicken to be sure, and one that had unusually big, front-facing eyes, but a chicken nonetheless.

In fact, he was the silliest thing Joseph had ever seen—and that wasn't just an aesthetic judgment. It was, unfortunately, an observation with concrete, real-world implications.

With his obvious physical limitations, the Binderian would find it hard to get others to take him seriously. In Joseph's mind, that cast doubts on Obal's ability to serve as a security officer.

After all, security personnel needed to command respect. They needed to inspire confidence. And the Binderian, well, didn't do either of those things particularly well.

Clearly, Joseph needed to do something about it. "Obal?" he said. "Could I have a word with you?"

Obal stopped in his tracks, turned to his superior again and replied, "Of course, sir. Right away." Then he waddled back across the room to Joseph's side.

The security chief took a moment to phrase his next remark. After all, he didn't want to hurt Obal's feelings. It wasn't the Binderian's fault he had been placed somewhere he didn't belong.

"You know," Joseph began, "the *Stargazer* is a big ship. A *very* big ship. It's got a whole range of career opportunities for a bright, young fellow like yourself."

Obal smiled at him. He didn't seem to have any idea what the security chief was suggesting.

"What I mean is," Joseph said, "there are lots of other sections where you could make a contribution."

This time, the Binderian spoke up. "That's good to know," he said. But he didn't say anything more.

Joseph tried again. "Sections that could profit immensely from your eagerness and your intelligence."

Obal's brow creased over the bridge of his nose. "You mean . . . you would like me to *work* in those sections? And apply my expertise to areas other than security?"

The security chief felt as if a weight had been lifted from his shoulders. "Yes! That's *exactly* what I mean."

The Binderian shrugged his scrawny shoulders. "I would be happy to do that, sir."

"You would?" said Joseph. "I mean . . . I'm glad to hear that, Obal, very glad indeed. I'll speak with the heads of the other sections the first chance I get."

"Excellent," Obal told him, clearly enthusiastic about the idea. "And when I return, I will be a better officer as a result."

Joseph's hopes fell. "When you . . . return?"

"Aye, sir. When I return to security."

The chief frowned. "To security."

"In fact, I will be happy to share what I've learned with my colleagues." Obal's brow creased again. "That is, unless you plan to lend *them* out to other sections as well."

It wasn't the response Joseph had been hoping for. Obviously, the subtle approach hadn't gotten him anywhere, so he decided to meet the matter head on.

"Obal," he said, "I was thinking you might want to transfer to another section *permanently*."

The Binderian's brow creased deeper than ever. Then, surprisingly, the smile returned to his face.

"Why would I want to do *that?*" he asked Joseph. "My heart is in security work. And I intend to do that work better than anyone who has ever worn the uniform."

This time, Joseph sighed out loud. He could request the transfer himself, of course. But he wouldn't do that until he had given Obal a chance to prove him wrong.

Not that the chief thought that would happen. "All right, then," he told the Binderian. "Welcome aboard."

"Lieutenant Simenon?"

Simenon looked up from his console in engineering to see who had called his name. There was only one person standing anywhere near him—a middle-aged, rather plump human with kind eyes and dark hair graying at the temples.

She was smiling at him. Obviously, the engineer reflected, she didn't know him very well.

"Yes?" he hissed.

"I'm Juanita Valderrama," she said. "The new sciences chief. You asked me to come see you . . . ?"

It was true. Simenon had wanted to show her something. "Join me," he said, beckoning the woman closer.

He tapped the keys on his console that would bring up the graphic he wanted. As Valderrama leaned over his shoulder, he pointed to the screen with a scaly finger.

"I've been working on amplifying our sensors with Beta Barritus in mind," Simenon explained. "We'll have better range, especially outside the visual spectrum. Here. Take a look for yourself."

Valderrama examined the screen. It took her a couple of minutes to absorb it all, since she wasn't an engineer by training.

When she was done, she turned to Simenon and said, "All right."

He thought she was kidding. "You're happy?"

"If you are," Valderrama told him, smiling again.

Simenon considered her a moment longer. Then he said, "Fine. Thanks for your input."

"Anytime," Valderrama told him. "If there's nothing else . . . ?"

"Nothing," he assured her.

"Then I'll be getting back to my section."

"Fine," he said.

So Valderrama made her way back across engineering and headed blithely for the exit.

Simenon shook his lizardlike head as he watched the doors close behind her. Cariello, Valderrama's predecessor as sciences chief, would *never* have let him off the hook so easily. She would have thanked him for his efforts, of course—but then she would have demanded even more of him, whether he could deliver it or not.

That was how *any* good science officer would have handled it. But not Valderrama. She had simply accepted the limitations laid out for her on the screen and let it go at that.

Simenon frowned. He could tolerate a lot of things, but indifference wasn't one of them. If Valderrama had been one of his engineers, she would have been on her way back to Starbase 32 already.

Starfleet was such a big place, he mused. Surely there had been a better science officer available *somewhere*.

Gilaad Ben Zoma gazed across the shiny black briefing room table at his new second officer.

Lieutenant Commander Elizabeth Wu was a small, wiry woman with short, dark hair. If Ben Zoma hadn't known her age, he would never have guessed that she was over thirty.

"I read your file," he said. "Your record is impeccable."

Her previous captain had called her "the kind of person who gets things done." But then, Ben Zoma could see that in the cast of her eyes and the way she carried herself.

"Thank you," Wu responded, neither discounting the praise nor wallowing in it.

"I can see why Captain Rudolfini wasn't happy to see you leave the *Crazy Horse*."

Wu's mouth pulled up at the corners—as close, apparently, as she came to a smile. "But I assure you, he understood. There wasn't any opportunity for advancement on the *Crazy Horse*. If I wanted to move up, I had no choice but to transfer."

A common motivation. "At any rate," said Ben Zoma, "I think you know why I called you here."

"Of course," she replied. "To brief me on the personalities of the people who will be reporting to me."

"Exactly." It was standard procedure. "Have you had a chance to read any of our personnel files?"

"I was just doing that when you called me."

"And whom have you read about so far?"

Wu thought for a moment. "Phigus Simenon. Your chief engineer, if I recall correctly?"

"That's right."

"He seemed capable enough," Wu remarked.

Ben Zoma smiled. "Simenon is more than capable, Commander. He's brilliant—the absolute best at what he does. But he's also as cranky as they come, so take that into account in your dealings with him."

Wu nodded, her expression indicating that she was filing the information away. "I'll do that."

"Have you gotten to Carter Greyhorse, our chief medical officer?"

She shook her head. "Not yet."

"Greyhorse is brilliant too, in his way."

"And cranky?" Wu suggested wryly.

"Actually," said Ben Zoma, "he's anything but. Greyhorse is always the same, always on an even keel, whether he's treating a splinter or third-degree radiation burns. He'd make a great poker player."

Again, the second officer looked as if she were filing his remarks away. "Noted."

Ben Zoma went on. "Idun Asmund, our helm officer?"

Wu's brow puckered. "Asmund, yes . . . I was halfway through that file. But I don't think the woman's first name was Idun."

"Her sister's name is Gerda."

The light of recognition went on in Wu's eyes. "Yes . . . Gerda. She's your navigator, I believe?"

"That she is," Ben Zoma confirmed. "And you won't find a more efficient officer in the fleet. Unless, of course, you bump into Idun, who happens to be her twin."

"Efficiency is to be commended," Wu said. "What else should I know about them?"

He smiled again. *How should I put this?*

"That they're not afraid of anything—and I mean *anything*. That they're perfectly loyal, dedicated to their work, and resourceful beyond any expectation. And that they were raised by Klingons."

That brought Wu up short. "Klingons?"

"Klingons. It's all in their files."

"I can't wait."

Who else? "Vigo?"

Wu shook her head. "Doesn't ring a bell."

"He's our weapons officer. A Pandrilite. Knows what he's doing inside and out. And he's eager to please."

"Sounds like we'll get along fine."

"I'm sure you will," Ben Zoma told her. He asked himself whom he had left out. It took a moment, but it came to him. "Then there's Pug Joseph, our security chief."

Unexpectedly, Wu's level of enthusiasm seemed to drop precipitously. "Ah, yes. Joseph."

Ben Zoma looked at her. "Something wrong?"

Wu sighed. "A few months ago, I heard some bad things about the *Stargazer*'s security section."

The first officer felt a rush of heat to his face. "Bad in what way?" he asked.

Wu shrugged. "Poor discipline, scheduling inefficiencies . . . generally, a lack of leadership."

"You don't say."

Wu's eyes brightened. "But don't worry. I'm going to crack down on Lieutenant Joseph. By the time I'm done with him, his section will be the best in the fleet."

Ben Zoma smiled halfheartedly. "I applaud your initiative, Commander. However, a few months ago, Pug Joseph wasn't the security chief on this ship. *I* was."

Wu's eyes opened wide. "I'm . . . sorry, sir. Believe me, the last thing I wanted was to offend you."

The first officer nodded. "It's all right. Really. But if I were you, I'd observe Mr. Joseph firsthand before making any judgments concerning his abilities."

"Of course," Wu responded crisply.

Ben Zoma went on with his list of command personnel. But as he did so, it occurred to him that Wu might not be quite the prize he had believed her to be.

Picard took a sip of his tea and gazed out the observation port of his ready room. The distant suns abeam of the *Stargazer* sped by him in long, straight lines of light.

Ben Zoma was sitting at the captain's computer terminal, going over the reports they had received from their section heads. For once, he wasn't smiling.

Out of the corner of his eye, Picard saw his friend push himself away from the desk and swivel his chair in the captain's direction. Picard turned to him.

"Finished?" he asked.

Ben Zoma nodded. "I see what you mean. Of our seven new crewmen, four seem to come with a bit of baggage. That's not a very good average, Jean-Luc."

Picard nodded. "An inescapable conclusion. And given what my friend Corey Zweller told me, I would not be surprised if it were more than a coincidence."

"You think McAteer stuck us with them on purpose? To give us a few distractions while we're hunting the White Wolf?"

"If you accept Corey's premise, it is difficult to ignore the possibility entirely."

Ben Zoma frowned. "I suppose."

"On the other hand," Picard said, "I'm not willing to give up on these crewmen just yet."

"You think we can help them?"

"A couple of them, at least. Ensign Nikolas, for instance. He has been labeled a discipline problem—"

"To put it mildly," Ben Zoma interjected.

"However," the captain continued, "he reminds me of myself before the incident at Bonestell that cost me my heart. He's young, brash, too full of himself to think about his future."

"But maybe, if we exercise a little more patience than Nikolas is accustomed to . . . ?"

"He may turn out to be a diamond in the rough. Precisely."

"Or," said Ben Zoma, "he may turn out to be what he's been labeled—a square peg in a very round hole."

"Then all we've lost," Picard countered, "is time and patience."

Ben Zoma didn't argue the point. Apparently, he had had enough of playing devil's advocate.

"And while we're at it," Picard said, "perhaps we can help Lieutenant Valderrama as well. True, she's been transferred twice in the last couple of years by disgruntled captains—"

"Who noted her exemplary service record but felt her level of dedication had eroded."

"Yes. But what did they do to get her motivated again? Did they challenge her or simply accept her deficiencies? That is the question, Number One."

Ben Zoma smiled. "And she's one of the easier ones. What do you think of Ensign Jiterica?"

The captain shrugged. "Apparently she was of rather limited utility in her previous assignment. Of course, we'll try to work with her. Given her people's status vis-à-vis the Federation, we don't have the option of doing otherwise."

"But you're not optimistic?"

Picard sighed. "Not terribly, no."

Given Jiterica's unusual anatomy, it was remarkable that she had come even this far. Living in the confines of that specially designed suit day in and day out, operating in an environment so different from her natural state . . .

It had to be hell.

But Picard wouldn't allow himself to mistake courage for potential. Unlike Nikolas and Valderrama, Jiterica showed no promise of fitting in on a Federation starship—not in the near term. Not *ever.*

"And Obal?" asked Ben Zoma. "From what Pug tells me, he's not especially suited to a position in security."

"That would be my judgment as well," the captain said. "Perhaps if Obal were encouraged to pursue a different sort of career . . . say, in the sciences section . . ."

"Pug's already tried encouraging him to do that. It seems he's got his heart set on being a security officer."

Picard took another sip of tea and savored it. Like Jiterica, Obal possessed a reach that drastically exceeded his grasp. "I will concede that there is a lot to be said for determination. But if I were Pug, I would try again."

Ben Zoma nodded. "I'll pass that on."

"Fortunately," the captain said, "there are the other three—Wu, Caber, and Ulelo. If McAteer had anything underhand in mind with regard to *them,* we have yet to see it."

A troubled look came over his first officer. "Actually . . ."

"Don't tell me—"

Ben Zoma dismissed the idea with a wave of his hand. "Nothing serious. It's just that Wu strikes me as a little . . . how can I put it?" He frowned for a moment, then said, "Overly enthusiastic."

"That doesn't sound so bad," Picard told him.

"It isn't," Ben Zoma agreed. "Forget I mentioned it. I'm probably just looking for problems where there aren't any."

The captain smiled wryly. "As if we did not have an ample supply of problems already."

"You know," his first officer said, "if Jiterica and the others don't pan out, you can take McAteer up on his suggestion."

"To transfer anyone with whom I'm unhappy?"

"That's what he said."

Picard thought about it. "I could do that," he agreed. "But I am not going to think about that for the moment. As far as I am concerned, a transfer is a last resort."

Because Ben Zoma was his friend, he knew better than to give the captain an argument on that count.

Chapter Seven

NIKOLAS SET HIS TRAY DOWN on the metal rack in front of the replicator opening and said, "Tuna casserole."

A moment later, the replicator went to work, transforming a small quantity of undifferentiated raw material to the parameters specified in a digitally stored molecular pattern matrix. The result was a black casserole dish full of something hot and steaming. Nikolas took it out, placed it on his tray, and looked around for an empty table.

Then he noticed Caber, who was in line behind him, looking at the casserole. Judging by the expression on Caber's face, he considered Nikolas's choice a less than desirable one.

But then, there were more than seven hundred fifty preset options on the *Stargazer*'s replicator menu, and a great deal more if one wanted to take the time to custom-program them. Tuna casserole was hardly the most exotic selection available.

"You sure you want to order that?" Caber asked.

"I know," Nikolas said. "You're surprised. Tuna casserole's for middle-aged guys in stellar cartography."

"Actually," Caber began, "I—"

"Best piece of advice I ever got," Nikolas explained, "was from an engineer on an Academy training ship. He told me replicators aren't all alike, and the worst of them are on *Constellation*-class deep-space explorers like this one. The best approach when you find yourself on one of these things is to start simple and work your way up—and what's simpler than a tuna casserole?"

"True," said Caber, "but—"

"If you're done discussing the finer points of replicator cuisine," said a blond woman waiting her turn behind them, "the rest of us would like to eat."

Nikolas frowned. "Come on," he told Caber. "I wouldn't want anyone to starve to death on my account."

Caber didn't address the woman, but neither did he seem inclined to rush. Turning to the replicator, he said, "Salmon steak. Medium rare. In béarnaise sauce."

Nikolas didn't get it. After he had given Caber the inside poop, he figured his roommate would go the tuna casserole route too. But something as tricky as salmon steak with béarnaise sauce? That was the exact opposite of what Nikolas would have recommended.

He saw the plate materialize in the replicator slot, its centerpiece a moist chunk of pinkish meat drenched in brown and translucent sauce. It looked good, all right—but thanks to that engineer on the *Copernicus,* Nikolas knew better.

There was only one explanation that he could think of. Despite appearances, Caber had allowed the woman in back of them to get him flustered. Obviously, he wasn't as self-possessed as he looked.

Nikolas found himself taking comfort in the observation. He knew he shouldn't, but he did.

"There's an empty table over there," Caber said, pointing to it with his chin.

"Sounds good," Nikolas told him. It was only after they sat down that he leaned toward his roommate and said, "You shouldn't have let that woman get you flummoxed."

Caber looked at him. "Flummoxed?"

Then, to Nikolas's surprise, Caber laughed. It was a deep, heartfelt laugh, the kind that said he hadn't been bothered by the woman at all—that, in fact, the whole idea was rather ludicrous.

"But," Nikolas asked, "if you weren't bothered by her, how did you end up ordering a salmon steak? Didn't you hear what I said about replicators on the *Constellation* class?"

"Sure," said Caber. "And I'd heard the same thing. But I checked the *Stargazer*'s specs before I came aboard, and it's been equipped with a different replicator system than the other *Constellation*-class ships. A more *advanced* system. It can handle a lot more than"—he glanced at Nikolas's plate with obvious sympathy—"the simple dishes."

Nikolas felt as if he had shot himself in the foot with a phaser rifle. The worst of it was that his roommate had tried to disabuse him of his error, but he hadn't listened.

"You don't say," he got out.

Caber shrugged. "It's only one meal. You can order the salmon for dinner if you like."

True, Nikolas thought. *But I'll still feel like a fool.*

Here he'd been thinking he had a leg up on Caber—an arena, no matter how small or insignificant, in which he could outshine the guy. *I should have known better,* he told himself.

Prodding halfheartedly at his casserole, Nikolas watched Caber dig into his salmon and lift a juicy-looking forkful into his mouth. "How is it?" he asked.

Caber nodded as he chewed. "Not bad," he said after he had swallowed and wiped his mouth with his Starfleet-issue cloth napkin. "I mean it's not the quality of the fish you get in Nova Scotia, but I've had a whole lot worse."

Nikolas knew of two places with the name Nova Scotia. Having never been to either one of them, he figured he had better ask. "Nova Scotia on Earth or on Dalarte Prime?"

Caber started to laugh. Then he seemed to realize it wasn't a joke. "There *aren't* any salmon on Dalarte Prime," he said gently. "The closest thing to it is called a second-sunset fish, and most people find it a bit too salty for their taste."

"Nova Scotia on Earth, then," Nikolas said, wishing he hadn't paraded his ignorance quite so successfully. So he hadn't traveled as much as the admiral's son, big deal. "What were you doing there anyway?"

"Ice-surfing," Caber told him, and a look of sublime contentment came over his features. "It's a passion with me. Ever try it?"

"Once," Nikolas replied.

To get a girl, he added silently. It was *always* to get a girl. But in the process, he had discovered that ice-surfing wasn't for him.

"Didn't love it?" Caber asked, taking note of his roommate's lack of enthusiasm.

"Not really," Nikolas said. "I mean, it was fun and all, and it never got as cold as they said it would, but it didn't make my toes curl. I like a sport where you're going head to head with someone, pitting your skills against someone else's."

"Winners and losers," Caber said, boiling it all down.

It sounded to Nikolas as if his roommate disapproved of the concept. But then, he reflected, an admiral's son might have a more "enlightened" view of such matters.

"So what do you play?" Caber asked.

"A lot of things," Nikolas said, steadfastly unashamed of his preference for competition. "Soccer, basketball, handball—"

"Handball?" Caber echoed, interrupting him.

Nikolas nodded, ready for what he figured would be a polite but condescending remark. "That's right."

His roommate's eyes narrowed. "Single wall?"

"It's the only kind," Nikolas said, eyeing Caber suspiciously. "Don't tell me you play?" He did his best to keep his incredulity out of his voice, but it came out anyway.

"Sure do," Caber told him. "Hell, I've been playing since I was nine or ten."

"But—" Nikolas was at a loss.

"What?" Caber prodded.

"I don't know. I guess I've always thought of single-wall handball as a street game."

Caber chuckled, his blue eyes gleaming. "And what makes you think I didn't grow up on the streets?"

Nikolas framed his answer carefully. After all, he didn't want to offend the guy. "Your father's an admiral. I figured an admiral's kid would spend a lot of time on starbases."

"He's an admiral *now*," Caber noted. "But when he was moving up through the ranks, I lived with my mother. In a place called Brooklyn."

Nikolas laughed. "You're kidding."

"Not at all. We had a place in Brooklyn Heights. The nearest courts were a few blocks away."

"I had a cousin in Brooklyn," Nikolas said. "Tommy Tsouratakis. He lived in Canarsie."

Caber leaned forward, his salmon seemingly forgotten for the moment. "I *know* Canarsie."

"I went to visit Tommy once," Nikolas recalled. It had been . . . what? Six years ago? Seven? "He wasn't into handball himself, but he took me to the courts near his house."

"Then," said Caber, "you had to see a guy named Red O'Reilly."

"Yes!" Nikolas was tickled by the coincidence. "You know Red O'Reilly? He was king of the hill, the guy to beat."

"Did you play him?" Caber asked.

"Once. He wiped the court with me. I scored two points, maybe three if I was lucky. I was just glad he didn't shut me out."

Caber's eyes lost their focus. "O'Reilly wiped the court with me too, the first half-dozen times I played him. But I kept trying, kept challenging him. After a while, I got to understand his game better. His strengths. His weaknesses, few as they were." His mouth pulled up at the corners. "And once, just once, I squeaked by him."

Nikolas couldn't believe it. "You *beat* Red O'Reilly?"

"Fifteen-thirteen," Caber recollected. "On a completely accidental lefthanded killer. Rolled off the wall so perfectly he couldn't have returned it in a million years."

Nikolas shared in the other man's vision for a moment, savoring it as if it were he who had made the shot. Then he said with absolute earnestness, "I'm impressed."

Caber made a dismissive sound deep in his throat. "Don't be. I never came close to beating him again."

But he didn't have to, Nikolas thought. He had already accomplished the impossible—scaled Everest, won the Academy Marathon. He had conquered Red O'Reilly.

"Small world," Nikolas remarked.

"Yeah," Caber said. *"Very* small."

As he said it, Lieutenant Commander Wu approached them on her way to the mess hall's only exit. Every bit as new to the *Stargazer* as Nikolas or Caber, she didn't look right or left as she passed the other diners. But then, she obviously wasn't expecting any greetings.

Nonetheless, she got one—from Caber. "Afternoon," he said.

Wu stopped and looked surprised. "To you too," she responded, her pleasure evident in her expression. She seemed to make note of Caber's face. Then she resumed her progress.

Nikolas looked at his roommate, more envious than ever. It would never have occurred to him to say anything to a command officer unless he absolutely had to.

"Now I'm *really* impressed," he confessed.

"With what?" Caber wondered. Then he seemed to understand. "That I said hello to Commander Wu?"

"Not just that you did it," Nikolas told him. "That you sounded so earnest about it."

"You can too."

Nikolas shook his head. "Coming from me, it would sound like mockery. I'm the wild child, remember? I don't mix well with command types."

"But you *could*," Caber insisted. "All you've got to do is make an adjustment in the way you look at them."

Nikolas looked at him askance. "An adjustment . . . ?"

"That's right. I mean, what's the difference between them and us, when you come right down to it? A couple of bars on their sleeves? A little bridge time we haven't accumulated yet?"

"The power to make us scour plasma conduits the rest of our lives?" Nikolas added.

Caber waved the notion away. "I'm telling you, they're the same kind of people we are—no better and no worse. All you've got to do is keep that in mind."

Nikolas frowned. "Easier said than done. For me at least."

"I'll tell you what," his roommate said. He looked around, as if to make sure that no one was eavesdropping on his conversation. Then he lowered his voice and went on. "I'll share a little technique I've found useful, if you promise to keep it to yourself."

Nikolas considered the offer. "Mum's the word."

"A couple of years ago," Caber began, "I was on Betazed for the wedding of a high-ranking Betazoid official. He knew my father pretty well, so he invited my whole family to the celebration. But rather than pull my mother away from work and my sisters out of school, my dad decided to just bring me."

A picture was starting to form in Nikolas's mind. "On Betazed? But don't they—?"

"That's right," Caber said. "They have naked wedding ceremonies. The bride, the groom, the guests, the guy who pronounces them soul mates for life . . . everyone. And in this case, there were also a few admirals and their staffs."

Nikolas tried unsuccessfully to suppress a smile. "Their staffs? You mean . . . their attachés?"

There was absolutely no one more stuck-up or supercilious than an admiral's attaché. They were always so straightlaced, so proper. So the idea of one of them standing there naked . . .

His smile turned into a laugh.

"Exactly," Caber said, his eyes crinkling at the corners. "They looked ridiculous. Stripped of their dignity, quite literally. And that's what gave me the idea for my technique."

Nikolas was beginning to understand what his roommate was getting at. "You think of people without their clothes?"

"Stark naked," Caber confirmed, "wearing nothing but what they were born with. Believe me, it makes it a lot easier to deal with the muckety-mucks of the world. It's hard to feel intimidated by somebody when they're standing there without a stitch."

Nikolas found it hard to disagree.

"Go ahead," Caber said. "Give it a shot."

Nikolas looked at him. "Now?"

"Why not?"

Nikolas frowned. Then he took in the mess hall at a glance, seeking a likely subject. Suddenly, one presented itself.

As the individual in question walked by, Nikolas got up from his seat and said, "Good afternoon, sir."

Chief Engineer Simenon looked up at him through slitted, ruby eyes, his scaly nostrils flaring. "Really."

Naked, Nikolas thought.

It wasn't a pretty sight. However, it had the desired effect. Whatever he might have found daunting about Simenon dematerialized along with his lab coat.

"Yes, sir," Nikolas assured him.

The Gnalish tilted his head as he regarded the ensign. "Whatever you say," he harrumphed. Then he trundled past, his tail impatiently switching back and forth behind him.

Nikolas sat down again in front of his casserole. "Not the friendliest individual I've ever met."

Caber didn't answer right away. When Nikolas turned to him to see why, he caught a glimpse of something hard in his roommate's eyes, something like disapproval but stronger.

Then the moment passed, and Caber turned to him with a smile on his face. "I've seen friendlier. But you've proven my point. You said hello to a high-ranking officer. You addressed him civilly, without even a hint of sarcasm. And you got *him* to speak to *you* civilly as well."

"If you can call that being civil," Nikolas quipped.

Caber glanced at the exit through which the engineer had departed. "That was Simenon," he said, "by all accounts the grumpiest, most mean-spirited officer on the ship. If you're going to offend someone, it's going to be *him.* And yet he left here without so much as a complaint. I'd say that constitutes success."

Nikolas saw the man's point. The technique had worked. And if Nikolas could approach Simenon, he could approach anyone—even the captain.

"And the best part," Caber told him, "is you don't feel you've kowtowed to anyone. You've still got your dignity."

Nikolas smiled. He did, didn't he?

"Thanks," he said.

Caber smiled at him. "Believe me, it's my pleasure."

Chapter Eight

PICARD HEARD THE SOUND of chimes and looked up from his terminal. "Come," he said.

The doors to his ready room slid aside with a soft exhalation of air, revealing the matronly, dark-haired form of Lieutenant Valderrama. Looking a bit tentative, the science officer came in and allowed the doors to close behind her.

"You asked to see me?" she said.

"I did indeed," the captain replied. He swiveled his chair around to face her. "Please have a seat."

Valderrama made use of the only other chair in the room, which was situated on the other side of Picard's desk. It occurred to the captain that the woman was old enough to be his mother, and for just a moment he felt awkward addressing her as a subordinate.

Then again, he mused, a great many of his subordinates were older than he was. Just not by quite so many years.

"I trust you've settled in by now?" he said, feeling the need to engage Valderrama in conversation before he began to get into anything more substantive.

"I have," the sciences chief assured him.

"Good. And your personnel?"

"Top-notch, as far as I can tell. I'm very much looking forward to working with them."

Picard nodded. "Excellent."

Valderrama seemed comfortable enough, both in her position and in his ready room. With that in mind, he put pleasantries aside and launched into the real reason he had summoned her.

Leaning forward in his chair, he said, "I hope you'll understand if I speak bluntly, Lieutenant."

Valderrama seemed to gird herself. She must have sensed this coming. "Aye, sir."

"Other captains have not been pleased with your performance of late. They have reached the conclusion that you are coasting—that you could do better if doing better still mattered to you."

Valderrama reddened. "They have said that, sir."

"However," Picard went on, "I don't care what conclusions other captains have reached. On the *Stargazer,* you'll be starting out with a clean slate."

It wasn't the kind of speech the lieutenant had expected. That much was clear from her bewildered expression.

He pressed on. "I fully expect that you will do an exemplary job here—a job of which you and I can both be proud. You will need to do no less, considering what we will soon be facing in Beta Barritus."

Valderrama stared at him for a moment. Then she lifted her chin and said, "I'm grateful for your confidence in me, sir. I'll try to be worthy of it."

"I'm sure you will," Picard replied.

Pug Joseph hadn't slept very well. He had been thinking about his new security officer all night long, turning the problem over and over in his mind and dreading the moment when he would have to confront the Binderian about his obvious inadequacies.

Maybe, he had told himself more than once in the wee hours as he lay staring at the ceiling, it would have been more merciful to nip Obal's hopes at the outset. Maybe it would have been less painful for the little fellow in the long run.

But he hadn't done that. He had shied away from what he couldn't help seeing more and more as the inevitable. And when the inevitable came, it would be that much more difficult for both of them.

As he thought that, he reached the doors to the security section. They slid apart in front of him and revealed an anteroom manned by two armed officers, Garner and Pierzynski. The officers inclined their heads and acknowledged him by name.

"Carry on," Joseph said, feeling a little silly.

Garner and Pierzynski were full lieutenants just as he was. And as soon as the captain found a permanent security chief, Joseph would be standing guard alongside them.

Beyond the anteroom lurked the hexagonal main security facility, where an officer named Horombo was sitting in front of a huge, concave bank of closed-circuit video screens. Each one showed him a different, strategically important portion of the ship—the bridge, engineering, the transporter room, and so on.

"Chief," said Horombo, sparing him a glance.

"Horombo," Joseph responded.

He proceeded across the hexagon to its opposite side, where an open doorway provided access to a short corridor. His office was located farther down that corridor. So was the *Stargazer*'s armory, which stood opposite his door and contained every phaser on the ship that wasn't currently in use somewhere.

The other doors that opened on the corridor led to a weapons diagnostics room, a weapons repair room, a target range and a storeroom full of communicators, palmlights, and other gear often needed by *Stargazer* away teams.

Joseph was so dull-witted and bleary-eyed from lack of sleep that he almost passed the diminutive figure hunched over a table in the diagnostics area without noticing him. Taking a step backward, he peered inside the room and saw that it was Obal seated there.

"Obal?" he ventured.

The Binderian turned to him. "Good morning, sir."

Joseph didn't get it. "You're not on duty for another six hours," he pointed out.

"True," Obal responded. "But I felt my time would be spent more wisely here in security."

The security chief could hardly object to such zeal. "So you've been . . . what? Testing the accuracy of our ordnance?"

The Binderian smiled at him. "Yes, sir."

"That's admirable," Joseph told him, "if unnecessary. Chief Ang made sure that was done before he left."

"In that case," Obal said cheerfully, "Chief Ang must have had something else on his mind at the time."

Joseph looked at him. "What do you mean?"

The Binderian held up the type-1 phaser in his hand. "This unit as well as several others exhibit targeting inaccuracies."

The security chief was understandably skeptical. He held out his hand and said, "May I?"

"Of course." Obal turned the phaser over to him.

Joseph placed it in the diagnostic device, closed the cover on it, and checked the digital readouts. Sure enough, the targeting mechanism was off—if only by a few hundredths of a millimeter.

"As I said," Obal noted, "there are inaccuracies."

Joseph turned to him and smiled. "Not serious ones, mind you. But I'll give you credit for finding any at all."

The Binderian inclined his head. "Thank you, sir."

"Now we've got to fix this thing. Why don't you—"

"Actually," Obal piped up, "that won't be necessary. I've already made all the necessary corrections, sir."

"You have?"

Obal nodded. "At least with regard to the type-one and type-two devices. I have yet to test the rifles."

Joseph looked at him. "You can't mean *all* the type-ones and type-twos."

"On the contrary, sir. That's exactly what I mean."

"But . . . between the type-ones and the type-twos, there are more than sixty phasers."

"Sixty-four, to be exact, sir."

"You're kidding."

"Not at all," Obal assured him.

The security chief chuckled appreciatively. "And you weren't even scheduled to be on duty."

"As I said," the Binderian reminded him, "I felt my time would be spent more wisely in security."

Under the circumstances, Joseph couldn't help but agree.

"After I check the rifles," Obal said, "I would like to take a look at the brig. In my experience, graviton polarity source field generators require frequent recalibration."

Joseph nodded. "Sure. Knock your socks off."

Obal smiled. "Thank you, sir."

The security chief left him in the diagnostics room and continued to his office, where he sat down in front of his computer screen. But before long, he found himself thinking about the Binderian again.

Sixty-four phasers, he mused. *And in his free time.*

Maybe he had been too quick to judge Obal, he told himself. Maybe the little guy was going to work out after all.

Vigo smiled to himself as he moved his tiny wagon across the winding blue ribbon of a river. Then he looked across the octagonal sharash'di board and saw Valderrama smile too, albeit a bit more ruefully.

"Looks like you've got me," she said.

Remembering his manners, the Pandrilite contained his enthusiasm. "I'll grant you, it looks that way. But it's not because you didn't pursue an interesting and effective strategy."

"It couldn't have been *that* effective," the sciences chief rejoined. "Otherwise, *you* would be the one conceding defeat."

"What hurt you," Vigo observed, "was your third-level defense. You should have chosen stone over sky."

"I would have," Valderrama told him, "if I'd had any large green stones left."

"You had two of them, actually. They were buried in the riverbed and obscured by ice."

To underscore his point, Vigo lifted the glassy overlay that represented ice and exposed the trough in the board that represented the river. It was filled halfway to the top with fine dark sand. Using a big, blue finger, he moved the sand around until he revealed a couple of smooth, blue-green stones.

"You see?" he said.

Valderrama looked surprised by his revelation. "But how did you know they were there?"

Vigo shrugged. "They had to be. When we left the first level, only three stones had turned up in the river. And on the second level, there weren't any at all. So—"

"So there had to be a couple of them on *this* level." Valderrama nodded in appreciation of his logic. "Well done, Mr. Vigo."

He inclined his head. "Thank you."

"And," she added with a gleam in her eye, "get ready for a rematch."

The remark caught Vigo off guard. "Really?"

"You don't think I'm going to just roll over and accept defeat, do you?" And with her challenge hanging in the air, Valderrama began to set up the board for another game.

The Pandrilite grinned.

He hadn't been happy about saying good-bye to Cariello, Valderrama's predecessor as head of the sciences section. Cariello was known for her drive and enthusiasm, her desire to get the most out of herself and others.

Vigo hadn't expected her replacement to be nearly as good. But fortune had smiled on the *Stargazer*, it seemed, because Valderrama was obviously made from the same mold.

"Well?" she said. "What are you waiting for?"

He chuckled. "Nothing, Lieutenant. Nothing at all."

Savoring the prospect of another match, he helped her put the game pieces back in place.

Ben Zoma forked half a stuffed grape leaf into his mouth and savored its aromatic flavor while he considered the list of Starfleet advisories on his padd.

It was midafternoon, and the *Stargazer*'s lounge was nearly empty, just as Ben Zoma liked it. Not that he wasn't the gregarious sort. On the contrary, he was probably the most gregarious person he knew.

But as the *Stargazer*'s first officer, he needed to digest everything that was happening on the ship—and in the case of a Starfleet advisory, everything that was happening *off* the ship as well. It was easier to do that in an empty lounge than in a full one.

"Commander?" someone said.

It took Ben Zoma a moment to realize that it was he who was being addressed that way. But then, he had only been a first officer for a week or so.

"Yes?" he said, looking up from his padd.

Wu was standing across the table from him, smiling politely. "Is this seat taken?" she asked, indicating one opposite Ben Zoma's.

He shrugged. "I don't think so."

"Good." Wu pulled the chair out and sat down, dispelling any notion Ben Zoma might have had about finishing his reading in peace. "I'm glad I found you here," she said. "I wanted to speak with you."

"What about?" Ben Zoma asked, putting down the padd.

Wu's brow knit. "Our last conversation included a rather . . . awkward moment. I wanted to address it."

Ben Zoma dismissed the notion with a wave of his hand. "You did that already. You said you were sorry."

"Yes," his colleague agreed. "But I wanted you to know that what I said was heartfelt."

He smiled. "I never had any reason to believe otherwise."

"You know, I *never* would have put my foot in my mouth that way on the *Crazy Horse*."

Ben Zoma understood. "Because you knew her personnel a lot better than you know the *Stargazer*'s."

Wu nodded. "Exactly."

The first officer was able to sympathize, since the *Stargazer* hadn't been his first assignment. "It's difficult getting used to a new ship and crew, especially after you've been in one place for a long time."

"It is," his second officer confirmed.

"So let's just forget what happened," he suggested. "In fact, I've forgotten it already."

Wu looked grateful. "Thank you."

"Don't mention it," said Ben Zoma. He glanced at his padd, which was sitting next to his plate of stuffed grape leaves. "And now, if I can ask *you* a favor . . ." He let his voice trail off meaningfully.

Wu seemed to notice the padd and the grape leaves for the first time. "Of course," she replied quickly. "By all means. Sorry to have distracted you from your work."

"No problem," he assured her.

She began to withdraw as quietly as she had approached him, but before she could leave, Ben Zoma tendered an invitation.

"Any time you want to talk . . ."

Wu smiled at him again. Then she crossed the lounge and made her exit through its set of sliding doors.

Ben Zoma smiled too, Wu's overzealousness at their first meeting as forgotten as he had promised it would be. Then he went back to his padd and its advisories.

Chapter Nine

JITERICA STOOD AMID A HERD of snub-nosed silver shapes, the overhead lighting glinting off their duranium hides.

"We've got a type-eleven pod, a type-twelve pod, and three type-thirteen pods," said Lieutenant Chiang, the gray-templed officer in charge of the *Stargazer*'s lone shuttlebay. His voice rang proudly from one end of the facility to the other. "We've got a type-three personnel shuttle, two type-four personnel shuttles, and a couple of type-five personnel shuttles, and right here is a type-eight heavy cargo shuttle fresh from the yards at Utopia Planitia."

The Nizhrak knew exactly what types the vehicles were. Shuttle design was one of the myriad subjects she had studied in her crash course at Starfleet headquarters.

"Of course," the short, stocky Chiang went on, "the type-twelve is in the process of being overhauled for the umpteenth time, so it's useless to us right now."

Jiterica saw a pair of uniformed legs sticking out from under the type-12, the exterior of which was virtually identical to the type-11. It was on the inside that the two shuttles were entirely different, thanks to the type-12's 500-millicochrane impulse driver engines and its three sarium krellide storage cells.

"As you can see," said Chiang, rapping his knuckles on the type-3, "we're not exactly cutting edge here from top to bottom. This little number can barely maintain warp speed over the long haul, so we'd only use it in a dire emergency like a full-scale evacuation."

"I understand," Jiterica responded.

She had been sent here to assist the shuttlebay crew for the time being. She had no objections to the assignment. An ensign was supposed to familiarize herself with as many aspects of starship operation as possible.

"We've got another type-five on order," Chiang told her, "but between you and me, I don't expect to see her any time soon. The way they ration out new shuttlecraft, you'd think there were a million ships all clamoring for them at once."

He chortled and looked to Jiterica, as if he expected some specific reaction from her. But not knowing what it might be, she remained silent and waited for a clue.

"Rrright," Chiang said at last. He rapped on the type-3 again. "Well then, let's see if we can't—"

Before the lieutenant could finish his sentence, he was cut off by a loud clanging noise. Chiang turned grim suddenly, no longer the affable tour guide. He shouted out some orders, then pointed to the double doors that comprised the shuttlebay's entrance.

"Let's go," he said to Jiterica.

She understood the reason for his sense of urgency. The loud sound she "heard" through her audio sensors was the signal for all personnel to respond to some immediate danger—loss of air pressure, exposure to radiation, or something equally inimical to humanoid life—by unhesitatingly evacuating the shuttlebay.

Jiterica wasn't sure why such an action was necessary. To her knowledge, the ship was not under attack. Nor was it in the vicinity of any dangerous phenomena. On the other hand, anomalies cropped up from time to time in the course of subspace travel, and the *Stargazer* might have encountered one of them.

In any case, it wasn't the Nizhrak's place to determine the reason for the evacuation. Her only responsibility was to leave the area as quickly as possible.

There had been half a dozen other crewmen in the bay besides Jiterica and Chiang—two humans, a Vulcan, a Bolian, a Carpathian, and a Vobilite. They all locked down their respective control stations and scampered for the exit.

But Jiterica couldn't scamper. Her containment suit wasn't equipped to let her move that quickly. All she could do was proceed at her usual deliberate, mechanical pace—a limitation that had never been an issue until that moment.

Chiang noticed Jiterica's difficulty, stopped halfway to the exit and came back for her. But her condensed mass was more or less equal to the lieutenant's, so he didn't have the option of picking her up and carrying her. All he could do was turn her around, grab her suit under its armpits and drag her toward the double doors.

Jiterica felt feeble and embarrassed. Had she been back in the roiling chaos of her homeworld, she would simply have altered her form and ridden one of the storm winds away from peril. Here, in this place of rigidly enforced geometric boundaries, she was forced to depend on a fellow crewman for assistance.

Little by little, Chiang pulled her in the direction of safety, the heels of her bulky white suit scraping on the floor. But the lieutenant wasn't moving quickly enough. According to the evacuation protocols Jiterica had studied, they had only twenty seconds to reach the exit before a duranium barrier descended from the ceiling and sealed off the shuttlebay.

Twelve seconds had already gone by, and they hadn't even cleared the last of the shuttlepods. At this rate, they wouldn't make it. They wouldn't even come close.

"Go," she told Chiang over the sound of the klaxon. "Leave me."

"I can't," he gasped into her audio sensors, his voice ragged with effort. "You're part of my crew . . . my responsibility . . ."

Just then, the ensign saw another crewman appear on her right and grab her by the arm. A moment later, someone else appeared to grab her by the other one. Pooling their strength with Chiang's, they dragged her with greater speed over the shuttle deck.

But it wasn't going to be enough, the ensign told herself. As the ceiling rushed past her, its details framed in her faceplate, she counted down the seconds in her mind.

Seven seconds. Six. Five . . .

"Leave me," she pleaded a second time.

This time, Chiang didn't respond. Looking back at

the man, Jiterica saw the rictus of strain on his face and realized he was struggling too hard to get an answer out.

Behind her, a heavy metal barrier started to descend from its slot in the ceiling. Once it closed, there would be no getting it open again. Whoever remained on the wrong side of it would be trapped.

Four, Jiterica thought. *Three. Two . . .*

The barrier was directly above, looming larger as it came down at her. At the last possible moment, she felt a jerk on her suit and saw herself shoot backward. When the sheet of metal hit the deck and locked into place, the bulky white feet of her suit were just inside it.

One.

She was safe, she realized. They were *all* safe.

Chiang and the others propped the ensign on her feet again. They were in the compartment that mediated between the shuttlebay and the corridor outside it, and one of Jiterica's colleagues was checking conditions in the ship on a computer terminal built into the bulkhead.

"Everything seems to be normal," the man said. "Power levels, hull integrity, air pressure . . ."

"Then why did we evacuate?" the Bolian asked.

That's when they heard the voice fill their compartment. "That was a drill, folks. I'm happy to say you passed."

It was difficult for Jiterica to discern one voice on the ship from another, but it seemed to her that it was Commander Ben Zoma speaking. One of the technicians alongside her, a Carpathian female, confirmed the speaker's identity.

"Ben Zoma," she said in an exasperated tone.

"Carry on," the first officer told them.

Then the duranium barrier began to slide up again, retreating into its slot in the ceiling. In the process, it showed them an undamaged and uncompromised shuttlebay, as clean and orderly as they had left it.

Jiterica turned to Chiang. He was the officer in charge of this section, and yet it seemed to her that he hadn't known about the drill. Otherwise, he wouldn't have worked so hard to get her on the safe side of the barrier.

The ensign hadn't had time to read much about drill protocol at Starfleet headquarters. She had been too busy learning more essential information, like how to walk and how to speak. However, now that she thought about it, it made sense that at least *some* drills would come as surprises even to the heads of the sections involved.

Perhaps there were drills that would even come as surprises to Commander Ben Zoma.

But it wasn't the propriety of the drill that gave Jiterica cause for concern. It was her reaction to it. Or more accurately, her *inability* to react to it.

If they had faced a real emergency instead of a false one, she would have been a burden to her colleagues. They would have been forced to risk their own lives to save hers.

Chiang wiped his brow with the back of his hand. "All right, everyone," he said, his voice echoing with something less than its usual resonance. He was still a little out of breath. "Let's get back to work."

As the others returned to their tasks, Jiterica approached him. "Excuse me, Lieutenant. I wish to speak with you."

Chiang frowned as he turned and regarded her. "Funny, Ensign . . . I was just going to tell you the same thing."

* * *

Greyhorse was sitting in his office, mulling what he had heard about Jiterica's misadventure in the shuttle-bay, when he saw Phigus Simenon crossing the sickbay and coming his way.

The engineer's scaly tail switched back and forth as he walked, making him look even more driven than usual—and his "usual" was already enough to bowl most people over. Obviously, he had something on his mind.

"What can I do for you?" Greyhorse asked.

He and Simenon had gotten to know each other rather well over the last few weeks. They were alike in many ways. For one thing, neither of them was exactly steeped in the social graces.

"You can pronounce Urajel fit for duty," the Gnalish told him, depositing himself in a chair opposite the doctor's. His ruby eyes were narrowed and demanding.

Urajel was an Andorian engineer who had broken her arm in one of their encounters with the Nuyyad. The limb had healed perfectly, but Greyhorse had wanted to give it a few more days to make sure. Those extra days were now over.

"You want her?" he said. "You've got her."

No doubt, Simenon had expected more of a fight. Little by little, the muscles around his eyes relaxed. But his tail didn't stop switching. Apparently, Urajel's situation wasn't the only thing that had been bothering the engineer.

"You look troubled," Greyhorse observed dryly.

"I am," Simenon told him.

The doctor knew he would regret asking, but he asked anyway. "Any particular reason for your discontent?"

"You know the new sciences chief? Valderrama?"

"Of course I do," Greyhorse responded. "I gave the woman a physical."

"So what do you think of her?"

Greyhorse looked at him askance. "Is this a trick question?"

The engineer scowled. "What do you *think* of her?"

The doctor shrugged. "I hadn't given her much thought. She seems efficient enough, I suppose."

Simenon harrumphed, obviously not happy with that answer. "Not as far as I'm concerned."

"Is there a problem?"

"I'd say so. Yesterday I showed Valderrama some sensor enhancements in anticipation of our encounter with Beta Barritus. What do you think she said?"

"I haven't the slightest idea," Greyhorse replied. "I'm a doctor, not an engineer."

"Give it a try."

Greyhorse rolled his eyes. "She thanked you for what you'd done and said she expected you to do better."

Simenon pointed to him triumphantly. "That's what you'd expect, right? For her to goad me into enhancing the sensors even more? That's what a science officer *does*."

Greyhorse frowned. "Am I to understand that Valderrama fell short in this regard?"

"She sure as *hell* fell short. All she did was smile and thank me for all my hard work, and go about her business. It was as if she didn't *care* how well the sensors worked."

"And this bothers you?"

Simenon's lips pulled back, exposing rows of small, sharp teeth. "It doesn't bother *you?*"

"Why should it?" Greyhorse inquired casually. "Your

people are probably working on the sensors even as we speak, regardless of Valderrama's reaction."

The Gnalish snorted. "Not probably."

The doctor held his hands up, palms facing the ceiling. "So why should I be bothered?"

"Because," Simenon said, "I'm not going to be there to pick up her slack all the time. *That's* why."

As the Gnalish's remark hung in the air, Greyhorse heard the shuffle of feet in the central exam area beyond his office door. Though he couldn't catch a glimpse of anyone from where he was sitting, he could venture a guess as to the newcomer's identity. Lieutenant Paxton was scheduled to come in for a routine physical.

"Paxton?" he called out.

"Right here," came the comm officer's response.

The doctor regarded Simenon and shrugged his massive shoulders. "Duty calls, I'm afraid."

The engineer nodded his lizardlike head. "Mine too." And he left without saying another word.

As soon as Simenon was gone, Greyhorse got up from behind his desk and went out into the central exam area. Paxton was sitting on a biobed, waiting for him.

"I hope I didn't interrupt anything," the comm officer said.

"Not at all," the doctor replied.

Then, putting everything else aside—Jiterica's problem as well as Simenon's—he focused on the matter at hand. After all, even a routine exam deserved his undivided attention.

And sickbay, Greyhorse resolved, would continue to

be a model of order and efficiency on the *Stargazer*—
even if some of the ship's other sections were not.

Idun Asmund sat cross-legged on the floor of her
quarters. Wisps of sharply scented smoke escaped from
a small iron receptacle in front of her, a receptacle
blackened by use and time, in which she had set fire to a
tiny chunk of *s'naiah* wood.

"Uroph, son of Warrokh," she intoned.

And she added, in her thoughts, *batlh Daqawlu'taH*,
meaning "you will be remembered with honor" in the
Klingon tongue.

For more than a thousand years, the warriors of Clan
Warrokh had recited the names of their known ancestors
before taking their evening meal. It was a tradition that
had been passed down from father to son and mother to
daughter.

"Weyto," she said, "son of Uroph."

Batlh Daqawlu'taH.

The list was nearly a hundred names long, but Idun
never forgot any of them. To do so would have brought
dishonor both to her and to the mother who taught her to
remember.

"Ukray'k, daughter of Weyto."

Batlh Daqawlu'taH.

They were the blood of her adopted father and
mother, not her own. Still, she considered them her fore-
bears, just as her father and mother considered her their
offspring—with all the rights and privileges accorded
progeny under Klingon law.

"Jitakh, son of Ukray'k."

Batlh Daqawlu'taH.

In Gerda's quarters, which were next to Idun's, her sister would be reciting the same litany of names. But then, Gerda had been raised in the same strict Klingon household, provided with the same exhaustive Klingon education.

"Hojeen, son of Jitakh."

Batlh Daqawlu'taH.

When she and Gerda were young and newly adopted, their family had spoken the names together, their father's deep, resonant voice a counterpoint to their high-pitched, childish ones. Idun could almost hear him now, giving an edge and a life to their heritage that she could never quite manage.

"Qerresh, son of Hojeen."

Batlh Daqawlu'taH.

She could feel her mother's gaze on her, full of pride and approval. Idun and her sister were truer warriors than many who had been born Klingon.

"Royyebh, daughter of Qerresh."

Batlh Daqawlu'taH.

"Dobrukh, son of Royyebh."

Batlh Daqawlu'taH.

"Rejjakh, son of—"

It was then that Idun heard something.

A chime. It alerted the helm officer to the fact that someone was seeking entrance to her quarters—and spoiling the sanctity of her meditation.

Idun frowned and opened her eyes. Her crewmates knew that she wished to be left alone at this time of day. If they were interrupting her, it had to be an emergency of some kind.

Rising to her feet, she said, "Enter."

The doors slid apart with an exhalation of air, revealing the small, wiry figure of Commander Wu. She was standing in the corridor with a data padd in her hand and a polite smile on her face.

Clearly, Idun thought, she had been wrong about the possibility of an emergency. It was just a matter of a new crewmate who was unaware of her meditation schedule.

"Commander Wu," she said. "Can I help you?"

"May I come in?" Wu asked.

Idun shrugged. "Of course."

The second officer entered Idun's quarters and looked around for a moment—first at the wood-burning artifact and the smoke issuing from it, then at everything else. There were chairs available, a couple of them designed specifically for human comfort, but Wu declined to make use of any of them.

Perhaps she was simply waiting for an invitation, Idun thought. "Would you like to sit down?" she asked.

"No, thank you," Wu replied. "This won't take long."

There was something in her tone that told Idun she wasn't going to like what her guest had to say. As it turned out, her suspicion was an accurate one.

"According to ship's records," Wu said, "you're nearly a week late in taking the requalification exam for helm duty."

At first Idun thought the second officer was making a joke—paving the way for what she had *really* come to say. Then she realized that Wu was absolutely serious.

The helm officer conceded the point. "That is correct. I *am* a bit late in requalifying."

It was something every officer was required to do in his or her area of specialization. But it wasn't a regulation that was strictly enforced—at least, not in Idun's experience.

She said so.

Wu seemed unimpressed. "Maybe that was true of your previous assignments. Maybe it was even true here on the *Stargazer*. But under my supervision, things will be different. Breaches of Starfleet regulations will not be tolerated."

It was so ludicrous that Idun was tempted to laugh. "We are in the middle of a hunt for a dangerous adversary. I can requalify as soon as it's over."

It seemed like an eminently reasonable course of action. Apparently Wu thought otherwise.

"My officers don't make their own rules," she said. "They comply with regulations. You'll either requalify immediately or you'll be removed from your post."

Idun couldn't believe what she was hearing. She felt a spurt of anger jump into her throat.

Somehow she managed to suppress it. Then she said, "That decision may not be in the best interests of this mission or this crew," pointing out what seemed to her to be the truth.

Again Wu appeared to see the matter in a different light. "Until further notice," she announced, "you're relieved of your responsibilities at the helm."

And without another word, she turned and left Idun's quarters, the sliding doors hissing closed in her wake.

For a moment, Idun was left speechless. Then she swore volubly and vividly in the Klingon tongue, filling her quarters with curses that threatened to blister the duranium bulkheads, and contacted Wu's superior via the *Stargazer*'s intercom system.

Chapter Ten

BEN ZOMA HAD JUST ARRIVED on the bridge to take over for Picard when he received Idun Asmund's impassioned call.

Her voice, normally so clipped and efficient, seethed with barely restrained anger and indignation—so much so that it attracted the attention of everyone present. Picard was no exception.

Ben Zoma frowned. Then he asked the helm officer to hold off for a moment and moved to the captain's side.

"A problem?" Picard asked.

He was beginning to look a little tense. A little grim. And Ben Zoma had no trouble understanding why that would be.

They were getting closer to Beta Barritus, closer to the White Wolf—and closer to McAteer's "trap," as Corey Zweller had described it. Picard was determined to buck the odds, to accomplish what a dozen other captains before him couldn't and turn the tables on the admiral.

But what if Picard didn't manage to complete his mission? What if he fell short and, in the process, showed everyone that Admiral Mehdi's faith in him had been misplaced?

The captain had been studying chart after chart of Beta Barritus, incomplete as they were. He had pored over every research paper he could find that dealt with the dynamics of Lazarus stars.

But what if that wasn't enough?

Then McAteer would have succeeded in his gambit—and Picard would never forgive himself for it.

Hence the beleaguered expression, the first officer reflected. In his friend's place, Ben Zoma would no doubt have looked a little beleaguered as well.

"Nothing I can't handle," he told Picard.

"I trust you are right," the captain said, easing himself out of his center seat. "But if you should require my assistance after all, you will find me in my quarters."

Ben Zoma nodded. "I won't. But thanks."

That seemed to satisfy Picard. Leaving his friend to deal with Idun's problem, he headed for his quarters and a much-needed rest.

Ben Zoma waited until the captain had left the bridge. Then he entered the captain's ready room, took a seat behind the black plastic desk, and said, "Ben Zoma to Lieutenant Idun Asmund."

Instantly the story spilled out of her, punctuated with denunciation and invective. It took the first officer a while to amass all the details and put them in what seemed like the proper order.

Then he said, "Let me get this straight, Lieutenant. Commander Wu relieved you of your duties as helm officer because you hadn't taken your requalification test?"

"That is correct," Idun responded, her voice trembling with fury she dared not release.

Ben Zoma didn't get it. "Was that the *only* reason?"

"It was the only reason she *gave* me."

The first officer frowned. It was highly unusual for anyone to be held that closely to requalification regs—especially while on a mission as potentially difficult as this one.

"I'll tell you what," he said. "For now, you'll have to comply with the commander's decision. But I'll speak with her first chance I get. And when I do, I have a feeling we'll clear this up to everyone's satisfaction—yours included."

That seemed to calm Idun a bit. "Thank you, sir."

"You're welcome," Ben Zoma replied. Then he sat back in his chair and considered what he was going to say to Commander Wu.

Pug Joseph had gotten into the habit of checking in with his monitor officer every so often, even when he wasn't on duty. Fortunately he had never caught one napping, even figuratively.

Until now.

Marching into the security section, he didn't nod to either of the armed officers standing guard in the little anteroom. He didn't even look at their faces. He just kept going until he reached the hexagon-shaped main security facility.

That's where he found Obal sitting in front of the big,

concave bank of monitors with its closed-circuit views of every strategically critical area on the ship. It was the Binderian's turn to stand watch over those critical areas.

And as Joseph had feared since his routine check-in several minutes earlier, Obal was fast asleep.

The security chief stood there for a moment, watching the little fellow's chest rise and fall serenely. Then, not too roughly, he took Obal by the shoulder and shook him.

The Binderian sat bolt upright with a little cry of surprise, his eyes blinking wildly. Still, it was a second or two before he realized where he was and who was standing beside him.

"Lieutenant Joseph," he said, his eyes wide as he began to grasp the nature of his circumstances.

"Sorry to have to wake you," Joseph told him. *In more ways than one,* he added silently. "But I can't have my monitor officer catching up on his sleep."

He might as well have driven an old-fashioned arrow into Obal's chest. "I—I'm sorry, sir," the Binderian bleated. "I don't know what came over me. Nothing like this has ever happened before."

"Maybe you've never stayed up half the night checking phasers before," Joseph suggested.

Obal swallowed. "That's true. Still, I feel terrible about this. Allow me to try to atone for it somehow."

By checking the phasers again? Joseph mused. *Or maybe the photon torpedo tubes this time?* "That won't be necessary," he said. "Just do the job you're assigned, all right?"

The Binderian couldn't possibly have looked more contrite. "Of course, sir. As you wish."

Joseph felt sorry for the little guy—he couldn't help

it. But he wasn't just a bystander here, he was Obal's superior. And as such, he couldn't just dismiss the incident.

Besides, if he had waited just a few more minutes to call in, one of the other officers might have discovered the Binderian before he did. Then the incident would have become the talk of the ship's lounge. And though he could have asked his people to keep it among themselves, the story might have leaked out anyway.

Joseph sighed. It wasn't just a matter of people respecting Obal anymore. Now it was a matter of people respecting *him*. Because when the captain read Joseph's report, he would be forced to wonder what kind of security section his chief was running.

"Am I relieved of my post?" Obal inquired humbly, wincing as he posed the question.

Joseph nodded. "I think that would be our best course of action under the circumstances."

Without another word, the Binderian slipped out of his chair, thrust out his scrawny chest, and stood there dutifully until his only slightly curious replacement could be called in. Then he left security and presumably made his way back to his quarters.

As Joseph watched Obal go, a sigh escaped him. He himself hadn't done a single thing wrong, but he felt every bit as bad about the incident as the Binderian did.

Maybe worse.

Picard eyed the viewscreen in front of him. It showed him a massive, dark bullet of a ship bristling with deadly armaments, half obscured by the roiling currents of Beta Barritus.

"Hail them," he said.

Paxton made the attempt at his comm console. There was no response—not that the captain had expected any.

"Sir," said Gerda Asmund, sitting at her customary spot behind the navigation controls, "they're powering weapons."

"Red alert," Picard snapped. "Shields. Phasers."

"Shields up," Gerda confirmed.

"Phasers ready," Vigo announced.

It was then that the captain noticed the two figures standing next to the weapons console, just behind his left shoulder. They comprised a mismatched pair if he had ever seen one.

One was an older man, his face lined, his hair all but gone. He wore simple, sturdy clothes, the sort one might don to work in the fields, and there were traces of dirt beneath his fingernails.

The other was a tall, athletic-looking fellow in the cranberry and cream of a Starfleet captain's uniform. His hair was thick and dark, only beginning to show signs of gray at the temples, and his smile was a beacon of confidence stretching across his face.

Or rather, across *half* his face. The other half was a charred, bubbling wound, the result of an explosion in a plasma conduit during his first and only encounter with the Nuyyad.

The fellow's name was Daithan Ruhalter. He had preceded Picard as captain of the *Stargazer*.

And the other man, the one with the plain, sturdy clothes and the dirt beneath his fingernails? He was a vintner, heir to a long line of vintners. And if he had had his way, his son Jean-Luc would have been a vintner as well.

"They're firing, sir," Gerda called out.

The viewscreen filled swiftly with a lurid barrage of phased energy emissions. A moment later the bridge bucked and shuddered with the force of the attack.

"Actually," said Maurice Picard, "I've never approved of this sort of technology. I believe man's place is on Earth, doing what his ancestors have done for centuries." He searched for a phrase. "Getting his hands dirty, if you know what I mean."

"You know," Ruhalter said judiciously, "I think you've got a point there. You can't rely too much on machines, even in a battle like this one. It's the human element that wins and loses wars."

"How so?" Maurice Picard inquired.

"Instinct," Ruhalter elaborated. "Either you've got it or you don't—and if you *don't,* no collection of sensors and shields and phaser banks is going to help you."

As if to underline the wisdom of his statement, the ship was bludgeoned again with a phaser volley. Holding on to his armrests, Picard felt his teeth rattle with the impact.

"Return fire!" he cried.

"Aye, sir!" came the crisp response.

The *Stargazer* lit up the sea of gases with a pair of ruby-red phaser beams. But somehow, though the enemy didn't seem to make any effort to evade them, they missed.

Picard's teeth ground together. "Torpedoes!" he bellowed.

Again, "Aye, sir!"

Packets of matter and antimatter plunged through

swirling currents, hungry to feed on their prey. But they missed as well and were rapidly lost to sight.

The crew of the *Stargazer* paid for the miss with another round of bone-jarring torment. The deck beneath Picard's feet jerked and shivered once, twice, and again.

"Fire again!" he roared.

But nothing happened. And when he turned to Vigo, all he saw was an expression of helplessness.

"Phasers and photon torpedoes are off-line," the weapons officer reported numbly.

"Shields down seventy-five percent!" Gerda snarled.

Picard felt his teeth grate together. "Evasive maneuvers!"

Idun sent them swerving to starboard. Ever so narrowly, they avoided the pirate's next burst of fury. But without weapons, there was no possibility of their winning this battle.

"Was it a good year?" Ruhalter inquired of his companion.

"It was an *exquisite* year," said Maurice Picard. "The grapes were sweet, succulent . . . the best I have grown in a long time."

"That's good to hear. I always liked good wines."

"Ah," the vintner sighed, glancing at his son, "but it's not enough to have a promising grape. It's what one does with it that makes for success . . . or failure."

He had barely gotten the words out when the enemy found them again. The *Stargazer* lurched hard to starboard under the force of the worst assault yet.

Without warning, Idun's control console exploded in a geyser of flame and sparks and the helm officer went flying backward. Even before Picard got to her, he could tell that she was dead.

"That's what happened to me," Ruhalter said.

The elder Picard screwed up his face in grim sympathy. "It looks terribly painful."

"Only if you survive," Ruhalter noted. "In my case, death came quickly and mercifully." He stroked the side of his face that had been reduced to blackened ruin. "Good thing I remembered to shave that day. I wouldn't have wanted to make a lousy-looking corpse."

He chuckled at his own joke. And after a moment, Maurice Picard chuckled with him. The sound of their laughter provided a bizarre counterpoint to the hissing of plasma and the exclamations of the captain's bridge officers.

Not the least of which were Picard's own raw-throated shouts. "Commander Ben Zoma," he cried, "take the helm! Get us out of here!"

His friend darted to one of the aft consoles and worked like a demon to transfer helm control. In the meantime, the pirate dealt them one savage blow after another, inflicting hull breaches and casualties too numerous to report.

"I knew he wouldn't be any good at this," said Maurice Picard. The lines in his face had deepened with disapproval. "He should have stayed at home, as I advised him."

"Doesn't seem that he learned much from me either," Ruhalter remarked. "Pity, isn't it?"

"The helm!" Picard cried helplessly, perspiration collecting in the small of his back. "Damn it, Gilaad—"

Finally Ben Zoma yelled, "Got it!" and brought the *Stargazer* about. But it was too late. Picard could see that. As he watched, spellbound, the enemy fired at point-blank range.

The volley filled the viewscreen with crimson light, turning everything and everyone on the bridge blood-red. And when it hit, it seemed to plunge everything into darkness.

Some time later—a second, or was it an hour?—the captain realized that he was lying on the deck. Raising his head, he looked around, but there was nothing but sparks and black smoke and the silhouettes of what had been his officers' control consoles.

Then they came walking out of the darkness and the sizzling flashes of light. Not his bridge officers, but *they*—the two who had no business being there.

They came to stand over him, both of them. And they had the same look on their faces—a look of heartfelt *disappointment*.

"He should have listened," observed Maurice Picard.

Ruhalter nodded. "I'll say."

"He had so much promise."

"Tons of it. He could've been a great captain."

"A great *man*."

"It was too soon," Ruhalter observed, a spurt of sparks illuminating the nightmare side of his face. "He was too damned young."

The elder Picard's eyes filled with pain, just as they had the day his son left Labarre to attend the Academy. He nodded in agreement. "Too young indeed."

The captain wanted to answer, but he couldn't. The words stuck in his throat, choking him like thick, sooty smoke, forcing him to gasp for air, for life—

Then he realized that he wasn't on the bridge at all.

He was sitting up in his bed, breathing hard as if he had exerted himself, his skin covered with a sheen of sour sweat. It seemed to him that he could hear his room echoing as if he had cried out when he woke, though he couldn't retrieve any of the words.

If there had even *been* words.

A dream, Picard thought, reassuring himself. All of it, a dream. But it had seemed so real while he was dreaming it.

So hideously *real* . . .

Chapter Eleven

NORMALLY CARTER GREYHORSE MINDED his own business. But every so often—as in the case at hand—he was compelled by duty to diverge from that policy.

"I'm fine," Picard said once the doors to his ready room had closed, giving him and the doctor some privacy.

"You don't *look* fine," Greyhorse told him. "You look like you've had something big and insistent running through your brain. Something with heavy spiked boots."

"Am I that transparent, Doctor?"

"I've seen viewports that are less so."

The captain frowned. Then he walked over to his observation port and stared at it. "I didn't sleep well last night."

"Nightmares?" the doctor suggested.

Picard turned to look at him, an echo of pain and confusion in his eyes. "*A* nightmare. Just one."

"It must have been a good one."

The captain's chuckle had a distinct lack of merriment in it. "It was. We had found the White Wolf and engaged him in battle. But we didn't fare very well."

"We lost him?"

"We lost *everything*," Picard told him.

"And that's it?"

"That's it."

Greyhorse had a feeling there was more to it, but he didn't force the issue. He just said, "Obviously, you're concerned about how we'll do when we find the White Wolf—particularly since we're operating with a new captain, a new first officer, and a new second officer."

"And that's not cause for worry?" Picard asked.

The doctor shrugged. "I'm not qualified to answer that question. What I *am* qualified to tell you is that such dreams are perfectly normal for men with command-level responsibilities—even when they're *not* about to face some legendary pirate."

"That's comforting." The captain smiled a little sheepishly. "I appreciate your putting the matter in perspective."

"It's my job," the doctor said.

"Nonetheless," Picard insisted.

Greyhorse did his best to ignore the expression of gratitude. Emotions tended to make him uncomfortable, and gratitude was perhaps the worst in that regard.

"If you have any more trouble sleeping," he said, "let me know and I'll prescribe something. Outside of that, just try to relax. I don't need to tell you that your getting all worked up won't increase our chances of success."

Picard nodded. "I'll try to remember that."

As he left the room, Greyhorse wasn't sure that he had actually accomplished anything, or that the captain would sleep any more soundly from that point on. But at least he had made the attempt.

Juanita Valderrama was examining the sensor profile of an asteroid belt on the outskirts of a nearby solar system when Lieutenant Paxton appeared in her office.

"Got a minute?" he asked her.

Valderrama swiveled away from her monitor to face him. "Of course. Please . . . have a seat."

Paxton came in and allowed the door to close behind him. Then he sat down in the seat next to hers. If his expression was any indication, it wasn't anything trivial he wanted to talk about.

It was something rather serious.

"Listen," he said, "I don't normally tell tales out of school. But in this case, I think it would benefit everyone concerned."

Valderrama regarded him for a moment, wondering what he was talking about. Then she said, "Go on."

"Just a little while ago," Paxton told her, "I overheard Chief Simenon talking to someone. It doesn't matter whom, really. He was saying that he'd had a meeting with you in engineering."

The science officer nodded. "That's right."

"You were talking about the sensors?"

"Yes. Mr. Simenon told me that he had enhanced them with Beta Barritus in mind. I thanked him."

Paxton smiled benignly. "But unless I'm mistaken, you didn't encourage him to do any better."

Valderrama's brow creased above the bridge of her nose. "He's the chief engineer. I didn't think—"

She stopped herself in midsentence. Judging by Paxton's expression, he believed he had made his point.

"I didn't think," Valderrama sighed.

"You see what I'm getting at, right?"

The lieutenant nodded. "I should have pushed him to do better."

It's what she would have done when she was younger and new to the fleet. But over the years, she had somehow stopped caring so much. She had developed some bad habits.

Habits she was about to break.

This was Valderrama's last chance to prove she still had what it took. The captain had placed his faith in her. It was up to her not to let him down.

"Thanks," she told Paxton. "I appreciate your going out on a limb for me like this."

He shrugged. "You'll do the same for me one day. Just keep it under your hat, all right? Or no one will trust me when I tell them they've got a secure channel."

Valderrama smiled. "My lips are sealed."

And they would be.

Pug Joseph was lost in thought—so much so that his colleague seemed to appear out of nowhere.

This would likely have startled him even if his colleague *hadn't* been more than seven feet tall and as blue as the sky on a summer day. "Geez," Joseph blurted, recoiling in his seat, "did you have to sneak up on me like that?"

Vigo, the *Stargazer*'s senior weapons officer, favored him with a broad and well-meaning grin. "I *didn't* sneak up on you. At least, that wasn't my intention."

Joseph blew out a breath and looked around the

lounge. None of the dozen or so crewmen present seemed to have noticed his jumpiness. Or if they had, they weren't making it obvious to him.

He looked up at Vigo again. "Sorry. I was just thinking."

"Deeply," the Pandrilite observed. He sat down on the other side of a low-slung table, his knees coming almost to the level of Joseph's shoulders. "Any particular reason for it?"

The security chief shrugged and lowered his voice. "I was just thinking about the new guy. *Obal.*"

Vigo's brow wrinkled. "Obal?"

"The little guy. The Binderian."

"Ah," said Vigo. "That one."

"I don't think he's going to work out."

"I'm sorry to hear that."

"Not half as sorry as I am," Joseph told him.

"You like him?"

"Sure. He's as eager as they come. If he wasn't so . . ."

The weapons officer shrugged. "So *what?*"

"So *silly*-looking. Then maybe I'd be more optimistic about his chances. But he looks like—"

"I know," Vigo interjected, sparing his colleague the need to describe the Binderian's appearance. "I have seen him. He is not your typical security officer."

"That's an understatement. I mean, if Commander Ben Zoma were still in charge of the section, maybe he could do something with Obal. But me, I'm new at this."

The Pandrilite frowned. If anyone could sympathize with Joseph, it was he. They had both received their battlefield promotions a scant few weeks ago, when the *Stargazer*'s clash with a race called the Nuyyad had ripped several links from the chain of command.

Of course, the weapons section wasn't very big, and its lone vacancy had been filled by a crewman from another part of the ship. So even Vigo wasn't exactly in the same boat as Joseph.

"Listen," the weapons officer said, "Commander Ben Zoma has faith in you or he wouldn't have given you the job in the first place. You're as qualified as anyone to help Obal." Vigo paused for a moment. "That is, if he *can* be helped."

It was a big *if,* Joseph told himself. "You're not just saying that to make me feel better, right?"

"I'm saying it," Vigo insisted, "because I believe it. Whatever the task, you are equal to it."

Joseph felt a pang of gratitude. He nodded. "Thanks for the vote of confidence. But I've still got to earn it."

"And you will. Now if I were you, I would stop worrying and spend my free time doing something enjoyable—something like, say, a game of sharash'di."

Joseph looked at him askance. "Sharash'di? You mean that game Charlie Kochman got for you?"

"Yes. I could set up a board right now."

The security chief considered it for a moment, then dismissed the idea with a wave of his hand. "No, thanks. I don't think I could concentrate on a game right now."

Vigo seemed on the verge of arguing the point with him, then seemed to think better of it. "As you wish," he said. "But remember what I said—you will be equal to the task, whatever it is."

Then he moved off in the direction of Greyhorse, who had just entered the lounge. Idly, Joseph wondered what Vigo was so eager to talk to the doctor about.

Worry about that later, Joseph told himself. *Right now, you've got to figure out what to do with Obal.*

But what *could* he do? If he kicked the little guy out of security, he would be crushed. And he would know that it wasn't just his lone indiscretion that had done him in, because every officer in the section made a mistake from time to time.

Joseph thought long and hard. He considered the problem from every angle he could think of. But despite Vigo's words of encouragement, he still couldn't come up with an answer.

"Mr. Simenon?"

The Gnalish looked away from his sleek, black control console and saw Lieutenant Valderrama approaching him. He knew the look on the science officer's face, having seen it many times over the years since he came to Earth to attend Starfleet Academy.

She was about to ask a personal favor of him.

What's more, he was uniquely capable of granting it. As the ship's chief engineer, he could make a significant difference in the quality of people's lives.

What was it? Simenon wondered. Had the lieutenant's replicator gone on the blink? Or maybe her sonic shower? Had the automatic doors in her quarters gotten jammed?

Well, Valderrama would have to wait her turn in the repairs queue like everyone else. Her status as a fellow officer didn't get her any privileges in *his* book.

"Listen," Simenon said, "I'm busy right now. If—"

"This won't take long," the science officer assured him.

He scowled, swiveled on his chair and gave Valderrama his full attention. "All right," he said. "I'm listening."

And she said, "I'd like to ask a favor of you."

I knew it, Simenon thought, inwardly congratulating himself for his infallible insight into the nuances of human behavior. "And what favor is that?" he asked.

"I'd appreciate it," she said, "if you would take another stab at enhancing our sensor capabilities. I've gone over what you did and I think you can do better."

Simenon straightened. "Better?"

"That's right. A *lot* better. You're one of the most experienced engineers in the fleet, and our sensor capabilities are going to be a key to this mission. We need more from you."

"I see," the Gnalish said.

"I'm glad," Valderrama told him. She smiled. "Keep me informed, will you? I'll be in the science section if you need me."

And with that, she made her way back to the exit.

Simenon's ruby eyes narrowed as he watched the doors slide closed behind Valderrama. Obviously, someone had told the woman how he felt about their earlier conversation. Either that, or her change of heart was a colossal coincidence.

And he didn't take much stock in coincidence.

But Greyhorse was the only one with whom Simenon had discussed the matter, and the doctor wasn't the type to get involved in other people's business. He didn't believe in making what he called "uninvited appearances" in his patients' lives.

So who, then? Who had tipped Valderrama off? Someone who had overheard his conversation with the doctor. . . . Paxton, maybe? Or one of the nurses on duty at the time?

Not that I care, Simenon reflected.

In fact, he didn't give a tribble's furry hide under what circumstances Valderrama's attitude had changed, or who might possibly have been responsible. All that mattered was that her attitude *had* changed—and that the science officer would be pulling her own weight from that point on.

With that happy prospect in mind, the engineer pulled down on the lapels of his lab coat, swiveled his chair around and returned his attention to his control console.

Jean-Luc Picard roused himself from his reverie, vaguely aware that someone had spoken to him as he sat in his center seat. He turned to his right and found himself staring at Lieutenant Iulus, one of the senior men in his engineering section.

Iulus had a padd in his hand. He offered it to the captain. "Those maintenance reports you asked for?"

"Yes," said Picard, "of course." Accepting the padd, he made a point of glancing at the data contained on its screen and nodded to Iulus. "Thank you."

The engineer assured him that it was no trouble at all. Then he left the bridge, leaving the captain to wonder how long he had been adrift in his thoughts.

A minute? Several? He cursed himself softly.

He had been thinking about the White Wolf. About what sort of commander the man might be, what sort of tactical capabilities he might have at his disposal.

Picard doubted that the White Wolf's vessel would be quite as well armed as the one in his dream. But certainly the pirate had to have some tricks up his sleeve to have remained free as long as he had.

It was unfortunate that Starfleet had given him so little to go on. Just a few snippets of other ships' sensor data here and there, and more than half of it of questionable reliability.

The captain felt his hand clench into a fist. If only he knew one thing about his adversary for certain. If only the White Wolf were more than a ghost to him, haunting him, taunting and tantalizing him like a cosmic will-o'-the-wisp.

Picard sighed. He would go over the other captains' logs once again. Then he would go over their charts of Beta Barritus. Perhaps there was something he missed, something that might prove of value when he confronted the pirate.

And he *would* confront him. The captain still had every confidence of that taking place.

Turning to Gerda, he asked, "How many hours until we reach Beta Barritus, Lieutenant?"

His navigator consulted her monitors. "Eighteen, sir. Unless you'd like to increase speed to warp nine—?"

Picard shook his head. "That won't be necessary."

It wasn't the White Wolf's way to try to outrun his pursuers. Starfleet had established *that,* at least. The pirate would go to ground like a fox, and the Beta Barritus system was his favorite foxhole.

Besides, the captain didn't want to exhaust his vessel's resources by maintaining too high a rate of velocity for too long. That was why they were cruising at warp eight and no faster.

But he couldn't wait to reach Beta Barritus.

Chapter Twelve

ADMIRAL MCATEER WATCHED the Pacific sun disappear behind a blood-red frond as he negotiated one of the many cunningly shaded paths in the expansive garden behind Starfleet Academy.

The place had looked quite different when the admiral was a cadet. Stodgy, geometric, cut-and-dried. Each path had been nothing more than a way to get from one building to another.

Then he had left the Academy to serve on ships that crisscrossed the galaxy. His objective, at least in theory, was the study of stars and their attendant planets. But in reality, he had studied the men and women with whom he worked—their strengths, their failings, the reasons they did what they did. After all, his thinking had gone, if he was to become an effective leader he would need to become an expert on the people he would be leading.

And he *would* become a leader, McAteer had assured himself. Even then, he knew with grim certainty that he would rise through the ranks and guide Starfleet into a new era someday.

Finally, after many long years of dedication and achievement, after entire decades' worth of care and planning and artful maneuvering, McAteer got what he had always envisioned. He stood on a height from which he could look out and see the end of his fated journey.

He was back on Earth, the planet of his birth. He was a Starfleet admiral, with all the trimmings. And most important, he was in a position to make his ideas about the fleet a reality.

One of the first things he noticed on his return was the Academy garden and how much it had changed. It boasted exotic plants, shrubs, and trees from dozens of alien worlds—vegetation that added life and scale and color to the place, lining each path and hiding long stretches of it from its neighbors.

It was a refreshment, an intrigue, a delight. One could walk for half an hour and not even come close to being bored.

McAteer had heard that the man responsible was someone named Boothby. A landscape architect, he had guessed, a highly trained professional who had touched this expanse with his genius and moved on.

The admiral admired the fellow for what he had accomplished—and fancied himself a like spirit. After all, what he was trying to do with Starfleet was very much what Boothby had done with this garden.

He had uprooted the old and introduced the new. He had pruned away whatever was holding him back and planted that which served his purposes. And if he had been forced to sacrifice some of the trees and hedges that had served here long and faithfully, his ruthlessness had gained him what nostalgia never could.

Soon, McAteer reflected, his garden would be free of useless undergrowth like Admiral Mehdi and unwanted weeds like that upstart Picard. It would only contain what he wanted it to contain, what he had handpicked and placed there personally.

He smiled just thinking about it. Picard had no chance to catch the White Wolf. *None.* He would look inept, in-adequate—and even more so when the pirate was brought to justice.

And he *would* be brought to justice. The admiral had absolutely no doubt of it.

Noticing a stone bench just off the path, he availed himself of it. As McAteer sat, he found himself charmed by a most unusual scent—a mixture, it seemed to him, of butterscotch and vanilla. He traced it to a generous cascade of pale-blue blossoms that fell from a nearby branch almost to the ground.

He didn't know the tree's name. But the blossoms were so fragrant, so eminently pleasing, he longed to smell one close-up. Plucking a single, fat specimen from among its companions, he held it to his nose and inhaled deeply.

Yes, McAteer thought, savoring the scent. Butterscotch and vanilla. He crushed it between his fingers to get more of the smell out. And maybe a trace of cinnamon as well.

"And what do you think *you're* doing?" someone de-manded.

The admiral looked around and saw a figure moving

toward him, alternately drenched in sunlight and dipped in shadow. It was a man, much older than McAteer, judging by his thatch of white hair and the lines in his face. He wore black overalls and a pale-blue pullover, and there was a spray can in his hand.

"I beg your pardon?" the admiral said.

"I asked you what you thought you were doing," the man snapped, his watery blue eyes fierce and warlike. "But if that was too subtle for you, how about this— *keep your hands off the cotton-picking flowers.*"

McAteer felt a spurt of anger. No—he reserved anger for enemies of equal strength. What he felt was indignation.

"Listen, old-timer, maybe your eyesight's not what it used to be." He held up his sleeve and pointed to it. "But if you can see these bars, you ought to have some idea to whom you're speaking."

The groundskeeper—for that's obviously what he was—chuckled dryly beneath bushy eyebrows. "You're an admiral. Big deal."

McAteer felt the color drain from his face.

"I see guys like you come and go twenty times a day." The older man moved past McAteer and inspected the branch that had yielded the flower. "And the vast majority of them know better than to pick blossoms off my *darro* tree."

"I don't think you understand," the admiral told him, his tone clipped and imperious. But then, he wasn't going to take that kind of talk from a mere gardener. "I could have you fired for speaking to me that way." He snapped his fingers. "Like that."

The groundskeeper chortled as if McAteer had said

something very funny. "Great. I could use a vacation. Haven't had one in longer than I can remember."

The nerve of him, McAteer thought, his teeth grinding together. *The unmitigated gall.*

He hadn't become an admiral to have a—a civilian tell him where to get off. "I'll be happy to oblige you, old-timer. Just give me your name and I assure you, you'll have nothing more to do with this place."

The old man sprayed a cloud of water at the injured branch, tilted his head to one side to see something McAteer couldn't, then turned an amused expression on him.

"The name," he said, "is Boothby."

And he walked away.

The admiral stared at the old man, sputtering. Then, no longer feeling quite so appreciative of the Academy garden, he returned to his office by the straightest route possible.

Simenon was still wondering about Valderrama's change of heart when he received a visit from Commander Wu.

"Don't tell me," he snapped in a preemptory tone. "You've spoken to Lieutenant Valderrama and you think I can do a better job of enhancing our sensor capabilities."

The second officer looked confused for a second. But *only* for a second. Then she seemed to regain her composure.

"I trust you know what you're doing here," she said.

Simenon didn't know what Wu was talking about, but he couldn't resist making use of the straight line. "We had better hope so, hadn't we? Otherwise, the warp core may blow at any time now."

He chuckled at his little joke. Unfortunately for Wu, she didn't see fit to join him.

"I'm not here about engineering expertise, Mr. Simenon. I'm here about violating Starfleet regulations."

It was another straight line, even better than the first one. "You're too late," the Gnalish said, moving along a bank of monitors. "The mutiny was last mission."

Again, he chuckled at his own jest. And again, the second officer appeared to be unamused.

"I mean it, Chief," she said as she followed him. "You're in violation of the regs."

"Oh?" he said, wondering exactly where she was going with this. "And which reg am I violating?"

"The one that says engineers are prohibited from working a double shift unless there's at least a yellow alert in effect. I count six men and women who are here for their second consecutive shift—and that's not including *you*."

Simenon looked at Wu, and saw by her frown that she was serious. "You're not kidding," he said, "are you?"

"Not at all," she confirmed.

Now it was his turn to scowl. "Look, Commander, we're trying to get something accomplished here— something that may make the difference between finding that damned pirate and going home empty-handed. If my people aren't complaining about working overtime to make that happen, why should Starfleet?"

It was as if Wu hadn't heard a word he said. "To comply with the regulation," she told him, "you'll have to—"

Simenon held up a scaly hand. He didn't have time for this nonsense. "I won't have to do a *thing*, Commander. This is my section and I'll run it any way I see fit—and if you've got a problem with that, you can take it up with the captain and Commander Ben Zoma."

Wu looked shocked by his declaration. Then her features screwed up into an expression of determination and she said, "Thanks for the advice, Chief. I think I'll do just that."

And she stalked off, presumably to find Picard or Ben Zoma.

Not that Simenon cared the least bit either way. Putting the incident aside, he took a look at the next monitor in line and muttered, "All right then . . . just where were we?"

Ben Zoma was about to get in touch with Commander Wu when Wu got in touch with *him.*

"I've just been to engineering," she told him over the intercom system, her tone one of restrained indignation. "Did you know that Chief Simenon's people are working double shifts down there?"

"I wasn't aware of that," the first officer admitted. "But it's not unusual for them to do that."

"Even in the absence of a yellow alert?" Wu asked. "Against explicit Starfleet regulations?"

It took him a moment to recall the sense of the regulation. "I see what you mean," he said. "But to tell you the truth, Commander, we often put minor regulations aside when they interfere with the smooth operation of the ship."

There was a pause. "Sir, regulations are designed to *ensure* the smooth operation of the ship."

Ben Zoma frowned. "Where are you now, Commander?"

Another pause. "I'm on my way to sickbay."

The first officer could just imagine what havoc the woman was bent on wreaking *there*.

He calculated the time it would take Wu to reach her quarters. Then he told her to meet him there in five minutes and terminated the link.

"Have you ever done this before?" Lieutenant Pierzynski asked.

It took a moment for the being in the gray-and-white containment suit to respond. "No."

"It's not difficult," the security officer assured her.

The ghostly expression behind the faceplate didn't change. "Perhaps you could demonstrate for me," Ensign Jiterica said in a flat, metallic-sounding voice.

Pierzynski shrugged, trying to act natural despite the strangeness of his visitor. "Sure."

Hunkering down on one knee, he swung open the metal plate that had been sitting flush with the bulkhead and exposed a compartment hardly bigger than his hand. Then he tapped a couple of square, colored studs inside the compartment and looked across the brig to the nearest of its eight cells.

It didn't look any different as a result of his efforts. Not yet, at least. But it would.

Jiterica leaned over in her suit to get a better look inside the compartment. "You pressed the yellow button?" she asked. "And then the red one?"

"That's right," the security officer told her. "And in that order. Otherwise, the emitters won't respond."

"I see," she said.

Pierzynski had been asked by Lieutenant Joseph to

show Jiterica around the brig. It wasn't the first time Pierzynski had briefed a brand-new ensign, though it was the first time time he had done so for someone in a containment suit.

He had heard about Jiterica's problem in the shuttlebay. By then, probably everyone had heard. *Unfortunate,* he thought. But in a way, it had been for the best. Better to find out the ensign's limitations during a drill than in a real emergency.

Anyway, nothing like that would happen in the brig. Commander Ben Zoma had given Joseph his word that there wouldn't be any evac drills as long as Jiterica was stationed there.

Pierzynski got up and walked over to the cell whose generators had activated. There was a padd set into the bulkhead just to one side of it. Tapping in the requisite code, he saw a force barrier spring into being, stretching itself like a translucent veil across the cell's doorless entrance.

"And that's how it's done," he announced. "If you want to turn it off, you just do the same thing in reverse. Or if you want to change the polarity of the fields, all you have to do is—"

Before he could finish his sentence, he heard something—a shuffling sound. Not sure what it meant, he shot a glance over his shoulder and saw Jiterica leaning against the bulkhead.

She was doubled over as if in pain.

"Are you all right?" he asked.

"I—" she began, but couldn't get any further. "I—"

The security officer didn't know what to do for her. He didn't even know what had happened. He had never had any experience with someone like Jiterica.

Tapping his combadge, he barked, "Pierzynski to sickbay! Something's wrong with Ensign Jiterica!"

"Not—" the Nizhrak said, her voice strangely flat and emotionless for someone who was so obviously involved in a struggle. "I can—"

Pierzynski didn't know what Jiterica was trying to tell him, but it really didn't matter. She needed help, and unless he was mistaken, she needed it quickly.

"Hurry!" he shouted, urging on the medical team.

Chapter Thirteen

JITERICA WAS SITTING on a biobed and peering at Grey-horse through the transparent faceplate of her contain-ment suit. "Interference?" she repeated quizzically.

"That's right," said the doctor. He turned to Simenon, who had apparently assisted in the ensign's recovery. "Perhaps my colleague here would care to explain?"

The Gnalish shrugged his narrow shoulders. "It's simple, really. Your suit is laced with a containment field—something like the barriers we generate in the brig to keep prisoners incarcerated. In your suit, though, the field is engineered to a rather exacting standard. In the brig, there's no need for such precision, so the fields there tend to bleed a bit."

Jiterica was beginning to understand. "When Lieu-tenant Pierzynski activated the barrier, it bled beyond its visible parameters . . . and interacted with the field in my suit."

"With the result that your containment field went down," Simenon told her. "At least, until we could figure out what had happened and drag you away from the barrier."

"But while you were without the assistance of the field," Greyhorse noted, "it was left entirely up to you to maintain your molecular density and keep your suit from exploding. That must have been quite a burden on your physiology."

It was indeed, Jiterica reflected. Of course, she had contained herself for short periods of time before—when she beamed up to the *Stargazer,* for instance. But in this case, the lapse in her containment field had been unexpected.

"Had there been more insulation in your suit," said Greyhorse, "this might have been avoided. But as it was . . ." He frowned.

"Needless to say," Simenon assured her, "this sort of thing won't happen a second time."

The ensign didn't doubt that he was right. But there were so many *other* things that could happen . . .

"And," said the doctor, "you can leave sickbay whenever you feel rested enough. With your suit functioning again, there's no reason to keep you here."

Jiterica slid off the biobed less than gracefully. "Then I will be going. Thank you," she said, "both of you."

And she made her way out into the corridor, beset by more doubts and uncertainties than ever before.

Ben Zoma was already standing at the entrance to Wu's quarters when the second officer showed up.

"Commander," she said, looking more than a little leery.

Ben Zoma acknowledged her with a nod of his head. Then he waited while she tapped the metal plate set into the bulkhead, opening her quarters to them.

As he might have expected, the place was impeccably if minimally furnished and unutterably neat. Following Wu inside, he took a seat and waited for her to do the same.

"Well," said Wu, with admirable efficiency, "here we are. What is it you wanted to speak to me about, sir?"

Ben Zoma chose his words carefully. "I take it the captain of your previous ship was a precise observer of regulations?"

She nodded. "Of course. Captain Rudolfini was an excellent officer."

Obviously, Wu wasn't going to make it easy for him—not that he had expected her to. "At the risk of being considered a *bad* officer," he said, "I have to tell you that we do things differently here on the *Stargazer.* We don't always adhere strictly to regulations, especially when they bump heads with common sense."

The second officer didn't say anything. She just sat there and listened to him.

"And as far as I can tell," Ben Zoma continued, "we're not unusual in that respect. Most captains will overlook minor violations if they don't interfere with overall efficiency—especially when they're seen in the context of a difficult mission."

Wu just looked at him.

"Therefore," he told her, "I would appreciate it if you let up on Simenon and Idun and whoever else among your subordinates may have been guilty of a minor infraction. Of course, if you see something seriously wrong, don't hesitate to correct it. But it's got to be more than a failure to requalify or the odd double shift."

Ben Zoma expected an argument from his second officer. To his surprise, he didn't get one.

"I'll obey your orders," Wu told him evenly, "if that's what they are. But I would be remiss if I didn't tell you that I sincerely and wholeheartedly disagree with them."

He sighed. He had been right about Wu, it seemed—she was going to be trouble after all.

Jiterica dutifully moved her containment suit along the corridor in the direction of her quarters. However, the suit wasn't the heaviest burden she had to carry with her.

When Lieutenant Simenon mentioned the similarity between the field in the ensign's suit and the barriers employed in the brig, he had only meant that they drew on the same technology. But Jiterica had come to the conclusion that the similarity extended well beyond that.

After all, her containment field was a means of incarceration as well, in that it kept her from assuming the form nature had intended for her. And there were other prisons into which she had blithely and willingly placed herself.

The *Stargazer,* for instance, in that it carried her far from the milieu into which she had been born. And the vows she had made as a member of Starfleet, for they kept her from living a life in which she could find meaning.

To this point, she had managed to fool herself. Despite mounting evidence to the contrary, she had convinced herself that she might thrive in Starfleet—that she might even manage to become a viable officer someday. But her experiences on the *Stargazer* had finally put an end to that notion.

First, there was the embarrassment in the shuttlebay, where she had placed others in peril by virtue of her very existence. True, it was only theoretical peril, but the next time it might be real.

Then she had suffered an even greater embarrassment by nearly exploding her containment suit in the brig. As Simenon had indicated, the situation wasn't likely to come up a second time, but how many other venues on the ship would prove inimical to her survival?

What further humiliation would she have to endure before she accepted the inevitable—before she resigned herself to the grim reality of her prospects on the *Stargazer?*

Just as Jiterica thought this, she saw someone round the bend in the corridor ahead of her. It was a human, older than most on the ship—a female with a greater body mass than the statistical average, her hair worn loose about her shoulders.

Jiterica didn't remember meeting the woman. However, it was clear that she was a lieutenant, because there was a spool-shaped device pinned onto the right shoulder and left sleeve of her uniform. It was also clear that she worked in the science section, because those same devices were at least partly gray in color.

A full lieutenant in the science section, Jiterica thought. That would be Lieutenant Valderrama. The woman had beamed up to the ship with the group that came after the Nizhrak's.

As Valderrama approached her, Jiterica could make out the expression on the lieutenant's face. It began with curiosity, reconfigured itself almost immediately into a mask of restraint, then evolved gradually into the inevitable look of pity.

Finally, Valderrama nodded. Jiterica inclined her helmeted head in response. Then the lieutenant was past her—mercifully so—and the Nizhrak was alone in the corridor again.

Valderrama was right to pity her, Jiterica thought. All her fellow crewmen were right to do so. She was, despite her best efforts, a pitiful excuse for a Starfleet ensign.

But they wouldn't need to pity her much longer. In the morning she would tell the captain that she was quitting the fleet and ask to be returned to her homeworld.

Jiterica wouldn't find any relief in that meeting—neither then nor later. No doubt, she would regret what had happened here and on the *Manitou* for a very long time.

But in light of all her failures, a quick departure was the only reasonable option open to her.

In the short time that Nikolas had known Joe Caber, his opinion had changed a hundred percent.

Not his opinion of Caber—*that* hadn't changed one iota. Nikolas still saw his roommate as the perfect Starfleet ensign, well on his way to becoming the perfect Starfleet skipper.

What had changed was the way Nikolas saw *himself.*

When he walked into his quarters the day before, he had already resigned himself to his fate. He was going to be a loose cannon, a thorn in the side of his superiors the rest of his Starfleet career—however long it might be allowed to last.

Now Nikolas believed there might be a different fate in store for him, one that involved some success in his chosen profession. He could even see himself becoming an officer someday.

And why? Because of Joe Caber.

Because the guy had encouraged him to look beyond his limitations. Because he had shown Nikolas that they had more in common than the ensign might ever have believed.

He might never be Joe Caber, admiral's son. But if he tried, if he managed to put aside his resentments and his insecurities, he might become someone almost as good.

"Hey," said Caber, "you going to hang there all day?"

Nikolas smiled despite the increasing strain on his arms and shoulders and regripped the horizontal bar one hand at a time. "Just until I feel comfortable," he grunted.

"You sure you've done this before?" Caber gibed in a good-natured tone of voice.

In fact, Nikolas was hardly an expert on the horizontal bar. But he didn't want to admit that in front of his roommate—especially after he had boasted about his gymnastic skills all the way here.

"Just step back," he said, "and try not to gasp in awe."

Then Nikolas began swinging back and forth, all the while maintaining his hold on the chalk-covered titanium bar above him. Ignoring the pain it cost him, he swung higher and higher, until his hips were well above the bar on his backswing.

Finally, when he couldn't take it any longer, he drove forward one last time. At the apex of his swing, he let go of the bar and threw himself backward into a tightly tucked somersault.

That was the easy part, he told himself. The hard part would be sticking the landing.

As fast as the room was spinning around him, Nikolas had no real idea what he was doing. All he could do was take a stab at it and hope for the best. With that approach in mind, he released his grip at what seemed like the appropriate time.

And somehow, as if by magic, managed to land on his feet.

There was an almost overwhelming moment of vertigo, when Nikolas had the feeling that he was standing more or less upright but couldn't be certain of it. Then the dizziness passed, and he realized that he had stuck the landing.

Stuck it perfectly, in fact.

"Nice job," Caber told him.

Nikolas grinned. "All in a day's work."

Then it was his roommate's turn. He eyed the bar, rolled a bar of chalk between his hands and put it down beside the apparatus. Then he leaped up, grasped the bar, and kicked forward into a swing.

In no time, Caber was swinging as high as Nikolas had. Then higher. And he was doing it with only one hand, first the right and then the left, never both at the same time.

In a burst of energy, he swung completely around the bar, cutting a perfect circle through the air—once, twice, and a third time. Finally, without warning, he released the bar and tucked himself into a rapidly spinning somersault.

But it wasn't the single flip that Nikolas had done. It was a double, with a twist for good measure. And when Caber landed, it was with flawless grace and balance.

Nikolas whistled involuntarily. And here he thought he had impressed his roommate with his relatively rudimentary performance. The guy was amazing. Absolutely amazing.

"Nice job yourself," Nikolas told him.

But Caber didn't answer. He was staring over Nikolas's shoulder, his face frozen in an expression of disbelief. His curiosity piqued, Nikolas turned and saw what had caught his friend's attention.

It was the Binderian—the one who had beamed up to the *Stargazer* in Nikolas's group. The ensign hadn't seen him since, but he had heard that the guy was in security.

What was his name again? Obert? Obizz? *No,* Nikolas thought, remembering at last. *Obal.*

When he last saw the little guy, it was in the transporter room. They had beamed up together, along with the new science officer.

At the time, Nikolas had noted how strange-looking the Binderian was, how awkward he seemed in his Starfleet uniform. Almost comical, the ensign had thought at the time.

Now Obal was wearing Starfleet-issue black gym shorts a couple of sizes too long for him and a blue tank top that accentuated his bony shoulders and arms, and he looked even more ridiculous than he had in the transporter room.

As Nikolas watched, the Binderian went over to the weight area and picked up a couple of barbells—the lightest pair on hand, perhaps three kilograms apiece. With an effort, he brought them to shoulder height. Then, taking a deep breath between clenched teeth, he began to push them toward the ceiling.

With each push, Obal grunted. No—it was less a grunt than a wheeze, Nikolas decided. And to add to the effect, Obal's face, which was already a bright pink, turned a lush crimson.

Nikolas was sorely tempted to laugh out loud—it was that funny-looking. But he knew it would hurt the Binderian's feelings, so he managed to refrain.

Then he heard laughter after all. It seemed to fill the gym. And it came from Caber.

"Boy," he said, "that's got to be the most pitiful excuse for a body I've ever seen."

Nikolas looked at him. It wasn't like his roommate to be so critical, even in jest.

Obal, on the other hand, didn't seem to mind the remark. He just smiled as Caber was smiling and went back to his lifting.

"Come to think of it," Caber went on, "I'm not even sure that *is* a body. Bodies have muscles, don't they? I've baited *hooks* with physiques more muscular than that."

Still the Binderian seemed not to take offense. He continued his exercises without a hint of animosity, without the least sign that he was bothered by Caber's comments.

But Nikolas was bothered by them.

It wasn't that he thought Caber was trying to hurt Obal's feelings. Anyone who knew the admiral's son knew he wasn't capable of that. He was just playing around.

But the remarks still felt wrong to Nikolas. Unsporting somehow, like hunting flies with a phaser rifle.

"Hey," he said, meaning to distract his friend, "all this exercise is getting me hungry. What do you say we hit the mess hall and pump some fried chicken?"

But Caber didn't even look at him. He was still too enthralled by the sight of the Binderian.

"I wonder what he looked like *before* he started working out." Caber snickered. "Must've been hard to see him *at all.*"

"Or some ribs," said Nikolas, pushing upstream with his suggestion. "I sure could go for some nice barbecued ribs. You *are* the guy who's always hungry, right?"

It was then that Caber finally seemed to notice him. "Yeah," he replied after a moment. "Ribs. That sounds good to me too."

Nikolas indicated the doorway with a tilt of his head. "So what are we waiting for?"

Caber glanced at Obal as if he were going to shoot one more comment in the Binderian's direction. But in the end, all he did was grin and shake his head and lead the way across the gym.

Nikolas followed him, relieved that the incident was over. But before he and his roommate could reach the exit, Obal piped up.

"Have a pleasant day," he said, his voice high-pitched and tremulous and nearly as silly as his appearance.

Nikolas sighed. "You too."

But Caber didn't say anything in return. He just broke out into another wave of laughter, filling the corridor outside the gym with it as he and Nikolas made their way to their quarters.

Chapter Fourteen

PICARD HAD NEVER SEEN a Lazarus star in person. And he wasn't unusual in that respect, considering the scarcity of such stars within the bounds of Federation territory.

Nonetheless, he had studied the phenomenon long and hard since their departure from Starbase 32. He had memorized the sequence of events in the life of a Lazarus star—its unremarkable creation, its placid red-giant phase, the violent scattering of heavy elements and blinding luminosity that accompanied its seemingly suicidal supernova, and the almost miraculous birth of a new red giant in the midst of its predecessor's ample debris.

Every recorded image that Picard had seen of a Lazarus star showed it to be gauzy and colorless, the reborn sun at its heart all but occluded by the cast-off material floating around it. But as Picard watched Beta

Barritus loom on his forward viewscreen, he saw that it wasn't gauzy and colorless at all.

It was a thing of sheer, unmitigated beauty—and a remarkably savage beauty at that.

The star itself was the fiery red eye of a cosmic god, glowering menacingly at the universe around it. It swam in a glittering sea of nested gases, a mammoth iridescence that boasted strands of emerald and lapis and amber.

And in the midst of that iridescence, hidden by that glittering sea, was the freebooter called the White Wolf.

Nor was there any question that he was in there. Gerda Asmund had identified his ion trail—the same sort of trail that Picard's predecessors had discovered and recorded in their sensor logs—and there was no corresponding trail to indicate the pirate's departure.

He was in there, all right. And at long last, Picard had his chance to fish the fellow out.

"Kind of takes your breath away," Ben Zoma remarked.

The captain forgot the White Wolf for the moment and again fixed his attention on the spectacle before him. "It certainly does, Number One."

Of course, Beta Barritus's beauty didn't make it any less dangerous to them. Those ionized gases surrounding it had the potential to wreak havoc with their mission.

He turned to Idun. "Reduce speed to half impulse."

"Aye, sir," said his helm officer.

"Shields at full," Picard directed.

"Shields at full," Vigo confirmed.

Slowly but surely, the system filled the viewscreen with its splendor, blotting out all evidence of more distant stars. Its outermost filaments of color blurred as the

Stargazer came closer and finally pierced them, sending a chill up Picard's spine.

It's not the first time you've ever entered a solar system, he chastised himself. On the other hand, it was the first time he had entered *this* one.

"Lots of debris, sir," Gerda reported, "just as we were warned. The pieces are too small to see, but they're there."

Picard wasn't surprised any more than Gerda was. His predecessors' reports had all mentioned the system's debris shell—a by-product of the star's initial, explosive demise, which had destroyed whatever planets originally circled it.

"The friction is causing an increase in hull temperature," Idun noted. She glanced over her shoulder at Picard. "It's as if we're entering a Class-M atmosphere."

"See if you can find a less debris-ridden entry path," the captain told her.

Idun did as he asked. But Picard didn't hold out much hope of her finding such a path. After all, no other helm officer had found one, and plenty of them had looked.

He said as much to Ben Zoma.

"Maybe we'll be the first," his first officer told him.

"Maybe," Picard conceded.

But after half an hour, Idun still hadn't had any luck.

If the captain had wished, his helm officer would have pressed on until she dropped from exhaustion. She had been trained by her adopted family never to admit defeat.

But Picard had been brought up by members of a more practical species, and he didn't see any point in placing Idun under such stress. Besides, it wasn't as if they couldn't get through the debris field without a path of less resistance.

They could do what the White Wolf's other pursuers had done—reshape their shields to minimize the friction and plunge through the region as best they could. But the *Stargazer* would pay a price for that approach, just as all the other ships had paid a price. And in the end, it would keep them from completing their mission here.

Clearly, they needed a different strategy—one that would get them through the debris field in better shape than their predecessors. Until they had that strategy in hand, they would have to hover here on the fringes of the Beta Barritus system.

And the White Wolf would remain free.

Frowning, the captain turned to Ben Zoma and said, "Convene the senior staff, Gilaad. We've got work to do."

Admiral McAteer gazed at the mantel clock sitting on his desk, the syncopated movement of its polished brass workings visible through its thin glass walls.

McAteer loved the clock, a gift from his grandmother on the occasion of her passing. Well, not exactly a gift, he reflected. More of an inheritance, really. But he thought of it as a gift.

Truth to tell, he hadn't liked his grandmother very much, nor had she liked him. But that didn't keep him from loving the clock. It was a symbol to him of precision, of efficiency—the kind that he would instill in Starfleet little by little, until it was the Starfleet he had always had in mind.

The admiral smiled as he watched the brass gears turn in perfect coordination. Timing was everything, wasn't it?

Take his plan for Picard and the *Stargazer,* and by extension for Admiral Mehdi as well. Its success depended on everything happening just when it should.

First, he had given Picard his assignment in front of every other captain in the sector. Next, he had foisted those seven new crewmen on him, to distract him and increase the level of difficulty. Finally, with all eyes on Picard, McAteer would pull the rug out from under him.

Not that he had any choice, really. Starfleet really *did* have to get that cargo back. And even if Picard had a lifetime to recover it, he would never be equal to the task.

Contrary to what Mehdi seemed to believe, the man just wasn't captain material.

And when that became as painfully obvious to everyone else as it was to McAteer, Mehdi would be exposed as well. He would finally be seen for what he was—a man who had been in power much too long and had begun to make choices to the detriment of Starfleet.

As McAteer looked on appreciatively, the brass insides of his clock spun and whirled, oblivious to everything but the march of time. Leaning back in his overstuffed chair, the admiral tapped his combadge with a forefinger and said, "Mr. Merriweather?"

"Sir?" came the response from his assistant, whose office was in the alcove beyond.

"Send a message for me," McAteer told him. "Subspace frequency."

"To whom, sir?"

The admiral smiled again. "To Captain Jean-Luc Picard . . . on the *Stargazer.*"

Captain Picard scanned the faces of the six officers who had followed him into the *Stargazer*'s briefing room. Ben Zoma, Wu, Simenon, Valderrama, Idun Asmund, and her sister Gerda barely fit around the room's black oblong table.

The captain indicated the hologram of Beta Barritus that floated above a projector built into the center of the table. The star looked like a drop of molten fire, the vast system surrounding it a shimmering blanket of fog.

"As you're aware from your study of this system," Picard began, "the other starships that have tried to deal with the problem of the debris field have all fallen short of their goal."

"Because all they did was reshape their shields to minimize the friction," Ben Zoma offered.

"That's correct," Picard said. "Unfortunately, this approach placed a great deal of stress on their shield generators and gradually wore out their energy reserves."

Wu spelled it out for them. "Which in turn reduced their chances of continuing their efforts."

The captain nodded. "What we need is a different approach—one that allows us to penetrate the debris field *without* depleting our energy reserves." He looked around the table. "Ideas?"

For a moment, no one spoke. Then Simenon shrugged and took a stab at the problem.

"We could use our phasers to blast a path for ourselves," he offered. But the words were barely out of his mouth before he shook his head vigorously from side to side. "No, that won't work."

"Too large an energy expenditure," Ben Zoma observed.

"Yes," said Simenon. "And it would take a ridiculous amount of time to clear enough debris."

"What about a tractor beam?" asked Wu. "We could move the debris out of our way as we proceed. And it would require considerably less energy than a sustained phaser blast."

"True," said Ben Zoma. "But it would also limit our rate of speed." He turned to the chief engineer. "How fast can a tractor clear a path through that stuff?"

Simenon snorted. "Not very." His eyes slitting, he made some rough calculations in his head. "We could proceed at fifty kilometers an hour, maybe a little better than that."

"So, if the shell is a thousand kilometers deep," said Gerda, "and our data tells us that it's at least that, we're talking about as much as twenty hours."

"And during that time," Picard noted, "our sensors will be completely blind. So if the White Wolf were to exit the system, we would have no way of knowing it. He might be eighteen hours gone by the time we get through the debris field."

"Assuming," said Valderrama, "that he has a way of getting through it in better shape than those who have hunted him."

"An assumption we have to make," Idun remarked. "Otherwise, he would not have concealed himself here so often."

"So we have ruled out phasers and tractors," said the captain. "What other options do we have at our disposal?"

Again, there was silence around the table. And this time, no one spoke up to relieve it.

Picard frowned. "It's late. Perhaps if we sleep on the problem and get a jump on it in the—"

He never completed his sentence. The word *jump*

had sparked a notion in his brain—one that he was even now turning over and over, inspecting it from all angles.

And the more he inspected it, the better he liked it.

"Sir?" said Wu.

"I believe I have a solution," Picard told her. "But it's not without a certain amount of risk."

"How *much* risk?" asked Simenon.

Picard planted a hand on the briefing room table, leaned toward the hologram of the solar system and pointed to a spot within its gray outer ring. "What I'm proposing is that we execute a very quick, very short subspace jump—which will, if it is successful, place us well beyond the debris field."

Glances were exchanged, some of them understandably skeptical. In fact, had someone else come up with the idea, the captain might have been skeptical as well.

"It's risky, all right," said Simenon.

"If we miscalculate," Wu told him, "we could find ourselves in the star itself."

"Yes," said the Gnalish. "Or some other inconvenient place."

Picard turned to Gerda. "How dependable is our data on the dimensions of the debris field?"

She considered the question. "Our predecessors' logs seem to differ somewhat. But they entered the system at different points, and the field may be thicker in some places than in others."

"Only a few of them ever reached the inner limits of the field," Wu chimed in, "much less explored beyond that point. For all we know, there's another debris field only a bit further in."

"If that's so," said Valderrama, "it would cut down our margin for error considerably."

"Yes," Simenon agreed. "And there's also the system's gravity well to take into account. It wouldn't be easy to pull this off inside the boundaries of a normal system. With a Lazarus star . . ." His voice trailed off ominously.

Picard turned to Idun. "What do *you* think, Lieutenant?"

The helm officer frowned at the hologram as if she were sizing up an adversary. "As Mr. Simenon says, it will not be an easy feat. There is much we do not know about this system."

"But can we do it?" Picard pressed.

Idun responded as if to a challenge, her eyes steely with resolve. "I believe we can."

That weighed more heavily in the captain's estimate than anything else that had been said. After all, Idun was the one who would have to execute the maneuver.

He looked around the table. "Any other comments?"

No one offered any. Not even Simenon, who still seemed more wary of the idea than any of the others.

"Very well, then," Picard said. "We execute the maneuver in one hour. Let's see to it that there are no delays."

Everyone got up and filed out of the room. At least, that's what Picard thought. It was only as he reached to switch off the hologram projector that he noticed someone lingering by the door.

It was Wu.

"A question?" he suggested, leaving the projector untouched for the time being.

"No question," she said. "Just an observation. It is a

significant risk you're taking. I thought you were some-what more conservative in your approach to command."

The captain smiled a wry smile. "You've been read-ing my personnel file, I see."

"Commander Ben Zoma made it available to me. I felt it was my duty to read it."

And so it was, Picard told himself. Nonetheless, know-ing Wu had read his file made him feel vulnerable in her presence—much more so than he would have imagined.

"I will concede that I am deliberate sometimes, Com-mander—perhaps to a fault. And I will also concede that I have the utmost respect for the obstacles placed in front of me. But make no mistake—I will not shy away from them."

Wu looked thoughtful. "I'll remember that."

Then she left him as well.

Picard looked back at the hologram of Beta Barritus. There was only one thing missing from the three-dimen-sional representation—the White Wolf that lay at the heart of the solar system, daring the captain to find him.

The muscles in his jaw rippled at the thought. *One step at a time,* he counseled himself. *That is the way to catch a White Wolf—one small step at a time.*

Then he reached across the briefing room table, switched off the little hologram projector, and returned to what would undoubtedly be a very busy bridge.

The man called the White Wolf sat in the captain's chair of his ship and drummed his fingers on his armrest.

"What is it?" asked Turgis, his Klingon second-in-command, who had come to stand beside him in the lurid red light of their bridge.

The White Wolf glanced at him, as slyly narrow-eyed as his namesake. "What do you *think* it is?"

His second-in-command's expression turned into one of disgust. "Starfleet," he spat.

The White Wolf nodded, a grim smile pulling his lips back from his teeth. "They're after me."

"You've picked them up on sensors?"

"Not yet. But I don't need sensors to tell me when someone's hot on my trail." His nostrils flared. "I can feel them stalking me, Turgis. I can feel the fire in their blood."

"You're the White Wolf," the Klingon reminded him. "Any Starfleet captain would give his soul to bring you in."

"No doubt."

"But none of them ever will. Whoever's come hunting us will go home empty-handed."

"Like all the others."

"And there have been many of them."

The White Wolf grunted softly. "You make it sound as if the outcome has already been determined."

Turgis grinned, exposing knife-sharp teeth. "Hasn't it?"

And they laughed, the bridge of their ship ringing loudly with the sound of their defiance.

Chapter Fifteen

IT SEEMED LIKE JUST A FEW YEARS AGO that Picard's mother had warned him about looking directly at the sun. Now, it seemed, he did nothing *but* look at suns.

Of course, the one that burned on his viewscreen at the moment wasn't any ordinary dynamo of nuclear fusion. It was one that would test the mettle of Picard's ship, Picard's crew . . .

And, of course, Picard himself.

The hour that he had given his command staff was about to elapse. Everyone was in place, every piece of equipment checked and rechecked. All he had to do was set things in motion.

But before Picard could open his mouth to do that, he heard someone say, "Captain?"

He turned to Ulelo, who was at the comm console. "Yes?"

"I have a message, sir. It's from Admiral McAteer."

From McAteer? "On screen," Picard said, and leaned back in his chair to see what the man wanted.

A moment later, the admiral's image stretched itself across the forward viewscreen. When he spoke, his tone was as unctuous as ever. "Greetings, Captain. I trust all is going well."

Picard didn't reply. It was just a message. At this distance from Starbase 32, two-way communication simply wasn't a viable option.

"I'll get right to the point," McAteer promised. "After dicussing the matter with Doctor Ibwasa of Starfleet Medical, I've been convinced that the cargo stolen by the White Wolf deserves a higher priority than I first assigned it."

"I don't like the sound of this," said Ben Zoma, who was standing alongside the captain.

"Nor do I," Picard agreed.

"Due to the increased urgency of your mission," said McAteer, "I've sent out three other captains and their crews to assist you."

But Picard hadn't heard the word "other." To him, it sounded as if the admiral had said "real." *I've sent out three* real *captains and their crews to assist you.*

Clearly, McAteer had decided that the *Stargazer* couldn't handle this assignment anymore. The conclusion left a bad taste in Picard's mouth.

A bad taste indeed.

"Help is on its way, Jean-Luc. In the meantime," said the admiral, "do your best. McAteer out."

And his image vanished from the viewscreen, giving way to the glory of Beta Barritus.

"Do your best," Ben Zoma echoed mockingly, just loud enough for his friend to hear him.

Picard scowled. "We'll do more than our best, Gilaad. We'll snare the White Wolf—and we'll do it *without* anyone's help."

His first officer glanced at him, a spreading smile on his face. "Now you're talking."

The captain took in his bridge crew with a glance. Everyone seemed intent on his or her console, unperturbed—at least on the surface—by the delicate nature of what they were about to attempt.

Satisfied, Picard turned to his helm officer. "Ready, Lieutenant?"

"Aye, sir," came Idun's reply.

The helm officer didn't have much to do anymore. Her real work, and painstaking work it had been, was already done.

Idun had programmed the warp engines to accomplish a feat no flesh-and-blood helm officer could hope to duplicate. They were to operate for precisely 0.0035 seconds—not enough time to breathe or swallow or even blink, but ample time for a vessel proceeding at warp one to clear an obstacle a thousand kilometers deep.

Picard could feel the muscles clench in his jaw. Even the slightest miscalculation could mean their doom. But he trusted Idun not to have made that miscalculation.

Ignoring the trickle of cold sweat making its way down his spine to the small of his back, he turned to the viewscreen again and pointed to the spectacle of Beta Barritus. Then he spoke a single word, eloquent in its simplicity: "Engage."

It was more than a command. It was a gesture of defiance, an announcement to himself, his crew, and the universe in general that he would accomplish his mission or die trying.

Because that was what Starfleet captains did, he reflected—the best of them, anyway. They did whatever it took to achieve their goals. They found a way.

And he would do the same.

At the helm controls, Idun tapped a single blue stud, and the *Stargazer* shot forward at the speed of light, her quartet of nacelles wildly spilling light as they carved a path through the mysterious realm known as subspace.

And then, with chilling suddenness, it was over. The warp engines were cycling down, their labors complete.

Picard released a breath he hadn't known he was holding. He felt his heart pumping blood through his body, just as it had done before he gave Idun the order to go to warp. He saw the bridge and his officers, all whole and uncompromised.

But where are we? he wondered. Where they had hoped to be, or somewhere else?

The viewscreen showed the captain the baleful eye of Beta Barritus, surrounded by a soft, pearlescent glow with bright, sharply defined tendrils of color pinwheeling through it. But it didn't tell him a thing he wanted to know.

"Report," he said, leaning forward in his chair, his voice echoing throughout the bridge.

There was a pause that seemed to stretch on forever. Finally, Gerda responded to his exhortation. "We made it, sir. We're on the other side of the debris field, approximately eleven hundred kilometers closer to Beta Barritus."

A cheer went up on the bridge among the officers at

the aft stations. Picard didn't take part in it, but by the same token he didn't feel the least bit inclined to rebuke those who did.

Even Ben Zoma was grinning from ear to ear. Glancing at the captain, he nodded his approval.

Picard nodded back. So far so good, he thought. "Scan for the White Wolf," he told Gerda.

"Aye, sir."

They weren't able to look very far. As they had been warned, the proliferation of gases and ion activity in the system made it impossible for their sensors to operate according to specs. But thanks to Simenon's enhancements, they were able to search a wider area than the ships that had come before them.

Not that it availed them anything. There was no sign whatsoever of the pirate. Of course, he hadn't gone unchecked and unfettered for so long by making it easy for his pursuers to find him.

"Chart a course based on his ion trail," Picard said. "Then we will proceed at one-half impulse."

"Aye Captain," Gerda told him, and set to work.

"One-half impulse," Idun acknowledged.

The captain settled back into his center seat. *At last,* he thought, *the chase is on.*

Gerda Asmund frowned as she studied her navigation console. She didn't like what she saw.

"It's getting worse," said her sister Idun, who was sitting next to her at the helm controls.

Gerda nodded. "So it would seem."

In fact, it had been getting worse for the last half hour, but now it was getting worse more quickly.

Not that it came as a surprise to Gerda. The reports they had read, filed by the captains who had approached Beta Barritus before them, clearly indicated that the sensor situation would deteriorate—that once they got past the debris field, the conditions inside the system would gradually make data gathering more difficult.

Of course, there was no way of knowing *how* difficult, because none of those captains had penetrated as far into the system as they would have liked.

Gerda had thought of suggesting the use of instrumented probes to expand their sensor horizon, but that would have been a bad idea from a tactical standpoint. Though such probes might help them locate the White Wolf, they might also alert the White Wolf to their presence here.

And they didn't want the pirate to know they were after him until it was too late.

"What is it?" asked Commander Ben Zoma, who had assumed the center seat in the captain's absence.

"Sensor range is decreasing," Idun told him.

The first officer nodded. Then he looked up at the intercom grid in the ceiling. "Ben Zoma to Mr. Simenon . . ."

Ben Zoma listened to the end of his chief engineer's long and impassioned speech. Then he said, "So what you're telling me is you can't do any better."

"What I'm telling you," Simenon rejoined impatiently, "is it's not *possible* to do any better. Our sensors are better tuned than any sensors in the history of Starfleet. They're operating at absolute peak efficiency. No—*above* peak efficiency."

"I see," said Ben Zoma.

"There is no way in the universe that I or anyone else could improve on their performance."

The first officer nodded. "So you've indicated."

Simenon's eyes narrowed. "Then why," he asked, "do you have that look on your face?"

"I have a look?" Ben Zoma asked.

"You certainly do. If I didn't know better, I'd guess you were going to ask me to enhance the sensors even more—even after I've *told* you that it can't be done."

"You know me that well, do you?"

Simenon scowled. "I'm afraid I do."

"And—just hypothetically—what if I *did* ask you to enhance the sensors, however unreasonably?"

The engineer's nostrils flared, an indication that he was growing increasingly annoyed. "Why bother to speculate? Having heard me say it can't be done, you would never ask."

"Yes," said Ben Zoma. "Of course. But . . . if I *did?*"

Simenon glowered at him, then took a deep breath and said, "I'll see what I can do."

The first officer watched him return to where some of the other engineers were standing and apprise them of their latest assignment. To their credit, they didn't grumble. They just got to work, no matter how daunting their objective.

And Ben Zoma went to tell his friend Picard that they had a problem—even if Simenon *did* manage to do the impossible and squeeze a little more out of the sensors.

* * *

"I see," said Picard, leaning back into the chair behind the desk in his ready room. "And what do you recommend?"

Ben Zoma, who was seated on the other side of the black plastic desk, frowned and shook his head. "Simenon has probably done all he can. If we're going to make any strides from here on, they'll have to come from the science section."

"From Lieutenant Valderrama?" Picard asked.

"That's right."

It wasn't normally the responsibility of the science section to work on engineering issues. However, the captain could appreciate his first officer's logic.

If they had come as far as they could with what they had—and it seemed that they had—they needed a new approach to the problem. They had to devise a way of "seeing" that transcended EM flux scans, neutrino imaging, and graviton spectrometry.

The ship's science personnel would have the greatest understanding of this environment. If anyone could devise a new strategy for obtaining information under the conditions imposed by Beta Barritus, it would be the people serving under Valderrama.

Part of Picard couldn't help wishing Cariello were still with them—that she were still available to solve problems like these. He knew what Cariello could accomplish, but Valderrama was still a question mark in his mind.

Unfortunately, Cariello was no longer an option. Now it was Valderrama's turn to show what she could do to justify the faith Picard had shown in her. With luck and encouragement, perhaps she would come up with what they needed.

"Speak to Lieutenant Valderrama," the captain told Ben Zoma. "Let her know what we require of her."

"Will do," his friend assured him. However, he didn't leave to carry out the order.

"What is it?" Picard asked.

"If we're going to ask something this important of Valderrama, we should provide her with all the help we can."

The captain nodded. "Agreed. Tell Valderrama that she can have as many bodies as she needs. She has my approval in advance."

"Immediately," said the first officer. Then he got up and headed for the exit.

Suddenly Picard got an idea—a way to kill two birds with one stone, so to speak.

"Number One?" he called.

Ben Zoma stopped and looked back at him. "Sir?"

"Let's include Ensign Jiterica among the crewmen assigned to the science section."

Picard didn't see the Nizhrak catching on in a demanding environment like weapons or engineering— not when she had had so many difficulties in less problematic environments. Perhaps she would have an easier time of it under Valderrama.

"Will do," Ben Zoma told him, and left the captain's ready room the way he had entered it.

Jiterica moved her containment suit in the direction of the double doors at the end of the corridor. As the doors slid apart for her, they revealed a hallway beyond.

There were three people standing in it. Only one of them looked the least bit familiar to Jiterica. That was

Lieutenant Valderrama, whom she had seen in the corridor near sickbay the day before.

As the lieutenant caught sight of the Nizhrak, she gave her companions some additional instructions—enough to send them on their way. Then she met Jiterica halfway.

"Ensign," she said in a warm, welcoming voice. "I was just informed that you'd be joining us."

Jiterica didn't know what to say to that. In the end, her response was simply, "Yes."

"We can use all the help we can get," Valderrama told her. She gestured for the ensign to follow her. "Come on. We'll find you a workstation and get you started."

"All right," said Jiterica in her tinny, artificial voice.

But she was far from optimistic that she would be of any use to Valderrama or anyone else on the ship. She also doubted that this latest assignment would change anything.

She simply didn't fit in here. Clearly, she would have to remain onboard for the duration of this mission. But the sooner she left, the better it would be for everyone concerned.

Nikolas looked around the hexagon-shaped space in which he found himself. It had pretty much the same dimensions as the main security facility through which he had passed a moment earlier, though it was equipped completely differently.

Wherever bulkhead met deck there was a sleek, dark computer terminal, its monitor alive with one graphic or another. The ensign counted twenty-four of the terminals in all, though none of them was anywhere near as elaborate as the multiscreen console in the other room.

"As you know," said Lieutenant Joseph, drawing the attention of Nikolas and the other dozen crewmen collected there, "we're hunting someone called the White Wolf. Unfortunately, we need meaningful sensor information to do that, and it's getting tougher for us to get that information the closer we get to Beta Barritus. Both the science and engineering sections are working on the problem now. But in the meantime, the captain wants more eyeballs on our incoming sensor data—so we don't miss any leads that *do* materialize."

"Which is where *we* come in," speculated Joe Caber, who was standing beside Nikolas.

"Exactly," Joseph confirmed. "You're our eyeballs. You'll be scanning from the time you get here to the time you leave—or the time you drop, whichever comes first."

It's a tedious job, Nikolas reflected archly, *but someone's got to do it.*

"Any questions at this point?" asked the security chief.

Naturally, Caber had one. "Exactly what kind of data are we looking for, sir?"

"I'd say an ion trail," Joseph told him, "but the odds of finding something like that are decreasing as we speak. Check for thermal hot spots, EM surges, unusual particle concentrations . . . anything that looks the least bit suspicious. And don't be afraid to waste the time of whoever's in charge of your shift. You never know what kind of reading might prove useful to us."

Caber nodded. "Thank you, sir."

"Find that pirate," said Joseph, "and I'll be thanking *you*, Ensign. In fact, we'll *all* be thanking you."

That inspired a chuckle from the assembled crewmen.

"To whom will we be reporting?" asked a woman

with curly, dark hair. The markings on her uniform identified her as a med tech.

The security chief seemed to hesitate, as if the question involved something more than a simple answer. Then he said, "He'll be arriving at any moment. His name—"

As if on cue, someone made his way into the hexagonal enclosure. Someone short and awkward looking in his crimson tunic, whose walk strongly reminded Nikolas of a duck's waddle.

The ensign bit his lip to keep from uttering an expletive. The crewman in charge of this shift—

"—is *Obal*," Joseph finished.

Nikolas saw a grin spread over his friend Caber's face. *Perfect,* he thought. *Just perfect.*

Chapter Sixteen

NIKOLAS TAPPED OUT A COMMAND on his keyboard and called up another graphic. This one was supposed to show him neutrino concentrations at a distance of a thousand kilometers or less, each concentration represented in red on a black background.

As it was, all the ensign saw was the black background. No red, no neutrinos. Or rather, they were there, but the sensors weren't strong enough to identify them that deep into the system.

And it was getting worse, Nikolas told himself.

Every few minutes, sensor range dropped in one key area or another. If they didn't come up with something soon, the *Stargazer* would be rendered blind—unable to "see" anything at all in this mess of ionized gases and subtle radiation fields—and therefore incapable of navigating. Then the captain would have no choice but to call off the hunt.

Nikolas had barely heard of the White Wolf before he embarked on this mission. But that didn't keep him from wanting to find the guy, and not just because he had stolen something valuable from the Federation, something that could help people.

It was the challenge—the idea of doing what no one before them had ever done. Back on the handball courts of Canarsie, Nikolas had itched to take on the legendary Red O'Reilly. Now he was itching to take on the White Wolf.

Which was why Picard and his people had to come up with a new sensor arrangement—and why Nikolas would try like hell to keep them in the running in the meantime.

"Look at him," said Caber, who was sitting at the next console.

Nikolas looked up from his monitor, still lost in the data he had been scanning. "Look at who?"

Caber was staring across the room. "Who do you think?"

Nikolas followed his friend's gaze. He found himself looking at Obal, who had raised himself onto his tiptoes to peer at a monitor over an ensign's shoulder.

"I can't believe they've got him overseeing us," Caber said, his voice tinged with irony.

"Believe it," Nikolas told him, pulling up another sensor graphic on his monitor.

"This is the most ridiculous thing I've ever seen. It's like taking orders from some kind of pest."

"He's still your superior," Nikolas reminded him. "You might want to remember that."

Silence for a moment. Then Caber said, "Watch this."

By the time Nikolas looked up again, his roommmate was walking across the room, headed right for Obal. *Oh man,* the ensign thought, sensing something bad in the offing.

Caber stopped when he got to the Binderian, over whom he towered the way an adult might tower over an eight-year-old. "Lieutenant?"

Obal turned and looked up at him. "Yes?"

What's he up to? Nikolas wondered.

"Sorry to bother you, sir," said Caber, "but I could use some help here." He jerked a thumb over his shoulder. "I'm not sure exactly what I'm looking at."

Obal glanced at Caber's console, then turned back to Caber himself. "We will take a look," he said agreeably.

They crossed the room together and Caber sat down in front of the screen. Unfortunately, he blocked the Binderian's view in the process, so Obal moved to the other side to see around him.

"You see what I mean?" Caber asked.

As he posed the question, he moved his chair around to the other part of the screen, again blocking Obal's view. Obal frowned, obviously a little frustrated, and moved back to his original position.

But by then, Caber had moved as well. "Sir?" he said, sounding completely innocent of any wrongdoing. "You *do* see what I'm talking about, don't you?"

Nikolas heard a sound and looked around the room. Some of his colleagues were watching Caber's antics and trying their best not to laugh at them.

"Sir?" Caber said again, provoking a snicker. He glanced back at Obal. "Can you help me, sir?"

It was only then that the Binderian got an inkling

of what was going on. Looking up at the big man, he said, "This is not appropriate behavior for Starfleet personnel."

Caber turned to Obal and assumed a serious expression. "I'm not sure I know what you mean, sir."

The Binderian regarded him for a moment. Surely, thought Nikolas, he's going to issue Caber a reprimand. Under the circumstances, it's the only thing he *can* do.

But Obal didn't do it. He didn't do *anything*. He just turned from his tormentor and walked away, leaving Caber unpunished and free to repeat his antics.

Nikolas sighed.

"Hey, Nik," Caber rasped at him. He was grinning his perfect, white grin. "Did you see the look on his face? If that wasn't priceless, I don't know what is."

Nikolas frowned as he watched the Binderian sit down at his monitor and return to his work. "Yeah," the ensign said with an empty feeling in his gut. "Priceless."

Pug Joseph stood behind one of his colleagues in the main security area and considered the big, concave monitor bank.

In actuality, Joseph was only concerned with a single screen at the moment. It was the one that showed him the other hexagonal room in security, where Obal was presiding over the dozen men and women assigned to special sensor duty.

The Binderian had seemed like the perfect individual for the job. After all, he had already demonstrated a knack for detail, he could hardly manage to fall asleep in the company of so many other crewmen, and—just as important—he would free up a security officer better suited to actual security work.

On the other hand, this was an important duty, one requested by the captain himself. Joseph didn't feel so confident in Obal that he was willing to let him operate without a little scrutiny.

The security chief had been reminded of a saying he had read back in high school in Colorado, when his class was studying Aristotle: *Who watches the watchers?*

In this case, he thought, I *do.*

And it was a good thing. Though the monitor allowed him only to see and not hear what was going on, he had witnessed enough of Obal's encounter with Ensign Caber to understand the gist of it.

The ensign had ridiculed Obal, and the Binderian's response had been no response at all. He had simply let it go.

Not good, Joseph thought. *Not good at all.* He hadn't been in charge of the security section for long, but even *he* knew that an officer couldn't let a subordinate get the best of him. It was the quickest way to lose control of a section.

He was tempted, as he turned away from the monitor bank, to relieve Obal of his assignment and put someone else in charge. But he didn't do it. Part of him wanted to give Obal a chance to redeem himself.

Even though the other part was sure he wouldn't.

Nikolas was about to tell his friend Caber that he didn't like watching Obal be ridiculed, that he wished like hell that Caber wouldn't do it anymore. But before he could get the words out, he caught a glimpse of what was on his screen.

Nikolas wasn't exactly an expert at interpreting sensor data, but what he saw looked like trouble—the kind he didn't think he ought to mull over for very long. He was about to call Obal over when he realized what it would look like—a replay of Caber's antics, which was the last thing the ensign had in mind.

Getting up from his seat, Nikolas crossed the room and leaned over beside the Binderian. Obal looked up at him and said, "Yes?" every bit as pleasantly as he had responded to Caber.

Nikolas jerked a thumb over his shoulder, indicating his monitor. "I think there's something here you ought to see."

Picard felt his jaw clench as he considered the rectangular viewscreen in front of him.

It showed him and his bridge officers what Ensign Nikolas had noted mere minutes earlier on his computer monitor—an army of vicious, twisterlike formations, each one appearing as an elongated diamond shape in a hue ranging from silver to dusky bronze. They looked as deadly as any phenomena Picard had ever seen.

"The vortices," Ben Zoma said.

The captain nodded grimly. "Yes." Their predecessors—that is, the three who had managed to venture this far—had described this obstacle in some detail.

Seeing no way around the twisters, they had attempted to negotiate a slow and careful path among them. Two of them, the captains of the *Mongoose* and the *Leningrad*, ended up turning back when the going got too rough. The third, the captain of the *Christopher*, had refused to give up until she lost a warp nacelle and no longer had a choice in the matter.

Ben Zoma frowned at the viewscreen. "Too bad we can't use your warp trick here."

"Because we don't know how far this region may extend," Picard elaborated.

"And," added Ben Zoma, "because the vortices are magnetic in nature. They'd wreak havoc with a subspace field. And then there's the problem of going to warp this close to a sun."

"Point taken," said Picard.

Ben Zoma looked at him. "Convene the command staff?"

The captain smiled, though he was hardly amused. "You must have read my mind, Number One."

Chapter Seventeen

AGAIN PICARD FOUND himself at the head of the long black table in the *Stargazer*'s briefing room, regarding six attentive officers.

"You are all aware of the problem, I trust."

Ben Zoma, Wu, Simenon, Valderrama, and the Asmund twins responded with nods and murmurs of confirmation.

The captain turned to the hologram hovering over the center of the table. It was different from the one he had called for last time in that the debris field and the outer precincts of the solar system had been stripped away, leaving the system's core and the vortex belt clearly visible.

"As you've learned in your readings," he said, "these magnetic vortices are what stopped the most enterprising of our colleagues. But they will not stop us. The question is: How can we get past them and continue to pursue our mission?"

Ben Zoma iterated his remark that a warp-speed jump was not an option. Then he called for suggestions.

Valderrama was the first to speak. "Magnetic forces of that intensity are going to tear up any shield they touch."

"But there's no way for us to avoid them," Wu noted.

"They're insubstantial," Gerda observed, "so we can neither punch a hole in them with weapons fire nor clear a path through them with a tractor beam."

"What about a competing force?" Idun asked.

Picard leaned forward. "What do you mean?"

"A magnetic emission of some kind," the helm officer expanded. "Something that will fight the vortices and reduce the threat they pose to our shields."

The captain looked around the table. Like him, everyone seemed intrigued by the nature of Idun's suggestion. However, no one seemed able to translate it into a workable strategy.

"It's beyond us," Ben Zoma said finally.

Picard nodded. "Let's move on."

That's when he saw the expression on his chief engineer's face. It was a surly look, a look of discontent.

The captain had seen it before. It meant Simenon was thinking about something. Thinking *hard*.

"Mr. Simenon?" he said.

The Gnalish turned to him and his ruby eyes blinked. But he didn't offer any other response.

"Mr. Sim—" Wu began.

But Ben Zoma stopped her by putting his hand on her arm. He too knew better than to interrupt Simenon when he was cogitating.

Finally, the engineer's eyes became animated again,

an indication that he was finished thinking. "I've got an idea," he rasped.

Picard frowned. "And . . . ?"

Simenon frowned back at him. "What if we were to change the polarity of our shields?"

For a moment, the idea hung in the air like a second hologram, inviting everyone's scrutiny. Then the group's reactions began to manifest themselves.

"Can you *do* that?" asked Ben Zoma.

Simenon nodded. "I think so."

"If you can," said Valderrama, "it should make the shields a lot less vulnerable to the action of the vortices."

Picard hadn't trained as an engineer. However, he had a rudimentary understanding of the principles involved, and Simenon's suggestion seemed to make sense.

"Even if Mr. Simenon's approach works," said Wu, "it will still be a dangerous passage."

"Yes," Ben Zoma agreed. "But not *as* dangerous."

"I would like to see a computer model," he said.

"No problem," the engineer assured him. "I can whip one up as soon as I get back to engineering."

Taking that as his cue, the captain nodded. "By all means, Mr. Simenon." He took in his assembled officers at a glance. "You're dismissed, all of you."

He looked forward to seeing what the Gnalish came up with. If luck was still on their side, Simenon's strategy would keep alive their hope of finding the White Wolf.

If not . . .

Picard caught himself. *There is no alternative,* he reflected. At least, not one he could live with.

* * *

Greyhorse was deep in reverie when he heard the captain's voice over the intercom system.

"What is it, sir?" he asked Picard.

"I've gone over Mr. Simenon's computer models and approved his plan for getting us through the vortex belt. Mind you, I believe we will come through with minimal damage. However, I want you to be on medical alert—just in case."

Greyhorse nodded even though he knew the captain couldn't see him. "Acknowledged, sir."

"Picard out."

The doctor's first thought was always the same: *Gerda*. Would she be endangered by what Simenon had proposed? Would he see her carried into sickbay on a gurney, her body broken and bleeding?

As he had on other occasions, Greyhorse forcibly put the unwelcome image from his mind. It was his duty as a physician and as a Starfleet officer to provide medical care for *everyone* on the ship, not just a single individual.

No matter *how* he felt about her.

As Picard emerged from the turbolift, he saw everyone on the bridge glance in his direction. His officers looked as determined as he was—an encouraging sign, to be sure.

"Mr. Simenon," he said, "this is the captain."

The engineer's voice flooded the bridge with its sibilance. "Simenon here. Time to give it a go?"

As Picard approached his center seat, his first officer abdicated it and exchanged glances with him. Ben Zoma's eyes crinkled at the corners, an expression of his particular brand of fatalism.

What could possibly go wrong? he seemed to say.

"Let us indeed give it a go," the captain told Simenon.

"Reversing shield polarity," the engineer announced.

Nothing changed on the forward viewscreen. The vortices still loomed ahead of them, savage twists of magnetic force daring ship and crew to try their luck.

Picard glanced at Gerda. "Lieutenant?"

She nodded. "He's done it, sir."

"Very well, then," the captain told her, his words ringing ominously across the bridge. "Let's proceed. One-quarter impulse."

The *Stargazer* started forward, heading for the narrow gap between the two nearest vortices. Picard felt the deck shudder beneath his feet as mighty forces reached out for them.

"Steady as she goes," he said.

Idun's best bet was to follow a course midway between the vortices, keeping the ship from being savaged by either one of them. She did this with unerring accuracy, even when the magnetic phenomena tore at the *Stargazer* and her shields, causing the vessel to slide and buck and creak in protest.

The captain trusted Idun as he had never trusted any other helm officer, and he wasn't the only one who felt that way. Captain Ruhalter had said once that his right arm was less precious to him than Idun's services at the helm.

If anyone could pull this off, it was she. Of course, the captain of the *Mongoose* might have felt that way about *his* helmsman. The same for the captain of the *Leningrad* or the *Christopher,* and they had been proven dead wrong.

So where did Picard get the gall to think he could

prevail over the vortices? To imagine that he and the *Stargazer* could succeed where all the rest had failed?

He didn't know. But he knew *this*—he wasn't going to stop until he had snared the White Wolf and brought him to justice.

As if in answer to his vow, the ship jerked suddenly to one side and then the other, jostling them in their seats and forcing a groan out of the deck plates. Someone cursed beneath his breath.

"Shields down eight percent," Vigo announced.

The captain frowned as the vortices on either side of them waxed immense on the forward viewscreen, two spectacular dynamos sizzling with magnetic energy. *Come on,* Picard urged his helm officer silently. *You can do it, Lieutenant.*

Sweat stood out on Idun's brow in beads. And not just Idun's brow, but Gerda's as well, for the *Stargazer*'s navigator was sifting through incoming sensor data and feeding her sister whatever tidbits she deemed most critical.

Slowly, with infinite care and patience, Idun guided them along the razor's edge. And finally, after what seemed like an eternity, the first two vortices fell away from them.

Only to reveal a great many more, rank upon rank as far as the eye could see.

Picard forced himself to take the sight in stride. After all, he was the captain now. He had to set an example.

Juanita Valderrama clung to the sides of her monitor in the science section and saw the same thing Captain Picard and his officers were seeing on the bridge.

One vortex after another muscled its way onto her

screen, majestic in its deadly, dazzling splendor. The ship shivered and jerked and reeled in the phenomenon's prodigious grasp like a fish caught on a very large hook. And then, through luck or skill, they managed to wriggle free of each vortex's influence.

But the battle had to be taking its toll on the *Stargazer.* It had to be sapping their resources, just as it had sapped the resources of the other vessels that had braved this passage.

Valderrama wished she had been able to do something to help their cause back in the briefing room. It wasn't that she didn't believe that Simenon's theory could work; in fact, she did think it could. It was that the captain had placed his faith in her, made her the chief of his science section, and she was letting him down.

When he had called for suggestions, she hadn't come up with one. All she could think to do was state the obvious—that the vortices were liable to tear up their shields. For all the good she had done, she might as well not have been in the room at all.

Suddenly, the deck shot out from beneath her feet. Valderrama tried to hang on to her monitor and stay upright. But just as she thought she might be able to keep from falling, the ship lurched again and she found the floor rushing up at her.

The science officer managed to get her hand between her face and the plastic surface, cushioning the blow. Still, she felt stunned for a moment. Then she heard someone say, "Are you all right?"

The voice that had asked the question sounded strange. Metallic, almost. Valderrama couldn't imagine why, until she turned to look up and saw the ghostly semblance of a human visage floating inside the clear-faced helmet of a containment suit.

"Are you all right?" Jiterica asked a second time.

"Yes," said Valderrama. She propped herself up on an elbow. "I'm fine, Ensign. Thank you."

By then, others had gathered around them. But it was Jiterica who gently grasped Valderrama's forearm and provided the counterweight that pulled Valderrama to her feet.

It was an eerie feeling, to have those gloved hands tugging at her. But the science officer didn't show it. After all, the ensign just wanted to help her.

And Valderrama knew how it felt not to be able to help.

"Thank you," she said a second time.

"You're welcome," Jiterica replied in her tinny, computerlike voice, and returned to her terminal.

Valderrama regarded the Nizhrak a moment longer. Then she looked around at the others who had ringed her and said, "I'm all right. You can go back to your stations."

One by one, the crewmen dispersed. Brushing herself off, Valderrama got a grip on her monitor again and tried to concentrate on the images she saw there. But it wasn't easy.

Not when she felt like more of a burden to her colleagues than ever.

Picard relaxed his grip on his armrests as the vortices they were passing slid off the sides of the viewscreen. They did so reluctantly, it seemed to the captain, as if they regretted not having torn the *Stargazer* to pieces.

Ben Zoma leaned closer to him. "Are we having fun yet?"

Indeed, Picard thought. But he kept the remark to himself. What he said instead was, "Report."

Idun was the first to respond. "Impulse engines still operating at peak efficiency."

"Shields at seventy-two percent," Gerda said.

It was better than the captain might have hoped. Simenon's approach seemed to be working.

Up ahead, another pair of vortices loomed in front of them, their whirling energies wild and hungry-looking. Idun began to steer the *Stargazer* between them.

But as she did, Picard caught a glimpse of the next group of vortices, deeper in, and they were significantly more tightly packed than any the *Stargazer* had already encountered. There was barely any space between them for a *Constellation*-class starship.

Idun turned to the captain, her unspoken assessment evident in her expression. "I agree," he said. "We'll see if we have a better chance of getting through elsewhere."

Turning back to her instrument panel, Idun backed them off the gap and moved them to starboard, since one of the twisters was blocking the way to port. Nor did she stop until she came to another opening that would give them sufficient leeway on either side.

But the story there was much the same. Even if the *Stargazer* managed to get through the breach at hand, she would be unable to get through the collection of vortices beyond that. The gaps were simply too narrow for her, too rife with destructive forces.

As before, Idun was compelled to slide them to starboard in search of something more promising. However, they hadn't gone very far before another twister became visible in the distance, threatening to cut off their lateral progress before long.

There was one more opening to starboard before they reached that point—one other chance to make it through both this set of vortices and the next one. The helm officer brought the *Stargazer* to a halt in front of that opening.

Leaning forward in his center seat, Picard took stock of the situation. The gap in front of them was certainly large enough to accommodate the *Stargazer.* However, the widest channel beyond it was considerably narrower, and considerably more daunting.

On the other hand, it was broader than any of the other second-rank openings the captain had seen. Perhaps even broad enough to grant them passage if they fought long and hard enough.

Idun was looking at him again. As before, Picard nodded. "Take us through," he said.

Punching in the requisite commands, the helm officer urged the ship forward. On the viewscreen, the whirlwinds before them appeared to grow larger, exerting more and more influence as the *Stargazer* sailed boldly between them. Smaller spirals of energy spun off from the main bodies, assaulting the ship.

The deck beneath Picard's feet kicked and rolled, balking at Idun's attempts to remain in control. An aft console sparked and gave rise to a slender plume of black smoke, requiring the attention of a crewman with a fire extinguisher.

And still the *Stargazer* plunged deeper into the jaws of pure, unbridled force.

Suddenly, something whipped them in the direction of the twister to port. Idun made the correction with a burst of thrusters, forcing them back on course. Moments later, they were rocked again by magnetic forces, but they managed to get through that setback as well.

Idun was getting better at this, Picard remarked to himself. She was navigating this corridor between the vortices with more skill and confidence than she had displayed in navigating the corridors that came before it.

Finally, the worst of the passage was over. The vortices began to peel away on either side of them, relinquishing their hold on the *Stargazer*—and revealing the even greater test that lay ahead of her.

"Shields at sixty-four percent," Gerda reported, even before the captain could ask.

Sixty-four percent, Picard repeated to himself. It was remarkable, given the challenges they had met. But would it be enough to see them through the challenge to come . . .

And what lay beyond it?

Picard eyed the phenomena between which they hoped to pass. They stood there like the gates of hell, pillars of cold fire that spun and undulated and writhed in what seemed to be the most hideous torment.

As the captain had always heard, misery loved company. The *Stargazer* had no choice but to give them some.

Picard could feel the tension on his bridge as Idun took them into the opening. It was a palpable sensation, like that of a violin string stretched to its breaking point.

And the trouble they had expected wasn't long in coming. First there was a rumbling, more felt in one's bones than heard. Then the *Stargazer* was wrenched hard to starboard, throwing the captain and everyone else to the deck.

The console next to Paxton's erupted in a fountain of

sparks, forcing the communications officer to recoil from it. As a crewman went to douse the fire, a second one broke out.

Picard staggered to his feet and eyed the viewscreen, where the image of the vortices had rotated a dizzying ninety degrees. Worse, the helm was unmanned. The captain started for it, ready and willing to put his once-considerable piloting skills to use.

But Idun managed to beat him to it. Dragging herself off the deck and back into her seat, she began tapping away at her controls. Little by little, she managed to right the ship.

But no sooner had the twisters turned vertical again on the screen than the *Stargazer* was bludgeoned anew. Wave after wave of magnetic energy broke over her bow, keeping her from advancing any farther.

Picard heard Idun growl as she struggled with her controls. Clearly, she needed more power.

"Mr. Simenon," he snapped. "All available power to the impulse engines!" And as he thought about it, he added, "Cut life support!"

"Aye, sir!" came the engineer's response.

The captain knew that they could survive on the air they had for as long as twenty minutes. Of course, the small amount of energy they saved might not make much of a difference, but it might also represent the margin between victory and defeat.

"Shields down to thirty-eight percent!" Gerda snarled.

Suddenly, the *Stargazer* began to make progress again. The walls of whirling energy seemed to crawl by on either side of them, yielding meter after grudging meter.

But they were far from free of the vortices' embrace. Picard felt his vessel vibrate and slew sideways, then shoot forward and veer in the other direction.

"Twenty-six percent!" Gerda announced grimly.

The captain began to doubt that they would make it—not that they had any choice but to try. They were more than halfway through now, too far to think about turning back.

The *Stargazer* lurched forward, fighting the good fight, though the vortices grabbed and tore at her with all their insane power. Yet another console began to spit sparks, and the smell of smoke became strong in Picard's nostrils, especially without the ventilation that was part of life support.

A little farther, he thought. *Just a little farther.*

And then he saw it.

Ben Zoma must have glimpsed it at the same time, because he pointed to the viewscreen and said, "Look!"

It was a narrow, vertical strip, seen between the seething near edges of the vortices. A ruddiness, as soft-looking as one of the clouds that stretched over the captain's native France at sunset.

It provided Picard and his officers with a glimpse of what lay beyond this strait—a hint that if they could only squeeze past these last two vortices, they could at last put this ordeal behind them.

"Shields at sixteen percent!" Gerda told her colleagues, inserting a note of reality into the captain's newfound optimism.

Picard felt his jaw clench. Once the shields were stripped away, there would be nothing left to protect them but their reinforced titanium hull, and no one could expect that it would last very long under such intensely adverse conditions.

"Six percent!" Gerda called out.

For just a moment, Picard had a vision of his ship being peeled like an overripe fruit, one section of hull at a time. Then, with an effort, he put the image from his mind.

Just in time to grab the back of his chair, because the vortices were clawing at them with renewed fury.

The *Stargazer* bucked and slid and bucked again, paying for every meter of headway with huge expenditures of energy. She shot forward, came up against what seemed like a tangible barrier, then pierced it and shot forward like an arrow.

And each time they made some progress, the scarlet strip ahead of them got noticeably wider, noticeably closer. *The end is in sight,* Picard assured himself. *We can do it . . .*

Gerda swiveled in her seat to look at him. "Sir," she said in a disgusted tone of voice, "the shields are down!"

The captain bit his lip. Their defenses were gone, and they were hardly out of danger yet. Had they dared too much after all? Would they falter just short of the finish line and be torn to pieces?

Picard shook his head, answering his own unspoken question. *Not today,* he insisted.

As if to dispute his conclusion, a wave of energy slammed into them head on. It sent the captain sprawling across his center seat, its armrests digging into his ribs. Then another wave hit them and another, each one fiercer and wilder than the one before it.

Without her shields to minimize the blows, the *Stargazer* was at the mercy of the vortices. She absorbed impact after impact, her lights flickering, her bulkheads keening as if in agony.

"Hull breaches on decks five, six, and seven!" Paxton announced. "Also, on decks ten and eleven!"

"Damage control teams!" Ben Zoma commanded.

There would be more breaches, Picard knew. Many more, if they lingered much longer in this confusion of colossal forces.

Get us out of here, he instructed Idun silently.

But the vortices seemed to have other ideas. They battered the ship's naked hull with assault after magnetic assault, as if they knew this would be their last chance to destroy the intruder.

And it seemed to Picard that it was just that. Never mind the damage they were taking—the ribbon of red had claimed nearly a third of the viewscreen and was claiming more with each passing second.

"Breaches on fourteen, fifteen, sixteen . . . !"

Suddenly, the lights went out and the captain felt the ship wrenched back and forth, shaken like helpless prey in the jaws of some titanic predator. He clung to his seat and watched the zagging image on the viewscreen, hoping Idun could straighten them out somehow.

Then, just as suddenly as the shaking had begun, it stopped. The lights came back on. And the viewscreen showed Picard a path all but free of the vortices.

He felt a single, small tremor, a final sickening reminder of what they had been through. But after that they were home free, sailing into the region of scarlet mist as calmly and effortlessly as if the vortex belt had never existed.

The captain drew a deep breath. Then he turned to his comm officer and said, "Casualties?"

"Nothing serious, sir," Paxton told him, relaying the latest information he had received from sickbay. "But there are hull breaches on *eleven* different decks."

"And we are defenseless," Gerda added, "until we can restore power to the shields."

"That too," said Paxton.

Picard nodded. They had taken a beating, one from which they would need time and considerable effort to recover. And somewhere beyond this placid sea of blood-red mists waited the White Wolf, who knew this system a good deal better than they did and might have come through the vortices a lot better fortified.

But they had made it through. They were alive. And for the moment, Picard reflected, that was all that mattered.

Ensign Jiterica got the news along with the rest of Lieutenant Valderrama's science section.

The ship had made it through the vortex belt. They had negotiated the system's second major obstacle without irreparable damage to the ship. It was a significant achievement, a tribute to the expertise of Chief Simenon and his engineers.

What's more, everyone in the science section seemed to agree with her. They were laughing and patting one another on the back. *Expressing jubilation*, the ensign observed.

Jiterica was capable of jubilation as well, maybe even more so than her colleagues were. But she wasn't jubilant at the moment. She was too intent on something that had begun to nag at her a moment earlier, something that lay just under the surface of her consciousness.

An idea. Or at least the beginnings of one.

Jiterica tapped out a command on her keyboard, and the image on her monitor changed, showing her a spectrographic analysis of the wildly churning gases surrounding the *Stargazer.* It was a different environment than the one that existed on her homeworld, but still . . .

The ensign tapped out another command and brought up a second analysis. It was encouraging enough for her to bring up a third analysis, and then a fourth.

It was still a raw notion, of course. Jiterica would have to examine it further to see if it held any real promise, and that might take a good deal of time. On the other hand, given the simplicity of her assignment here in the science section, time was something she seemed to possess in great abundance.

Chapter Eighteen

Captain's log, supplemental.

  Having completed our passage through the vortex belt, we have at last begun to pierce the heart of this solar system. However, we have paid a price for our progress. We have managed to resurrect only the flimsiest of deflector defenses, and it will be some time before our shields or any of our other tactical systems are back to full strength. At the same time, sensor range is steadily diminishing because of the gases through which we are compelled to travel. And we are strictly on our own now, lacking our colleagues' advice, since no other Federation vessel has managed to get this far in pursuit of the White Wolf. Of course, we have a vague idea of what to expect here, but none of it is extraordinarily promising.

* * *

STUDYING IDUN'S CONTROL PANEL over her shoulder, Ben Zoma frowned. "Then that's it?" he asked, already knowing the answer but wanting to hear it from his helm officer.

"I do not see any alternative," Idun said.

Ben Zoma nodded. "All right. I'll inform the captain."

Picard had spent the last three hours in his quarters trying to catch up on some much-needed sleep. Ben Zoma didn't like the idea of waking him. However, the captain had asked to be apprised of any significant development, and this one certainly qualified.

The first officer looked up at the intercom grid embedded in the ceiling. "Ben Zoma to Captain Picard."

No response.

"Ben Zoma to Captain Picard," he repeated.

This time he got an answer. "I heard you the first time," Picard said, his weariness evident in his voice.

"Sorry," Ben Zoma told him, smiling sympathetically. "But I thought you should know—"

"I had a dream," the captain interjected. "A wonderful dream. We had figured out a way to make the sensors work, long- and short-range, interference or no interference." He yawned. "We were hot and heavy on the trail of the White Wolf."

Ben Zoma's smiled tightened a bit. "Then this is a rude awakening in more ways than one. According to Idun, sensor range has diminished too precipitously for us to continue our forward progress—especially with our deflectors in such sorry shape."

A long pause. "I see," said Picard, his voice unmistakably full of disappointment.

It had to be a bitter pill for his friend to swallow, Ben

Zoma reflected. Having come so far, only to be stymied by what was really a mere technical problem . . .

"All stop," Picard commanded, "until we can devise a way to see in this muck."

The first officer turned to Idun, who looked utterly disgusted with the situation—like any Klingon denied a confrontation with her enemy. "You heard the captain," he said. "All stop."

"Aye, sir," she told him, and cut impulse power.

Without the application of braking thrusters, the *Stargazer* would continue to drift forward on momentum alone. But she wouldn't go very fast or get very far that way.

Ben Zoma swore under his breath. For the moment, it seemed, the hunt for the White Wolf was on hold.

The man called the White Wolf pushed his sensor screen away on its swivel and leaned back into his captain's chair.

"You've found them?" asked his second-in-command, the ruby-red light casting his blunt features into sharp relief.

"I have," the White Wolf told him. "They've survived the twisters in one piece."

Turgis's expression was one of grudging respect. "Really."

"Yes. But they've stopped moving. Either they've lost impulse power or their sensors have finally failed them."

"Their sensors, most likely."

The White Wolf nodded judiciously. "Most likely."

He himself had had trouble in that area for a long time. And when he finally came up with a solution, it had been a product more of good fortune than of expertise.

"They'll linger there for a while," Turgis speculated disdainfully, "then turn around and go home—and brag about how close they came to capturing us."

The White Wolf cast a sidelong look at him. "You think so? None of their colleagues have gotten even *this* far."

The Klingon sneered. "There's a big difference between beating the twisters and beating *us*."

The pirate smiled. "There is indeed."

And they laughed, as they had before whenever the subject of their pursuers came up. But this time, the White Wolf couldn't work himself up to Turgis's level of enthusiasm.

Their situation had changed. For the first time since they had begun lifting cargoes from Federation vessels, there was a chance they might have to defend themselves.

Not that the pirate had any doubt as to the outcome of an all-out encounter—especially when he had an ace wearing a Starfleet uniform up his sleeve.

Lieutenant Ulelo peered past the half-hidden form of Marion Sears, his repair-team partner, into the depths of a state-of-the-art subspace field generator.

Sears reached back, open palm extended. "Hyperspanner," she said, her voice muffled by its confinement.

"Hyperspanner," Ulelo repeated, and selected one from the assortment of handheld tools laid out in front of him. Then he laid it in his partner's palm.

"Thanks," said Sears, and pulled the hyperspanner into the shadowy nether regions of the field generator.

Ulelo had never had an opportunity like this on the

Copernicus—a chance to inspect a key component in the deflector system at close range. And even if he'd had such an opportunity, it wouldn't have been nearly as valuable. Field generators on *Oberth*-class ships were a full level of sophistication below the *Stargazer*'s.

Sears made an unintelligible noise.

"Did you say something?" Ulelo asked her.

"No," said the engineer. "I just banged my head is all."

Ulelo didn't comment further. He just went on scrutinizing what he could see of the field generator, trying to file away everything he could about it.

According to the specs he had pulled up shortly after his arrival on the ship, the *Stargazer* boasted eight of the devices in all. Two were located on deck 10, two more on deck 26, and one in each of the ship's four warp nacelles.

Each field generator consisted of a dozen graviton polarity sources feeding a pair of 500-millicochrane subspace field distortion amplifiers. At least, that's the information Ulelo had gleaned from the pertinent computer file.

When the magnetic vortices had battered the shields down to nothing, the engineering section was left with two tasks. The first was to repair and replace whatever power linkages had been damaged. The second was to reinitialize the field generators.

Ulelo, who had received precious little training as an engineer, had been assigned to the generator initialization team. So had a number of other non-engineers—crewmen from sections as disparate as security and weapons and even sickbay—which was why this compartment was crawling with more uniformed personnel than it had seen since the *Stargazer* was commissioned.

But then, this was where the captain had decided everyone was needed—here and in the other generator compartments or in the science section. Because they couldn't complete their mission if they couldn't find a way to navigate in the gases that surrounded them, and they didn't dare move until they got their shields up.

Of course, Ulelo had a mission of his own—one that was completely different from Captain Picard's. And with that mission in mind, he dutifully resumed his studies.

Jean-Luc Picard had never been a pacer.

Certainly, he had been plagued by moments of impatience like anyone else. But he had almost always managed to find a way to channel his nervous energy into something useful.

Or, if not useful, at least diverting.

But now, with the fate of his ship and crew resting squarely on his inexperienced shoulders, he was forced to rely on others to be useful—and diversions held no appeal for him.

And without realizing it, he had begun pacing from one end of his ready room to the other.

The captain had just caught himself and resolved to discontinue the activity when he heard the sound of chimes outside his door. "Come," he said, wondering who might be calling on him.

It turned out to be Lieutenant Valderrama.

"Sit," he said. "Please." He deposited himself in the chair behind his desk, glad for the interruption.

Valderrama sat down as well. Then she smiled and said, "I think I may have come up with the solution to our problem."

It took a moment for Picard to process the information. "Our problem?" he repeated inanely. Then it sank in, making his heart beat against his ribs. "You mean our *sensor* problem?"

"Actually," said Valderrama, "I haven't been able to come up with anything regarding the sensors."

The captain's hopes fell precipitously. "I see. Then what *have* you come up with?"

"A way to see in this gas soup, sir. But it doesn't have anything to do with our sensors."

Picard looked at the science officer, making no attempt to conceal his confusion. "I'm afraid you've lost me."

"Sorry," said the lieutenant. "What I mean is, there's a data-gathering option we've overlooked. It's a bit antiquated, I'll admit, but I think it's perfectly suited to this environment."

The captain leaned forward in his chair. "I would be interested in hearing more," he told her.

Valderrama went on to explain her theory in considerable detail. Partway through the process, Picard found himself smiling. It was a brilliant idea she had come up with, and one that wouldn't be at all difficult to execute.

"And that's it," she said finally.

He nodded. "Let's put it to the test."

Obviously pleased with the captain's reaction, Valderrama said, "Aye, sir. Right away."

Picard looked up and addressed the intercom grid. "Captain Picard to Chief Simenon."

"Simenon here."

The captain glanced at his science officer. "Lieutenant Valderrama has suggested a novel alternative to our sensor scans. I would like you to assist her in implementing it."

"And what exactly *is* this novel approach?" the engineer wondered.

Picard shrugged for the science officer's benefit. "Why don't I let her tell you herself? Picard out."

Valderrama took that as her cue to stand up. "Thank you, sir," she told the captain.

Picard knew what she meant, but he shook his head. "No, Lieutenant. Thank *you*."

He watched her depart, then sat back in his chair and experienced a surge of satisfaction. *And why shouldn't I?* he asked himself. He had shown faith in someone, and that faith had been rewarded.

Picard was proud of Juanita Valderrama. In fact, he was proud of them *both*.

Ensign Nikolas rubbed his eyes, cursed softly to himself, and focused again on his monitor screen.

He was studying the same sensor graphics as before. Except now, the areas in question were much smaller, much more proximate to the ship. And they weren't changing, because the *Stargazer* hadn't gone anywhere in the last few hours.

Still, there were reasons to keep up their watch. They didn't know enough about this system to predict what it might throw at them. And even if nature didn't come after them with a vengeance, the White Wolf might not be so accommodating.

"Tired?" asked Caber.

Nikolas shrugged. "No more than anyone else."

He wasn't sure anymore what to make of Caber. The guy couldn't have been nicer to him or more supportive. In fact, Caber seemed to be that way with *everyone*.

With one notable exception, Nikolas added silently.

He glanced across the room and saw Obal hard at work, absorbed in whatever graphic was occupying his screen at the moment. Nikolas didn't understand why Caber had it in for the Binderian. He had asked, but Caber didn't seem inclined to offer an explanation.

Maybe there *was* no explanation. Maybe it was just a matter of chemistry. But quite clearly, there was something about Obal that rubbed Caber the wrong way.

Fortunately, Nikolas had exacted a promise from his roommate—no matter how Caber felt about the Binderian, he would leave the little guy alone. No more mocking, no more instigation.

And until then, Caber had been as good as his word.

"I could use a break," he said.

"A break?" Nikolas chuckled as he turned back to his screen. "While we're sitting here without a stitch of protection? You like to live dangerously, don't you?"

"Come on," Caber rejoined. He leaned back in his chair and stretched. "The White Wolf's not even thinking of coming after us."

"How do you know that?" Nikolas asked.

"Because he knows this system and we don't. All he's got to do is stay where he is, nice and cozy in his hiding place, and we'll eventually have to give up and go home."

Nikolas frowned at the notion as he called up another graphic. "And you think that's what's going to happen? You think we're going to leave here empty-handed?"

"Don't you?"

"I don't get it," said Nikolas, forcing himself to concentrate on his work. "Aren't you the guy who kept chipping at Red O'Reilly until you finally beat him?

And now you're willing to give up on the White Wolf halfway into the mission?"

"Red O'Reilly was known to lose a game here and there," Caber told him, swiveling his chair to face his roommate's. "The White Wolf has *never* lost. And believe me, when the day comes that he's caught, it won't be at the hands of a captain a couple of years older than *we* are."

Nikolas could feel his blood rising into his face. He wasn't a quitter, and he didn't like talk of quitting. And besides, Caber was distracting him from what Nikolas still considered important.

"Listen," he said, "let's talk about this later, all right? *After* this shift is over."

Caber made a sound of disdain. "This shift will *never* be over. Not as long as our captain thinks he can—"

"Ensign Caber?"

Nikolas knew who had spoken even before he turned and saw Obal waddling toward them. What's more, the ensign had a pretty good idea of what the Binderian wanted.

Caber didn't get up to acknowledge Obal's superior rank. He just folded his arms across his chest. "Yes?"

Obal frowned as he stopped in front of the big man, who looked down on the Binderian even though he was still seated. Obal looked as earnest as Nikolas had ever seen him.

"You do not appear to be approaching your assignment with the proper diligence," he observed.

"Don't I?" Caber responded.

The Binderian's frown deepened. "If we are to succeed in our mission, we must all do our part."

"Normally," said Caber, "I'd agree with you. But I just don't feel very motivated today."

Puzzled, Obal tilted his head. "And why is that?"

Caber shrugged. "I don't know. Maybe I feel funny taking orders from someone who looks like Thanksgiving dinner."

Nikolas wasn't sure if Obal knew what Thanksgiving was, much less what kind of meals were associated with it. However, he seemed to understand that he had been insulted. For a moment, he stared at Caber as if trying to decide what kind of charges to level against him.

And charges certainly seemed to be in order. Nikolas hadn't witnessed this kind of arrogance, this kind of insubordination, since the day he entered Starfleet.

But to his surprise, Obal didn't say anything about filing a report. He didn't even tell Caber that he was out of line. He simply said, "Try to be more attentive to your duties, Ensign," and walked back in the direction of his workstation.

Caber watched him go, a smile spreading across his face. Then he turned to Nikolas. "Came down on me pretty hard, didn't he?"

Nikolas sighed. "Listen, Joe—"

"The guy rules with an iron hand," Caber went on. He laughed. "I'll sure think twice before pulling *that* again."

"Joe," said Nikolas, "that's *enough.*"

His voice had an edge to it that even he hadn't expected. Hearing it, Caber was brought up short. Then he grinned.

"Don't worry," he told Nikolas. "Our pal Obal's not going to take offense. He hasn't got a sensitive bone in his body. In fact, he hasn't got a bone in his body, *period.*"

And Caber laughed again, making sure it was loud enough for Obal to hear him, even across the room.

But the Binderian didn't do anything about it. He just settled into his seat and regarded his screen as if nothing had happened—as if he hadn't been ridiculed in front of everyone present.

"Guess it's time to get back to work," Caber said, and swung around to face his monitor again. But the damage had been done, Nikolas reflected, and Caber knew it.

Nikolas shook his head. He didn't know with whom he was more disgusted—Caber for the abuse he was heaping on his superior, or Obal for not fighting back.

Chapter Nineteen

PICARD SAT BACK IN HIS CENTER SEAT and eyed his forward viewscreen, with its deep, daunting vision of blushing plasma seas and their continually swirling currents. He could barely make out the glowering red orb of Beta Barritus in the center of it all.

"Are we ready?" he asked.

"As ready as we'll ever be," said Ben Zoma, who was standing in his usual place beside the captain.

"And Lieutenant Valderrama?"

"On her way."

Picard had deemed it fitting that Valderrama join them on the bridge at this juncture, as it was her brainchild that had set this effort in motion.

Just as he thought that, the turbolift doors hissed open behind him. Looking back over his shoulder, the captain could see Valderrama come out onto the bridge. She was smiling, albeit a bit nervously.

"Welcome," Picard told her.

She nodded as she took up a position beside him, on the opposite side from Ben Zoma. "Thank you, sir."

The captain glanced at Gerda. "Launch probe, Lieutenant."

The navigator ran her fingers over her controls. Then she turned to him and said, "Probe away, sir."

On the viewscreen, Picard could see the probe shoot through the nest of misty, wine-colored gases. It didn't take long before it was gone—or at least, seemed to be gone, at this level of magnification.

He turned to Lieutenant Valderrama. The science officer looked tense, hopeful, and perhaps more than a little proud of herself. But then, she deserved to feel that way after she had given them their best chance to locate their prey.

Valderrama's idea had been a wonderfully simple one. The plasma soup surrounding the star made it impossible to get any more useful information out of the ship's active sensor systems.

Sensor systems consisted of proton spectrometers, gravimetric distortion scanners, and gamma ray imagers. What Picard needed—and what Valderrama had prescribed—was a sensor technology that predated the *Stargazer* by hundreds of years.

A technology called *radar*.

Radar was just a matter of bouncing ultrahigh-frequency radio waves off a distant object. And as Valderrama had so astutely pointed out, certain frequencies of radio waves could make it through almost anything, including the veils of hydrogen gas that surrounded the star in this system.

It was with this in mind that Simenon's people had spent the last day or so working on the navigational deflector and lateral sensor arrays, rerigging them so that the former could emit radio waves, which the latter could then receive and analyze.

And to enhance their prospects of success, the Gnalish had added a touch of his own. He had outfitted the probe they had just launched with radar capabilities as well.

Programmed to follow a course parallel to the *Stargazer*'s, the probe would give them additional input from a remote source and, as a result, substantially better odds of finding what they were looking for. Nor was it likely to tip off the White Wolf with its presence, since it was flying parallel to the *Stargazer* and not ahead of her.

For now, however, the probe would serve a different purpose. Its communication facilities temporarily deactivated, it would present Valderrama's idea with its first test.

"Activate radar assembly," Picard said.

"Activated," Gerda told him.

He looked forward again. "On screen."

Instantly, the image of the plasma sea gave way to a rigid green-on-black grid—the same one Gerda saw every day on her navigational console. Unfortunately, there was nothing remarkable to be seen on the grid. In fact, there was nothing at all.

Radar, Picard knew, was ploddingly slow compared to the other sensor technologies at their disposal—technologies which had, for all their quickness, proved useless here.

This might take a while, Picard told himself. Not that

he minded. What they were doing here was important. No, he thought—*critical.*

Then he saw it—a bright red dot in the upper left quadrant of the grid. It flashed at the captain triumphantly, bringing a smile to his face. Nor was his smile the only one.

Unfortunately, it wasn't the White Wolf. It was just the probe. But if they could find a probe, Valderrama had reasoned, finding the pirate would be just a matter of time.

"Congratulations," Picard told the science officer. "It appears that your theory has panned out."

Valderrama's sense of accomplishment was evident in her voice as well as her expression. "Thank you, sir," she told him. "I'm pleased I could make a contribution."

So am I, the captain reflected.

Phigus Simenon hated the idea of what he was about to do. He absolutely *hated* it.

Fortunately, it wasn't difficult for him to locate Valderrama. She was standing right there in the science section, her hand on a junior officer's shoulder, lending him encouragement, it seemed, as she pointed something out on his sensor screen.

No doubt she was telling him what to expect of her radar arrangement—the one she had thought of when Simenon himself had despaired of devising any further sensor innovations. The one that would more than likely guide them to the White Wolf.

And that, of course, was what he had come to speak to her about.

Noticing his approach, Valderrama said, "Mr. Simenon. To what do I owe this pleasure?"

The engineer winced at her congenial tone. She wasn't going to make it easy for him, was she?

"I came," he said, "to . . ." It was difficult for him to get the word out—as difficult as he had imagined it would be.

Valderrama's brow creased, but she remained patient. He would have felt better if she had nudged him a little, or maybe even folded her arms and tapped her foot.

But of course, she didn't do that. She was too nice, too much like someone's mother to provoke him that way.

Simenon took a breath and started again. "I came to—" With an effort, he finally squeezed the word out: "—*apologize.*" He paused. "That is, for what I said about you."

Valderrama didn't pretend not to know what he was talking about. There was that consolation, at least.

"You mean," she replied, "about my . . . apparent lack of interest in enhancing the sensors?"

Simenon nodded. "Yes. That."

"It's all right," the science officer told him. "As it happens, you were correct. I was being lax in the performance of my duties. But I'm not going to be lax anymore, I assure you."

"Good. Then . . . you accept my apology?" he asked, hoping she would say yes so he could end this debacle.

"I do," she said.

Simenon breathed a sigh of relief. "Excellent. I'll be in engineering if you need me." And he began to retreat toward the exit.

But he hadn't gotten very far before Valderrama called after him. Stopping dead in his tracks, the engineer wondered what further torment he would have to endure.

But all she said was, "How are the repairs going?"

"We're almost done," he told her. "Shields should be back to full strength within the hour."

The science officer smiled. "That's good news."

"So it is," Simenon mumbled. Then he made his way out of the science section before Valderrama could think of some *other* way to prolong his agony.

Nikolas wasn't sure at what point he realized that he had responded to the intercom greeting.

But he *had* responded to it. The ensign knew that in a distant, instinctive sort of way. Otherwise, there wouldn't have been a feminine voice in his room speaking to him as if there had already been an exchange of salutations.

"I hope I haven't disturbed you," the voice said. "I know you've been working long hours."

Nikolas sat up with an effort, shook off the warm, welcome weight of sleep, and tried to remember where he was and who in blazes was talking to him.

Stargazer, his mind said, sifting through its haze for the pertinent facts. *Commander Wu.*

"Ensign?" said the second officer.

"Yes, Commander," Nikolas responded a little shakily. He ran his fingers through his hair and suppressed a yawn. "Here. And no—you haven't disturbed me at all."

"I just wanted to assure you that your contribution has not gone unnoticed. In fact," Wu told him, "it's been brought to my attention more than once."

"It has?" the ensign said. Despite his attempt to speak clearly, he slurred the words a bit.

"Indeed," Wu replied. "Mr. Joseph informed me that you were the first to detect the vortex belt down in the security section."

That was me, all right, Nikolas thought.

"However," the second officer continued, "it was Ensign Caber who filed a report providing the full details of your diligence. Given the dedication you've shown, the seriousness with which you seem to have undertaken your assignment, I'm not surprised you were able to get wind of the vortices well before any of your colleagues."

"Ensign *Caber* said that?" Nikolas wondered.

"I know," Wu said. "It's rather unusual for an ensign to file an unsolicited personnel report, especially when it involves a crewman of equal rank. However, Mr. Caber seems possessed of a rather extraordinary sense of fairness."

And an extraordinary hostility toward a certain Binderian, Nikolas added inwardly. But all he said was, "Yes, sir."

There was a pause. "I've gone over your personnel file, Ensign, and I couldn't help noticing the strikes against you. The disciplinary action for fighting, in particular."

Nikolas felt a rush of warmth in his cheeks. "That wasn't my fault, Commander. I was just defending myself."

"Unfortunately," said Wu, "your captain saw it otherwise. Hence the disciplinary action, which didn't exactly ensure you of a successful career path."

The ensign frowned. There was nothing to be gained by arguing the point, especially with someone who had begun their conversation on a positive note.

"No, sir."

"Nonetheless, Mr. Nikolas, people change. They improve. They put their pasts behind them. And from what

I've seen of your efforts so far on the *Stargazer,* you've done all those things."

Nikolas smiled. "Thank you, ma'am."

"Keep up the good work," Wu advised him. "Don't lose focus. And get some sleep, Ensign. You'll need it."

Nikolas stifled a groan. "I'll do that, Commander."

"Wu out."

Their exchange over, the ensign finally had a chance to take stock of himself. He looked down and saw that he had gone to bed still dressed in his uniform.

And his roommate, who was possessed of that "rather extraordinary sense of fairness"? There was no sign of him. Obviously, Caber hadn't been as tired as Nikolas was.

The ensign felt the urge to yawn again, and this time he gave into it. Funny, he thought. This was the last problem he had expected to have on the *Stargazer*— being woken out of a dead sleep by the second officer, who just couldn't wait to praise his devotion to duty.

Maybe Caber was right, he told himself as he slumped back against his bed and closed his eyes. Maybe he could prove those Academy guys wrong after all.

That is, if he didn't screw things up by returning to his old tricks. But he wouldn't do that, he vowed. He would be as patient and cooperative as anyone who had ever served on a Starfleet vessel.

Lieutenant Nikolas, he thought. *Captain* Nikolas. He smiled at the prospect as he drifted off.

Picard was on his way to the bridge when the doors to his turbolift compartment opened and admitted Lieutenant Valderrama.

He smiled. "Lieutenant."

She smiled back. "Sir." As the doors closed again, she said, "I understand the shields have been restored."

"Very nearly," the captain told her. "Enough for us to get under way again, so we can finish what we have begun."

Valderrama nodded. "That's good to hear."

"But we would still be in a hole if not for your brainstorm." He favored the lieutenant with a look of admiration. "Using radar in this day and age—it was an inspired idea, to say the least."

"Thank you, sir," said Valderrama.

It seemed to Picard that she was somewhat less enthusiastic than he had seen her on the bridge. But then, the novelty of her discovery and its success were probably beginning to wear off.

It occurred to him to ask Valderrama about his *other* project in her section. "Incidentally," he said in a softer voice, "how is Ensign Jiterica faring?"

The lieutenant didn't answer right away. "Unfortunately," she replied with obvious reluctance, "Ensign Jiterica could be doing better, sir. She seems listless, uninterested in the challenges we're tackling . . . even withdrawn at times. If I may be allowed to venture an opinion . . . ?"

"By all means."

"I don't think we're doing her a favor by continuing to try to make her fit in."

Valderrama sounded understandably sympathetic. She had been considered a misfit herself for the last few years.

"I'm sorry to hear that," Picard said. "I was hoping her situation would improve—for the Federation's sake as well as her own. Nonetheless, I appreciate your candor."

"I'd prefer to have been candid about *good* news," the science officer told him.

The captain smiled wistfully to himself. "Perhaps next time, Lieutenant. Carry on."

"I'll do that," Valderrama promised him.

By then, they had reached her destination—deck 6, which housed the ship's science section. The doors opened and the lieutenant departed, leaving Picard with something to think about.

In his head, he began to compose an advisory to Starfleet Command. It would contain a recommendation that Ensign Jiterica be given her unconditional discharge.

Under the circumstances, Picard reflected, it was the only humane choice open to him.

Idun Asmund heard the hiss of the turbolift doors as they parted to admit someone. *The captain,* she thought without turning. He had said he was on his way.

"Helm," said Picard, confirming her suspicion. He took his seat behind her. "Activate impulse drive."

"Aye, sir," Idun responded. Her long, slender fingers tapped the requisite studs on her control console. "Ready."

There was a pause, as if the captain was savoring this moment. And no doubt he was. "Full impulse," he said finally.

"Full impulse," she confirmed.

"Engage," Picard ordered, his voice the crack of a whip.

Idun sent them hurtling through the gases and ion clouds of Beta Barritus, depending on a kind of sensor operation she had never heard of before this mission. Not that it mattered that she was unfamiliar with this thing called *radar*.

If it got them closer to their prey, Idun Asmund was all for it.

The White Wolf frowned as he peered at his personal sensor screen, where a single blue dot was drifting slowly across a white grid. "They're moving again," he announced. "Obviously, whatever problems they had have been solved."

His second-in-command's thick brows met over the bridge of his nose as he considered the news. Then, with a curt backhanded gesture, he dismissed the threat posed by their pursuer.

"I'm *glad* they're moving," the Klingon snarled. "I'm tired of hiding here like a mewling *p'takh*."

The White Wolf shook his head slowly as he studied his screen. "There are no cowards on this ship, Turgis. If there were, I would've gotten rid of them a long time ago."

The Klingon rumbled on as if he hadn't heard his captain's comment. "My heart yearns for battle—for *blood!* It's been too long since I raised my hand against an enemy!"

The White Wolf saw others on the bridge turn to Turgis, wary of the edge in his voice. On the other hand, he mused, some of them probably felt the same way.

"We're not operating a warship," he insisted—and not for the Klingon's benefit alone. "We're privateers. Our victory comes in not getting caught."

A sound of disgust tore from Turgis's throat. "That's no victory! That's mere *survival!*"

The White Wolf's eyes narrowed as he turned to look at his second-in-command. "What are you saying? That you've had enough of this life? Of what we do here?"

It put the Klingon on the spot. But then, that was exactly what the pirate had meant to do.

"Well?" he asked.

Turgis turned red in the face, but he contained his fury—just as the White Wolf had expected he would. He hadn't shared a bridge with the Klingon all this time without getting to know him a little.

As Turgis stalked off to drown his defiance in a bottle of bloodwine, the pirate turned to the others. "What are you looking at?" he asked them. "The hunt's on again—and we've still got work to do."

One by one they went back to their business. And a moment later, so did the man known as the White Wolf, for he had played a poker game or two in his day.

And he knew that a hidden ace wasn't always a guarantee of victory.

Chapter Twenty

CHIEF COMMUNICATIONS OFFICER MARTIN PAXTON wasn't a stickler about much, but he did have a thing about punctuality.

So when his relief had yet to show up a full ten minutes after Paxton's shift had ended, it bugged him. And it bugged him even more that the tardy officer was Ulelo.

He had taken Ulelo off the graveyard shift sooner than any other comm chief would have. He had treated the new guy with warmth and respect. In Ulelo's place, Paxton would have made damned sure he didn't bite the hand that fed him.

Finally, the comm chief had had enough. Tapping his insignia, he said, "Paxton to Ulelo."

There was no answer.

Again he said, "Paxton to Ulelo."

Still no response.

"Computer," he said, "locate Mr. Ulelo."

The computer's soft, feminine voice informed him that "Mr. Ulelo is in the shuttlebay."

The comm chief frowned. "Paxton to Ch—"

"Mr. Paxton?" someone said over the comm link. But it didn't sound like Ulelo.

"This is Paxton," he said. "Who's this?"

"It's Andarko, sir. Technician first class. I'm speaking into Mr. Ulelo's communicator."

"And why isn't Mr. Ulelo speaking into his communicator?" Paxton inquired, figuring it was a reasonable question.

"He took off his tunic to work on one of the shuttles with Lieutenant Chiang," said Andarko. "But when I heard a voice coming from his communicator, I came over to see what was going on."

"I see," said Paxton.

Had he spoken directly into the intercom grid, Ulelo's name would have rung throughout the shuttlebay. But, not wanting to embarrass Ulelo any more than was necessary, he had chosen to use the more private method of communicator-to-communicator, so Andarko was the only one who had ended up hearing him.

"Would you be so kind," Paxton asked the technician, "as to get Mr. Ulelo for me? I need to speak with him right away."

"Actually," Andarko said, "he's right here, sir."

A moment later, the comm chief heard a voice that he recognized as Ulelo's. "Sir?"

"Mr. Ulelo," Paxton said evenly, "are you aware of the fact that you were supposed to report to the bridge almost fifteen minutes ago?"

"Actually," a third voice chimed in, "it's my fault Ulelo's late."

It took Paxton a moment to place it. "Chiang?"

"That's right," the shuttle chief confirmed. "And I'll take the blame for Mr. Ulelo's tardiness. You see, he asked for a look at the newer shuttles. And while we were going over them, he found a comm problem with the type-eight. I asked if he could stay awhile and fix it, and, unfortunately, we both lost track of the time."

"Sorry, sir," said Ulelo.

"Same here," Chiang added. "I didn't mean to keep your man that long."

Under the circumstances, Paxton could hardly be angry. It wasn't as if Ulelo had been goofing off. He had been working—just not where he was *scheduled* to be working.

"Don't give it a second thought," said the comm chief. "Just tell me when to expect him."

"Immediately," Ulelo assured him. "I'm done with the shuttle. Mr. Chiang shouldn't have any more problems with it from here on."

"I wouldn't even have known it *had* a problem," the shuttle chief remarked, "if Ulelo here hadn't mentioned it."

"Then it's a good thing he was there," Paxton said. "See you later, Chiang. Paxton out."

With a private chuckle, he turned his attention back to his comm console. Chiang was lucky Ulelo was so curious by nature. In fact, they were *all* lucky.

Considering the dangerous nature of their mission, the last thing they needed was a shuttle malfunction.

* * *

As Gilaad Ben Zoma entered his captain's ready room, he saw a figure standing on the other side of the room, gazing out the observation port. For just a moment, he could have sworn that the figure was that of the late Daithan Ruhalter.

But of course, it wasn't. It was that of Jean-Luc Picard.

Strange, the first officer thought. Picard wasn't as tall as Ruhalter or as broad, and Ruhalter's hair had been gray where Picard's was still brown. And yet, for just a moment, Picard had put him in mind of their former captain.

It was something about Picard's bearing, Ben Zoma decided. Something about the set of his shoulders. Ruhalter had been a confident man, a confident captain. It seemed to Ben Zoma that his friend was becoming a confident captain as well.

And why not? They had already accomplished what no one else could. They had gotten through the debris field and the vortex belt, and now—thanks to Valderrama—they had come up with a way to see in a place where standard sensors were of no use to them.

With a little luck, they would accomplish one more task—the one they had come here for. They would catch the infamous, elusive White Wolf.

"You're staring out that port again," Ben Zoma noted.

Picard chuckled grimly. "I find I do my best thinking here."

"You used to do your best thinking in the shower," said the first officer. "Or so you told me."

"That," said the captain, "was *before* I had an observation port to stare out of."

Ben Zoma found himself smiling. "So what's on your mind at this advanced hour?"

"Our approach to catching the White Wolf. I think we need to reconsider it."

The first officer pulled up a chair. "I'm all ears."

Picard made a fist with his right hand and used his left forefinger to describe a circle above it. As he spoke the circle moved down until it described an equatorial orbit.

"Right now," Picard said, "we are descending toward Beta Barritus in a shallow spiral—the textbook approach to finding something in a solar system under less than optimum sensor conditions. The virtue of that approach is the likelihood that we will eventually come across the White Wolf's position."

But there was a downside as well. Picard articulated it.

"Unfortunately, this may take a very long time. And if the White Wolf is hiding on the other side of the star, which he may well be, catching him will take even longer."

Ben Zoma nodded. "No argument there."

"What I'm considering," the captain told him, "is going directly to Beta Barritus—a trip that should take no more than three hours at full impulse. Then, when we've come within perhaps a thousand kilometers of the star, we can follow an *upward* spiral."

"Because the White Wolf is probably hiding as close to Beta Barritus as he can," the first officer noted thoughtfully. "I mean, that's what *I* would do—make it as difficult as possible for my pursuers to reach me, much less find me."

"Precisely. And if it happens that his sensor capabilities are superior to our radar and he finds *us* before we find *him,* he will probably take flight in an outward direction."

"Which will eventually flush him out of the system—and make him easy prey for McAteer's armada." Ben Zoma grinned appreciatively. "Obviously, you've done more than consider this. You've thought it through pretty damned thoroughly."

"I have," Picard admitted as he took the seat behind his desk. "So what do you think?"

Ben Zoma shrugged. "What I think, Jean-Luc, is we ought to put your strategy into action."

The captain looked pleased with his friend's response. "I am glad to hear you say that, Number One." He tapped his communicator. "Helm, this is Picard . . ."

And he gave the order to head directly for Beta Barritus.

"Aye, sir," said Idun.

Ben Zoma glanced at the observation port and saw the ruddy glare of the star grow more intense. Idun was bringing them about, putting them on the course Picard had described.

The captain noticed as well. "There," he said, and turned back to his friend. "That's done."

Ben Zoma regarded the man on the other side of the desk. "You know," he remarked, "I'm glad to see you feeling so enthusiastic. For a while there when we first entered this system, you were frowning so hard I thought your face would crack."

Picard looked skeptical. "Really."

"Really," said the first officer.

"Well," said the captain, "I do feel more in control of the situation. Though, to be honest, I'm anything *but* in control. I still don't know what tricks our adversary may be holding in reserve."

He had a point, Ben Zoma conceded. It was hard to

know how to fight someone when you knew so little about him.

"Funny," Picard went on. "I thought our battle against the Nuyyad was our baptism of fire—a fight to the death against a ruthless and powerful enemy. Yet I feel so raw, so untested."

"Maybe that's the way a captain *always* feels," Ben Zoma suggested. "No matter *how* long he's been in command."

Judging by the expression on Picard's face, that possibility hadn't occurred to him. "Perhaps," he allowed.

The two of them sat in unhurried silence. Finally, it was the captain who spoke up.

"I should take another look at what we know of the White Wolf. I may find something I have overlooked."

Ben Zoma shook his head. "You've gone over those logs for days on end. It's enough. You may be the man in charge here, but there's nothing more you can do."

"There must be *something* I can—"

"Go to bed," Ben Zoma advised him. "That's what Captain Ruhalter would've done."

The captain mulled it over, then rejected the notion. "Perhaps not just yet, Gilaad."

Ben Zoma's eyes narrowed suspiciously. "You just can't stay away from those logs, can you? You're going to stay up into the wee hours trying to find something you missed."

"Not into the wee hours, I assure you."

"You'll turn in shortly, then?"

"Absolutely. In just a few minutes."

"Scout's honor?"

"Without question."

Ben Zoma leaned back in his chair and folded his arms across his chest. "Good. I'll wait."

Picard began to protest. "There's no need to—"

His friend stopped him with a raised hand. "Honestly, what kind of first officer would I be if I didn't look after my captain's health and well-being?"

Picard shook his head. "Gilaad, I—"

"And what kind of friend would I be if I let you sit here all by yourself, trying to find a needle's worth of something useful in a haystack of command logs?"

The captain sighed. "Believe me, I'm not looking forward to it. I would go to bed if I could."

"I'm sure you would," Ben Zoma replied evenly. But he didn't move out of his chair.

Picard was reminded again of why he held his first officer in such high regard. "Can I at least offer you something to drink?" He indicated the half-empty cup on his desk. "Tea, perhaps?"

Ben Zoma shook his head. "No, thanks. Puts me to sleep. How about a cup of black coffee?"

The captain rose from his chair to fill his friend's request. "Coming right up."

Gerda Asmund watched the seething red expanse of Beta Barritus slide off the edge of the viewscreen. She didn't think she would miss it, either—not after staring at its steadily swelling girth for the last three hours.

The star's lurid light was replaced by cottony clusters of soft rose and lavender, too dense for Gerda to see through. Fortunately, she didn't have to see anything. Valderrama's radar was working like a carefully honed *bat'leth,* slicing through anything and everything in its way.

Soon, the navigator thought, they would find the White Wolf. She could feel it in the marrow of her bones. They would find him and put an end to the myth of his invincibility, adding to the glory already associated with the name *Stargazer.*

And glory was what made the difference between bloodwine and water, between life and mere existence. Any Klingon knew that.

Gerda was in the process of refining the course she had laid out for her sister when she noticed something on her radar monitor, something represented by a green blip on the otherwise black field.

There weren't any planets or moons in this solar system. There weren't even any asteroids. They had all been reduced to ions when their original star went nova.

And it couldn't be their radar-assist companion probe because that was elsewhere. So if there was an object out there, it was neither one they had brought with them nor a naturally occurring body.

Which left Gerda with just one inescapable conclusion.

She turned to her sister and saw that Idun had noticed the green blip as well. Her eyes, which were locked intently on her monitors, were alight with a warrior's anticipation.

The navigator looked to the intercom grid. "Captain Picard, this is Lieutenant Asmund."

"Picard here," the captain said a moment later.

He sounded tired to Gerda. But then, none of them was getting much sleep these days.

"There's something on radar," she told him.

A pause. "I'll be right there," the captain replied. And he no longer sounded the least bit fatigued.

Chapter Twenty-One

PICARD WAS A STEP AHEAD of Ben Zoma as they emerged from his ready room and crossed the bridge.

"How far?" he asked as he approached Gerda's console.

"Slightly more than a million kilometers," his navigator told him.

"Is it a ship?"

Gerda nodded. "I believe so, yes."

Picard looked up at the viewscreen. All it showed him was a nest of blood-red gases.

Then he peered past his navigator at the screen on her console that had tipped her off. It showed him a black field with a green blip prominently displayed on it.

There was something there all right, Picard thought. Something that might be the White Wolf. And thanks to Valderrama's radar, the *Stargazer* could track it down.

"Red alert," he said.

"Raise shields and power weapons," Ben Zoma added.

"Shields up, sir," Vigo assured him from his weapons console. "Phasers and photon torpedoes ready."

Of course, the torpedoes were a last resort. Picard still wanted to bring that cargo home intact—and the White Wolf as well, if he could.

"Bring us closer," he told Idun.

She saw to it. "Aye, sir."

His helm officer made the necessary adjustment in their heading. Nothing changed on the viewscreen, but Gerda's monitors told the captain a different story. There, the object of their attentions was getting closer by the second.

"Four hundred thousand kilometers," Gerda announced.

If it *was* the White Wolf, he didn't seem to know he had company yet—and that meant Picard held a big advantage. He could get even closer before his prey knew it was being hunted.

Unless it's a trap.

Picard's mouth went dry at the unwelcome thought. Could that be it? Could his adversary be biding his time, every bit as aware of the *Stargazer* as the *Stargazer* was of him?

"Three hundred thousand kilometers, sir."

Still no reaction from the White Wolf—if it *was* the White Wolf. The captain was beginning to harbor some doubts.

"Two hundred thousand," Gerda reported.

"Fire when ready!" Picard barked.

"One hundred thousand . . ."

And their adversary woke up.

The White Wolf's phaser salvo seemed to erupt from

out of nowhere. It loomed rapidly on the main viewer, growing in volcanic splendor and magnitude until it blanched the entire screen.

"Evasive maneuvers!" Picard called out.

But it was too late.

The phaser attack bludgeoned the *Stargazer* with bone-rattling force, causing the deck to lurch beneath the captain's feet. Grabbing the back of Gerda's chair, he managed to stay upright, but only barely.

As Idun sent them twisting away from the enemy, Vigo launched a counterstrike. The *Stargazer*'s phased energy bolts vanished into the crimson haze, reaching for their unseen enemy.

"Missed!" Gerda hissed, consulting her radar in conjunction with a computer model of their phaser strike.

A second time, a ruby-red barrage loomed on their viewscreen. But this time, it swept past them without taking a toll. Obviously, Idun's helm work was baffling the enemy's weapons batteries.

Vigo unleashed another volley of his own. The captain tracked it on Gerda's monitor, watching it stab across the screen at the green dot that represented the enemy ship. It was as true an attack as a phaser cannon could make.

But at the last possible moment, the White Wolf banked sharply and escaped unscathed.

At that point, the pirate might have turned tail and tried to shake them. But he didn't do anything of the sort. He switched back and went for the *Stargazer*'s throat.

Picard glanced at Idun. She was accepting the enemy's challenge, refusing to change their heading a single degree. But then, she had been raised by

Klingons, and Klingons didn't flinch when an adversary attacked them head-on.

As a collision became imminent, the captain wished his helm officer had been raised in a slightly less aggressive culture. And he wished so even more when the White Wolf's vessel became visible on their viewscreen, no longer an abstraction but a fact.

And yet, for a fact it seemed remarkably ethereal—a ghostly specter emerging from a sea of blood and fire, swimming up from an impossible red depth. Not a massive black bullet like the ship of his nightmare, but a slender, pale wraith.

And like Idun, the vessel's helm officer wasn't flinching. The pirate was on a course that threatened to ram the *Stargazer* into oblivion.

"Fire!" Picard barked.

But the White Wolf had already foiled him by veering off to starboard. And as he darted past the *Stargazer,* he unleashed a series of phaser blasts at close range.

The captain was sent sprawling by the fury of the attack. Somewhere behind him a console exploded, spewing sparks and billows of smoke, and he could hear groans of pain.

But Ben Zoma would see to the console and the injured, Picard thought as he dragged himself to his feet. It was the captain's job to see to it they didn't absorb such punishment a second time.

"Report!" he commanded.

"Shields down thirty-eight percent!" Gerda growled.

"Casualties on decks seven, ten, and eleven!" Paxton reported. "Hull breaches on twelve and thirteen!"

Picard cursed under his breath. They had taken a

beating. And to that point, they hadn't even dealt the enemy a glancing blow.

The problem was that the pirate was more maneuverable than the larger and more powerful *Stargazer.* The White Wolf might not have been able to match their firepower or their defenses, but he could certainly fly rings around them.

Clearly, they needed a new tactic. Gritting his teeth, Picard tried to come up with one.

But all he could think about was Daithan Ruhalter—not the heroic and inspirational human being under whom he had served, but the strangely wistful Daithan Ruhalter of his nightmare. The latter's words came to the captain anew, surging from the depths of his memory . . .

Instinct, the nightmare Ruhalter had said. *Either you've got it or you don't. And if you don't, no collection of sensors and shields and phaser banks is going to help you.*

Picard could feel a bead of sweat meandering down the side of his face. He felt as if all eyes were upon him, waiting for him to say the words that would turn the battle around.

But he had no such words at his disposal.

It was too soon, the nightmare Ruhalter had said of Picard. *He was too damned young.*

No, thought the captain. He glared defiantly at the viewscreen, which showed him nothing more than billowing scarlet gas clouds. *I am* not *too young,* he insisted. *I* will *beat the White Wolf.*

And suddenly, it came to him how he would do it.

Turning to Idun, Picard said, "Retreat! Full impulse!"

His helm officer looked at him with an expression of horror on her face. It seemed to him that she was about to protest, right there in the middle of their encounter with the enemy.

But in the end, she kept from commenting on his choice of tactic. She simply worked her helm controls and carried out her captain's command.

A moment later, he saw the gas clouds ahead of them swing to port. Idun was bringing them about, moving them away from the enemy as fast as their impulse drive would take them.

Joining Gerda at her navigation console, Picard inspected her radar monitor. It showed him that the pirate wasn't content to let them go—not after they had smoked him from his lair. He was following the *Stargazer,* pursuing her as quickly as she was running away.

And why not? The White Wolf had already proven his tactical superiority. He wanted to end this hunt and end it quickly, just as Picard would have done if their roles were reversed.

The captain gauged the distance between the two ships—a bit too far for effective phaser fire, he judged. But that could change—and with a grim smile, he demonstrated just how quickly it could happen.

"All stop!" he bellowed. Then, to Vigo: "Fire phasers!"

Everything happened so quickly, Picard couldn't be certain at first whether his gambit had worked or failed. The White Wolf's ship seemed to surge out of nowhere, looming impossibly large on the viewscreen, even as the *Stargazer* stabbed it with two seething red phaser bolts at appallingly close range.

The twin energy lances sent the pirate ship skittering past them at a terrifyingly oblique angle. Picard could almost imagine the White Wolf's hull scraping that of the Federation vessel. But the miss, narrow as it may have been, was unquestionably a miss. The *Stargazer* and what was left of her shields remained intact.

Which was more than the captain imagined could be said of their adversary. Of course, without traditional sensor readings, he had no way of knowing how badly he had damaged the White Wolf. But there was a way to find out.

"Go after him!" Picard commanded Idun. Then, as the helm officer's fingers flew over her controls, the captain glanced at Vigo and added, "Ready phasers!"

The gas clouds slid sideways on the viewscreen as the *Stargazer* came about and offered pursuit. Turning to Gerda's monitor, Picard saw the green blip in full flight.

"Range?" he asked.

"One hundred twenty-five thousand kilometers," his navigator informed him.

Farther than they would normally have attempted weapons fire, even with their normal array of sensors in operation. However, the White Wolf wasn't bobbing and weaving at this point. His attempt at escape was straight and unswerving.

Picard gave the order. "Target and fire!"

A moment later, his forward phaser banks belched crimson fury. It pierced the softly tinted gas clouds ahead of them and was almost immediately lost to sight.

However, the phaser beams hadn't ceased to exist. With luck, the White Wolf would soon find that out.

"Fire again!" the captain said.

As before, two seething beams of phased energy poured out of the *Stargazer* and buried themselves in the sea of gases. And as before, he could only imagine their effect.

But this time, Gerda gave him something more concrete than his imagination. "The enemy is slowing down," she announced triumphantly. "Half impulse at best."

Glancing at her monitor, Picard could see the gap between them and their prey diminishing precipitously. One hundred thousand kilometers. Eighty thousand. Sixty thousand.

"Match their speed and fire!" he said, his voice sounding stentorian in the narrow confines of the bridge.

Idun slowed them down, and the *Stargazer*'s phaser batteries poured destruction into the roiling clouds. As the captain watched them vanish, he was joined by Ben Zoma.

"How are we doing?" the first officer asked.

Picard kept his eyes on Gerda's radar monitor. "Better than before, Number One. *Much* better."

"So what made you think of that stop-and-fire tactic?"

What indeed? "I was thinking of Captain Ruhalter. We used to fence, as you know, and one of his favorite moves was something called a stop-thrust. It often began with a retreat."

Ben Zoma seemed impressed. "I see."

"We must have hit them again," Gerda said. "They've slowed to a crawl, sir."

Indeed, the behavior of the green blip bore out her observation. The pirate was hardly making any progress at all.

"Looks like he's had it," Ben Zoma remarked.

Something occurred to the captain. "Unless our friend the White Wolf is laying a trap for us."

Ben Zoma looked at him. "Feigning disability to

bring the *Stargazer* in closer, so he can let us have it with both barrels?"

Picard nodded. "Precisely."

"Our regular sensors aren't *completely* dead," Ben Zoma reminded him. "If we get within fifty kilometers of the bastard, I'll bet we can get a full scan of him."

The captain considered the option. If the White Wolf attacked them with phasers at a range of fifty kilometers, it could leave the *Stargazer* a shambles. But they had a mission to complete, and they weren't going to complete it by hanging back.

"Slow to one-eighth impulse," he said.

"One-eighth impulse," Idun confirmed.

Picard watched Gerda's radar screen. The pirate ship's behavior wasn't changing one iota. She was still moving through gas-drenched space at a snail's pace.

When they got within sixty kilometers, the captain called for thrusters only. At fifty-six kilometers, some of the traditional sensors began to kick in. By the time they reached fifty-two kilometers, they had enough information to know where they stood.

The White Wolf's shields were down, her weapons were off-line, and her propulsion systems were all but useless. The *Stargazer* had won. Her prey was hers for the taking.

The White Wolf swept away some of the smoke issuing from his helmsman's flaming control console, situated just ahead of his captain's chair. Then he peered at the still-functioning radar screen attached to his armrest.

Their pursuer, represented by a blue icon on a white grid, was creeping closer to them by the moment.

"Damn them," growled Turgis, who had been injured and was using the back of the center seat to hold himself up.

"Yes," said the pirate. "Damn them indeed."

His vessel was absolutely helpless, rendered so by their Starfleet enemy's surprise tactics. There was nothing he could do to keep his hold from being emptied of its stolen cargo, or his crew from being tried at the nearest starbase.

The prospect left a bitter taste in his mouth—even more bitter than the acrid taste of burning plastic.

But he had still had his hidden ace. As long as that individual hadn't come into play yet, there was still a chance that the White Wolf would come out on top.

Picard was tempted to smile as he savored his victory.

But he couldn't, of course. There was still work to be done and lots of it. For one thing, he doubted that he could tractor the pirate's ship back through the obstacles Beta Barritus had thrown at them, so he would have to board the pale, slim vessel in order to remove her crew and cargo.

And the captain couldn't depend on his transporters. The gas clouds and free-floating ions in the vicinity were creating too much interference for that. So the only way to remove anybody or anything—

"Captain?" said Gerda, interrupting his thoughts.

He looked at her. "What is it, Lieutenant?"

The navigator pointed to her radar screen, which now showed not one blip but two. "Sir," she said, her voice low and grim, "radar shows a *second* ship in the area."

Chapter Twenty-Two

PICARD TURNED TO BEN ZOMA. "A *second* ship?"

They had been expecting only one ship when they went after the White Wolf. If there were two or three of the pirates or perhaps even more, it would mean trouble.

Ben Zoma frowned. "Doesn't sound good."

"Evasive maneuvers," the captain told Idun.

But as the *Stargazer* began to swing around the White Wolf, Paxton spoke up from his comm console.

"They're hailing us," he informed Picard.

The captain felt a muscle spasm in his jaw as he considered the situation. "Discontinue maneuvers," he told Idun. "But be ready to resume them on my command."

"Aye, sir," came the helm officer's response.

Picard glanced at Paxton. "Return their hail, Lieutenant."

Paxton turned to his console and did as he was told. A moment later, he turned around again, an unmistakable look of disbelief on his face. "Sir," he said, "it's the *Cochise.*"

Picard wasn't ready to believe it. "Are you certain?" he asked his comm officer.

Paxton shrugged. "That's what they claim, sir."

"Then they should be able to show me Captain Greenbriar," the captain concluded. "Tell them I want to see him. *Now.*"

Paxton went to work again at his console, and before Picard could draw another breath, the craggy visage of a Starfleet captain filled his viewscreen. It was static-riddled and it wavered occasionally, but there was no question that it was Greenbriar.

"Picard," he said, "are you all right?"

"I am," the captain told him. He looked around his bridge at the damage it had taken. "Though somewhat the worse for wear."

"And the White Wolf?"

"Disabled, apparently. We were about to put together a boarding party when you arrived."

"That's good news," said Greenbriar.

Picard should have been happy to see his colleague, happy to have a little support in such a perilous setting. But something about the *Cochise*'s presence here felt wrong to him.

Before the *Stargazer,* no one had ever managed to get this far. Not in dozens of previous attempts. *No one.*

Yet here was the *Cochise,* basking in the proximate, ruddy light of Beta Barritus. It seemed like an awfully big coincidence—a little too big for Picard to swallow.

"I hadn't expected to see you here," he told Green-briar.

"I hadn't expected to *be* here," Greenbriar replied in a comradely tone of voice. "At the last minute, Admiral McAteer changed his mind and dispatched us to back you up."

"Yes," said Picard, "I knew that. I meant I didn't think you would be able to penetrate this far into the system."

As he spoke, his mind raced headlong. *What is going on here?* he demanded of himself.

Picard's friend Corey Zweller had warned him that McAteer wanted to see him fail, so that Admiral Mehdi could be seen to fail as well. But how badly did McAteer want it?

Badly enough to take the lives of Picard and his crew?

And if the *Stargazer* and all its hands were to be lost here, in this dangerous place, who would question it? Who would know that the *Cochise* had followed her in?

No one but the captain and crew of the *Cochise*—and Admiral McAteer, of course.

Suddenly, the captain realized what he was saying—and rejected the idea. *I'm being paranoid,* he thought. *I've been on edge so long, I've begun tilting at shadows.*

McAteer might have been a lot of things, but he was also a high-ranking Starfleet officer, a man trusted implicitly by other men of good judgment. It was unthinkable that he would sacrifice the *Stargazer* just to further his personal ambitions.

Wasn't it?

As he asked himself that question, he noticed Ben Zoma leaning over Gerda's console. A glance told him that Greenbriar's ship had come within their limited sensor range—although it wasn't as limited as the *Cochise*'s sensor range, since Greenbriar's instruments hadn't been enhanced by the *Stargazer*'s Chief Simenon.

Ben Zoma was scrutinizing the *Cochise* intently, examining her power levels, her structural integrity, her crew, anything that might have told him something was wrong. And Gerda was following his every move.

Inwardly, Picard smiled. It seemed he wasn't the only one wary of Greenbriar's appearance here.

"How *did* you make it this far?" he inquired of Greenbriar.

"The same way you did, I expect," came the man's reply. "We warp-jumped the debris field, then altered the polarity of our shields to make it through the vortex belt. And when we couldn't see in this muck, my chief engineer came up with the idea of—"

Without warning, Gerda whirled in her seat. "Captain," she said, her eyes hard and angry, "the *Cochise* is powering up her weapons!"

Picard didn't even have time to utter a curse. "All available power to the shields!"

They made the adjustment just in time to ward off a blinding red phaser barrage. Nonetheless, the impact sent everyone on the bridge reeling hard to starboard and tore one of their plasma conduits free of its moorings.

"Return fire!" the captain bellowed as the conduit whipped back and forth capriciously, spraying superheated plasma at a bulkhead.

Vigo punched back at the *Constellation*-class *Cochise* with his forward phaser banks, but Greenbriar's ship was already executing evasive maneuvers. Only one of the energy beams managed to strike her.

And a moment or two later, Picard's colleague came about for another pass at him.

"Shields down fifty-four percent," Gerda noted.

The captain absorbed the information. His ship was at a distinct disadvantage. She had already been battered by the White Wolf, whereas Greenbriar's vessel was all but unscathed.

And Greenbriar himself was one of the most experienced captains in the fleet, while Picard had been given command of the *Stargazer* only a few short weeks ago.

A lopsided match if ever there was one, Picard thought. He had to find a way to pull off an upset.

"Evasive maneuvers," he told Idun. Then he glanced at Vigo and said, "Fire at will."

Picard's helm officer moved them off the bull's-eye, giving the *Cochise* a running, twisting target. And as soon as Greenbriar's ship came within range, Vigo greeted her with a sizzling phaser salvo.

But the *Stargazer* was brutalized as well. The captain was thrown back into his chair as an aft control bank erupted in flames.

"Shields down seventy-six percent," Gerda reported.

"Casualties on decks seven and eight," Paxton added. "Sickbay is sending out teams."

Picard felt a familiar hand on his shoulder. "We can't just trade volleys with them," Ben Zoma said, his voice so low that only his friend could hear it. "That's what Greenbriar *wants* us to do."

The captain frowned as he considered his options. In the meantime, the *Cochise* wheeled and came at them again with full fury. As before, Idun made it difficult for Greenbriar to hit them, but he still got in a solid phaser shot.

"Shields down eighty-seven percent," Gerda announced, a hint of frustration in her voice.

And the *Cochise,* her captain undaunted, was coming about for another charge at them.

The *Stargazer* could withstand only one more barrage before she lost her defenses altogether. If Picard was going to turn the tide, this would be his last chance to do so.

Perspiration collected in the small of his back. He had to do *something.* But *what?*

And then it came to him. *Of course,* he thought. It was so simple, he was amazed that he hadn't thought of it before.

"Mr. Vigo," Picard said.

The weapons officer turned to him.

"Target the center of the *Cochise*'s navigational deflector and hit it with the narrowest, most intense beam you can manage. And don't let up until I tell you."

Vigo smiled, a sign that he had some idea of what his captain was up to. "Aye, sir."

The captain glanced at his helm officer. "Give us a good look at our target, Lieutenant."

Idun nodded, as steady as ever. "I will, sir."

As they closed with Greenbriar's ship, Idun banked sharply and unexpectedly, taking the *Stargazer* across the *Cochise*'s bow. It seemed like a reckless move in that it exposed their flank to their adversary's phasers for an awkward amount of time.

And the *Stargazer* paid for it.

Raked by Greenbriar's directed energy beams, she

lost more than what was left of her shields. She suffered hull breaches and severed power linkages and ceased to function in a thousand small ways.

Picard didn't need to hear the damage reports. He could feel what had happened in his bones.

But Idun's maneuver also gave Vigo the opening he needed. The *Stargazer*'s powerful crimson phaser beams plunged mercilessly into the heart of their adversary's navigational deflector, cutting through layer upon layer of graviton-contained spatial distortion in the merest fraction of a second.

Fortunately, they didn't have to take out the entire deflector. Their objective was the small, long-range signal emitter at the center of it, a shallow, bowl-like structure currently being used for one purpose and one purpose only . . .

To transmit the special-frequency radio waves that drove Greenbriar's radar system.

As Obal rushed into the shuttlebay with the other members of his security team, he took in the scene as calmly and objectively as his Academy trainers had advised him to do.

There were three crewmen down. *No,* he thought, as he came around a cargo shuttle and saw another pair of legs protruding beyond it, *make that four crewmen down.*

Racing across the bay as fast as he could, he reached the unidentified legs and saw the body to which they were attached. It belonged to Lieutenant Chiang, the chief of this section.

The man was unconscious, bleeding from a cut on his forehead. There was blood on the shuttle next to him as well. Apparently, Chiang had struck his head on it during one of the phaser impacts the *Stargazer* had suffered.

It was Obal's job to get him out of here, just as his comrades were removing the other crewmen in the bay. Of course, Chiang was much bigger and heavier than the Binderian, but he believed he could manage.

He had already hooked his hands under the man's armpits and begun to drag him toward the exit when he noticed something—a red light on the lonely-looking console not twenty meters away.

It gave Obal pause. If he recalled correctly, a red light only came on in case of trouble, and very specific trouble at that. It signaled that the semipermeable force field between the bay and the tinted sea of gases outside was about to fizzle out.

If that happened, all the air in the bay would rush out into interplanetary space. And along with it would go any crewmen and equipment that happened to be present at the time.

Could the light have gone on due to a circuitry malfunction? It was certainly possible, with all the punishment the ship was taking.

Or, Obal asked himself, a chill running down his spine, might it be that the light was working perfectly? In that case, the problem would be in the mechanism that maintained the force field.

"Lands of fire," he breathed, invoking an image from his people's most primitive belief system.

He couldn't take the chance that it was a simple short circuit. He had to do something, and do it quickly.

Easing Chiang to the smooth, hard surface of the

deck, Obal darted in the direction of the console. But even as he did this, he saw the barrier begin to buckle and spark, and felt the tug of something hideously powerful.

Was he too late? he wondered. Would everyone in the bay, rescued as well as rescuers, be sucked out of the ship?

No, he vowed. *I won't let it happen.*

Gritting his teeth, Obal hunkered down and drove his slender legs as hard as he could. Little by little, he made his way across the bay to the freestanding control console.

He ignored the cries of his fellow security officers as they realized what was happening. He even managed to ignore the sight of Lieutenant Chiang sliding toward the failing barrier.

Slowly but insistently, Obal plied the last couple of meters of his journey and reached the console. Then he hung on to it against the pull of space as he surveyed its colored studs and touch-sensitive pads.

In his Academy class he had had no trouble remembering which stud did what. Now, with so much riding on his actions, he found the task a bit more difficult.

That one, he decided at last, singling out a square blue stud. And he pushed it down as hard as he could.

For a moment, Obal feared he had made the wrong decision. Then he felt a let-up in the force that had been tugging at him. Looking up in the direction of the force field, he saw by the silver gleam along its perimeter that the back-up emitters had been activated.

There was a second force field in place, stopping the air from leaving the bay—along with everyone and everything in it. Obal drew a deep breath and expelled it. He was just glad he had noticed the red light in time.

Releasing the console with an understandable reluctance, he returned to Lieutenant Chiang's still-unconscious form. Then he began dragging the man toward the exit again.

Jean-Luc Picard looked around his bridge at the devastation he and his officers had endured—the flaming control panels and the clouds of black smoke and the persistent blasts of white plasma—and hoped it had all been worth it.

He turned to Vigo. "Did you get it—the signal emitter?"

The Pandrilite shrugged his massive shoulders. "I don't know, sir. I think . . ." But he couldn't finish his sentence. All he could do was shrug a second time.

Picard turned to Gerda's control console, which had survived the battle to this point. Her radar monitor still showed the movements of the *Cochise* as a green blip.

But unless the captain was mistaken, the *Cochise* wasn't coming around for another pass at its finally defenseless adversary. In fact, Greenbriar's ship wasn't going anywhere at all.

Picard looked to Gerda for confirmation. Looking up at him, she said, "They're dead in the water, sir."

And there could be only one reason for that. The *Stargazer*'s phaser assault had disabled the *Cochise*'s signal emitter. Greenbriar's ship, though still well shielded and well powered, was completely and utterly blind.

Instinct, he thought. *Either you've got it or you don't.*

The captain nodded in recognition of Gerda's remark, then turned to Vigo. "Well done, Lieutenant."

The weapons officer smiled at him. "Thank you, sir."

Picard took in his other officers at a glance, settling on Idun last of all. "Well done, all of you."

His helm officer nodded, a glint of satisfaction in her eyes. This was the sort of thing she lived for—she and Gerda both.

Finally, the captain considered the viewscreen, which had reverted to an image of the gas clouds surrounding them. "Mr. Paxton," he said, "see if you can raise Captain Greenbriar."

In a matter of moments, Greenbriar appeared on the viewscreen. For a man who had just lost a space battle, he didn't look very disappointed. He seemed as pleasant and easygoing as if he and Picard were standing around the punch bowl at McAteer's cocktail party.

"Good shooting," Greenbriar told him. "My compliments to your weapons officer."

Picard didn't feel inclined to join in the jocularity. "What's going on here, Captain?"

The other man frowned, accentuating the lines in his seamed face. "I guess there's no point in trying to conceal it any longer."

But Greenbriar's tone of voice belied his expression of resignation. It suggested that he was stalling for time, still looking for a way to secure the victory.

Picard glared at him. He was through playing games, especially the sort that put the welfare of his ship and crew at risk. "The truth, Captain. And I mean *now.*"

Greenbriar regarded him for a moment. Then he nodded soberly, appearing to accept the fact that he was out of options.

"I'd appreciate it if we could speak in private," he said.

Picard considered it for a moment. Then he turned to

Ben Zoma. "I'll be in my ready room. You've got the bridge."

His first officer nodded, though he would no doubt have preferred to hear what Greenbriar had to say. "Aye, sir."

Casting a last wary glance at the viewscreen, Picard repaired to his ready room.

241

Chapter Twenty-Three

PICARD SAT BACK IN HIS CHAIR and studied the same craggy visage that he had seen on the viewscreen. Except now, it filled the computer screen on his desk.

"You must be a little confused," Greenbriar said.

"To say the least," Picard responded. "Try as I might, I cannot imagine why you would attack a Starfleet vessel, unless you have aligned yourself with a pirate who has become the bane of this entire sector. And if you have, that begs yet an even *greater* question."

Greenbriar nodded. "It's difficult to explain. Maybe it would be better if I let the pirate speak for himself."

Picard shrugged. "If that is what it takes."

A moment later, Greenbriar's image was shunted to the left side of the screen, making way for the image of another man on the right. *The White Wolf,* Picard thought.

But the pirate wasn't at all what the captain had expected.

For one thing, his hair wasn't white; it wasn't even gray. And he wasn't the crafty old veteran he was cracked up to be. The White Wolf was a baby-faced young man, barely out of his twenties if Picard was any judge of such things.

"Captain," said the pirate in a soft, cultured voice. "I wish I could say it was a pleasure to meet you. But under the circumstances . . ."

Picard frowned. "Captain Greenbriar promised me an explanation. I'm waiting to hear it."

The White Wolf nodded. "Of course. My name is Carridine. And contrary to what you may have heard about me, I'm more of an exobiologist than I am a pirate."

It sounded familiar. *"Emil* Carridine?" Picard asked.

The pirate looked at him. "I see you've heard of me."

"If I recall correctly, you come from a wealthy family on Earth. Some years back, you embarked on a series of planetary surveys in a previously unexplored part of space—"

"And was never heard from again," the White Wolf said. "But I hadn't disappeared. Not really. I had only assumed a different identity."

"So I gather," Picard told him. "The question is, *why?*"

Isn't it always? Carridine's expression seemed to say.

"During one of my routine planetary surveys," he said, "I found a world I called Daribund. It was ridiculously rich in latinum—a huge prize for anyone with a yen to get rich quick."

The White Wolf's eyes lost their focus as he remembered. "If it had been a barren world, I wouldn't have thought twice about it. But Daribund was populated by a pre-sentient species with an extremely fragile niche in the planet's ecosystem. Any mining enterprise on that world would have doomed that species to extinction."

Picard saw the problem. "And you wanted to prevent that."

"In the worst way," Carridine told him.

"And he couldn't go to the Federation," said Greenbriar, "because the planet's dominant species was a pre-spaceflight culture."

Picard nodded. "The Prime Directive."

"So," Carridine continued, "I bought a ship and put a crew together and took the matter into my own hands."

"And defended this world on your own," Picard concluded.

"Not that it was easy. I wasn't Starfleet, so it was difficult to acquire much in the way of firepower. So I took a different tack."

Carridine went on to describe his boyhood fascination with Earth's twentieth-century buccaneers—men like Bluebeard and Jean Lafitte. Inspired by them, he set out to create a situation that would keep unsavory characters from strip-mining Daribund.

"If I became a pirate," he said, "if I raided the ships of Federation member worlds, Starfleet was bound to come after me eventually. And if Starfleet was focusing its attention on this part of space, what pirate in his right mind would try to horn in?"

Picard followed the reasoning. "And as long as real pirates stayed away, Daribund's pre-sentients would remain safe."

It was a clever scheme. And more important, it had

worked, up to then. The *Stargazer*'s presence here was evidence of that.

Picard regarded Greenbriar. "And just how did *you* become involved in this enterprise?"

Greenbriar shrugged. "I caught the White Wolf, just as you did. But as I was about to take him in, he told me the story he's telling you—and I changed my mind."

Picard frowned. "You let him go."

"He did more than that," said Carridine.

"I became his ally," Greenbriar told them without remorse. "I became his informant. Whenever Starfleet sent a ship after him, I let him know about it in advance. Until now, that was the extent of my involvement. By making it here, you compelled me to do more."

"To attack a colleague," Picard said.

Greenbriar nodded. "Yes."

"Unfortunately," Carridine said, "I've now been apprehended a second time, and I don't imagine you'll be as open-minded as Captain Greenbriar was. It seems Daribund is about to lose its defender."

He paused, no doubt waiting for his comment—and its implications—to sink in. When he spoke again to the captain, it was as one reasonable man to another.

"On the other hand, Captain Greenbriar saw the injustice in apprehending the White Wolf. I hope you will see the injustice as well, Captain—and act accordingly."

Picard looked at him. "You're suggesting that I let you go? After all we've gone through to apprehend you?"

"What I'm suggesting," said Carridine, "is that you follow the impulses that led you to become a Starfleet officer in the first place. No more, no less."

Picard frowned. He hated the idea of deceiving his su-

periors as Greenbriar had. He hated even the suggestion
of it. He had taken a vow when he entered Starfleet, and
he had every intention of remaining true to it.

And yet . . .

It was difficult not to see Carridine's point. The man
was protecting something worthwhile, something no
one else was inclined to protect, and harming no one in
the process.

The White Wolf was on the side of the angels, strange
as it seemed. And if Picard wanted to be on the side of
the angels as well, there was only one choice he could
make.

With a sigh, he tapped his communicator and summoned Ben Zoma. Then he tapped it again and said, "Picard to Simenon."

The reply came a moment later. "Simenon here."

"I'd like to see you in my ready room," Picard told
him. "You and I have an important matter to discuss."

"What's that?" asked the engineer.

"In my ready room," the captain maintained.

Simenon grumbled. "As you wish."

Picard turned to Carridine. "I'm going to arrange a
shutdown of the *Stargazer*'s impulse engines. An *accidental* shutdown, of course. It will present only a minor
inconvenience to my engineering staff, but its timing
will be most unfortunate, as it will allow the legendary
White Wolf to slip through my fingers."

Carridine smiled in relief. "Thank you, Captain."

"But there's a condition," the captain added. "I want
the Federation's cargo returned. I don't care how."

The White Wolf nodded, only too glad to comply.
"Whatever you say. I've got no use for it anyway."

Greenbriar nodded approvingly. "You're a good man, Picard. Just as I had heard."

Picard took some solace in the knowledge that he had at least one true ally among his fellow captains. Also, it occurred to him, he understood something he only *thought* he had understood before.

"People are often not what they seem," he said, quoting Greenbriar word for word.

The other captain smiled. "You've got a hell of a memory."

"Yes," said Picard. "But this is one day I may want to forget."

Idun didn't know anything about Picard's conversation with Captain Greenbriar. She didn't know why he had summoned Ben Zoma and Simenon and then dispatched them again.

But when Picard finally emerged from his ready room, the helm officer was certain that his orders would involve phasers and boarding parties and the incarceration of all who had committed crimes against the Federation.

That is, until the captain actually spoke.

"You know," he said, "this is not a good situation."

She looked at him. "I beg your pardon, sir?"

"I was referring to the impulse engines," Picard told her. "This is a very bad time for them to have shut down."

Idun looked at her console, trying to figure out what the captain was talking about. As far as she could tell, the ship's impulse engines were working perfectly.

"Sir," she said, "I don't see any problem with the—"

The helm officer stopped in midsentence. Suddenly,

all her monitors were flashing, indicating that they had lost impulse power. She turned to Picard again.

"I don't understand," she said. "How did you—?"

"In fact, the timing couldn't have been much worse," Picard remarked, his voice now loud enough for everyone on the bridge to hear him. "No doubt the White Wolf will take advantage of this unexpected opportunity to escape us. And without working impulse engines, there's no possibility of our offering pursuit."

Idun didn't understand. The captain didn't seem very disappointed, considering how hard they had worked to find the pirate and disable his vessel. Then she realized what he was doing.

He was letting the White Wolf go.

"Had another starship tracked us down and joined the fray," Picard continued, "it might have been a different story. However, we faced the pirate alone." He looked around at his bridge personnel, eyeing each of them in turn. "Completely alone," he added for emphasis.

Idun didn't know why the captain was doing this. But clearly, it had something to do with what he had learned in his ready room.

She had been raised by Klingons to be a warrior, and a warrior didn't allow a defeated enemy to slip through her fingers. Her every instinct cried out against this.

Yet she remained silent, because it was Captain Picard who had implicitly asked her to do so. Her respect for him went beyond instinct, beyond protocol, beyond her understanding of right and wrong.

If Picard wanted to allow the enemy to escape, Idun wouldn't do anything to stand in his way. Nor, she decided, would she include any of this in her helm report.

Her sister darted a glance at her from her place at navigation. Judging from Gerda's expression, she felt the same way.

"It's too bad," Lieutenant Paxton said, taking his cue from the captain. "We came so close."

"So *very* close," Picard sighed.

"I guess we have no choice but to repair the engines and go home with our tail between our legs," Vigo said.

"No choice at all," the captain agreed.

He looked around the bridge, waiting for one of his officers to object. No one did.

Least of all Idun Asmund.

Obal was taking his turn at the big concave bank of security monitors when Pug Joseph approached him.

"Mr. Obal," said the security chief.

The Binderian turned to him and smiled. "Good morning, sir."

"How's it going?" Joseph asked, though that wasn't exactly the question he had come to ask.

"Fine, sir," said Obal. "I understand the impulse engines are running perfectly again."

"Uh . . . yes, I guess they are. I'm told we'll be leaving Beta Barritus before we know it."

Obal shrugged his narrow shoulders. "It's a pity the White Wolf got away. But at least we managed to recover the stolen cargo."

Joseph looked at the Binderian and couldn't tell if there was any irony in his comments or not.

"Listen," the security chief said, feeling the need to change the subject, "I wanted to tell you what a great job you did down there in the shuttlebay. If not for you, we might have had a real tragedy on our hands."

Obal smiled. "I was happy to help. But then, isn't that what a security officer does—provide help in times of crisis?"

Joseph didn't have the heart to tell the Binderian that he still didn't have what it took, or to reprise his advice that Obal's talents would be better served elsewhere. Not now, after he had made such a hero of himself.

Unfortunately, there was more to security work than cataloging phasers or securing the shuttlebay. One had to have the respect of others, and Joseph just didn't see how Obal could earn that respect.

"Yes," the chief replied grudgingly. "That's what a security officer does."

Picard smiled when he saw the stars.

They were long, bright streaks rather than points of brilliance, a function of the *Stargazer*'s faster-than-light velocity. But they were a welcome sight nonetheless.

"You know," said Ben Zoma, who was standing at the captain's side, "I could go a long time without missing Beta Barritus again."

Picard nodded in agreement. "A *long* time."

"Sir," said Gerda, putting a damper on the moment, "sensors are picking up a vessel."

Picard turned to her, his eyes narrowing. "What *kind* of vessel?"

His navigator consulted her monitors. "It's a Federation starship—the *Antares*. Two hundred million kilometers and closing."

Normally, Picard would have treated this as good

news. Or at the very least, not *bad* news. But after his experience with the *Cochise,* he couldn't help feeling a little gun-shy.

"Hail them," he said.

"Actually," Paxton told him, "they're hailing *us.*"

Picard nodded. "On screen."

The viewer filled with the image of a Starfleet captain—a swarthy man with a neat dark goatee. Picard believed he had seen the fellow at the admiral's soiree on Starbase 32.

"This is Captain Vayishra of the *Antares,*" the man said. "The *Grissom* and the *Reliant* will be here within the hour."

"I see," Picard replied.

Vayishra looked sympathetic, in a vaguely condescending sort of way. "Had trouble getting in, did you?"

Picard shrugged. "Some."

"Don't take it too hard," Vayishra told him. "From what I've heard, it's a mess in there."

"That it is," Picard confirmed.

"When we're all here," said Vayishra, "follow our lead. We'll find the White Wolf no matter what it takes."

"Actually," said Picard, "we already found him."

The other captain looked skeptical for a moment. Then he laughed. "Of course you have. You've got him in your brig even as we speak."

"I'm afraid we don't," Picard told him. "However, we *do* have the cargo he lifted."

Vayishra's brow furrowed. "You're being facetious, of course."

"I'm not," Picard assured him.

Vayishra shook his head. "But how did you—?"

"It will all be in my report. Picard out."

As Vayishra's perplexed expression vanished from the screen, giving way to the field of streaming stars, Ben Zoma moved to the captain's side. "That was more fun than you deserve," he said.

"Is it?" Picard responded. "I *am* the only captain who's ever cornered the White Wolf."

"Also the only one who's ever let him go."

Picard glanced at his first officer. "You would have done the same thing in my place."

Ben Zoma smiled. "Probably."

"Which makes us . . . what?" the captain wondered. "Soft touches?"

His friend considered the question for a moment. "I prefer to think of us as men who can tell where orders end and justice begins."

"Very poetic," Picard said appreciatively. "But what kind of captain ignores his orders?"

"In this case?" Ben Zoma said. He clapped his friend on the shoulder. "The best kind."

Chapter Twenty-Four

As OBAL WORKED OUT with a set of weights in the ship's gymnasium, he reflected on how happy he was.

He had pleased Lieutenant Joseph with his work in the shuttlebay. And if Lieutenant Joseph was pleased, Obal was pleased. In fact, he was smiling to himself when he heard a hiss and saw the doors to the gym slide apart.

They revealed someone in exercise togs. Someone tall and muscular. Someone obviously human.

Caber, he thought.

The ensign didn't notice the Binderian right away. He was too intent on something, too wrapped up in his own thoughts. In fact, he was halfway to the parallel bars when he seemed to realize that there was someone else in the room.

Caber turned to see who it was. When he caught sight

of Obal, a grin spread across his face. A *cruel* grin, if the Binderian was any judge of such things.

The human stood there for a second, staring across the room. Then, like a predator who has caught the scent of his prey, he started in Obal's direction.

The Binderian wasn't surprised. Caber had taken advantage of every opportunity to ridicule and belittle him. Why would he miss out on this one?

Obal eased his weights to the ground and sighed. He wasn't looking forward to the abuse that was sure to follow. He wasn't eager to be humiliated again. However, he had tolerated his treatment to this point for the sake of decorum—and, for the sake of decorum, he would continue to do so.

His superiors had more important things to do than mediate petty differences between crewmen. Obal was determined not to be a burden to them. He would endure whatever he had to for as long as he had to.

And eventually, Caber's hostility would wane. At least, that was the Binderian's plan.

But as the human approached him, the curl in his lip seemed to undercut Obal's expectations. "Imagine finding *you* here," he spat.

The Binderian didn't say anything at all. He just stood there, stoic and uncomplaining.

"Nothing to say?" Caber laughed. It was a short, ugly sound without any humor in it. "Funny, you seemed to have *plenty* to say when we were in security."

Seeing he hadn't gotten a reaction, the human bent down and poked a rigid forefinger into Obal's bony chest.

"Where the hell do you get off telling me what to do?" he demanded through clenched teeth. "Where does a squirt like *you* get the gall to lord it over some-one like *me?*"

The Binderian's chest hurt where he'd been poked, but he managed to remain silent.

It only made Caber that much angrier. "You don't even have the guts to stand up for yourself. You think you deserve to give orders to people who *do?*"

Again he poked Obal in the chest. This time, it was all the Binderian could do to keep from crying out.

"Why don't you find yourself another ship?" Caber demanded, his saliva striking Obal in the face. "One where they *like* taking orders from skinny little cowards?"

Another poke, stabbing deep into the Binderian's flesh. His eyes watered from the pain, but he kept it to himself.

"You hear me?" Caber snapped, his voice echoing, his eyes mere inches from Obal's. "You get your scrawny butt off this ship or I'll make you wish you *had!*"

As the gym doors slid open, Nikolas caught sight of Caber. He was about to offer an excuse for his lateness when he realized that his friend wasn't alone.

Obal was with him. And it looked as if Caber were trying to ram his forefinger right through the Binderian's anatomy.

"You hear me?" Caber snarled, either oblivious to Nikolas's presence or purposely ignoring it.

"Hey, Joe!" Nikolas snapped. He loped across the gym to intervene before the situation could deteriorate any further. "Come on, leave the poor guy alone!"

Caber didn't respond. Instead, he poked Obal in his scrawny chest again and said, "Get lost—and I mean now!"

Nikolas felt a spurt of anger. Obviously, his room-mate had let his feelings about the Binderian run amok. Grabbing Caber's arm, he spun him around.

"You can't do that," Nikolas told him, meeting his friend's red-rimmed gaze with equal intensity. "He's a crewman on this ship, just like you and—"

Before he could finish, Caber's fist came flying at him. Nikolas couldn't believe it. The next thing he knew, he was lying on his back, his jaw feeling as if it had been broken in a dozen places.

Caber came to stand over him, the angle accentuating the difference in their sizes. He pointed a thick, trembling finger at Nikolas and growled, "Stay out of this!"

"I can't," Nikolas insisted, his words slurred by the pain and stiffness in his jaw. He began to get up, hoping he could still keep Obal from harm.

But Caber had other ideas. As Nikolas got his feet underneath him, the other man launched a kick at his friend's face. Nikolas was too surprised by the unrestrained viciousness of the attack to defend himself. All he had time to do was turn his face away.

Caber's kick wound up smashing Nikolas in the side of the head with the fury of a phaser blast, putting him on his back again. For a moment, the ensign was too dazed to move. Then, his ear a fiery agony, he rolled over on his belly in an attempt to get up and stop the other man.

But it seemed that Caber was done with him for the moment. He was going after Obal again, his finger pointed at the helpless Binderian in an unmistakable promise of violence.

Nikolas groped for his combadge, found it, and tapped it. "Security to the gym," he mumbled through his pain, his voice sounding strange and distant, as if it were someone else's.

Then he thrust himself up onto all fours. It would take security a few minutes to get there, he told himself. In that time, Caber could inflict on Obal what he had inflicted on Nikolas.

Or worse.

Staggering to his feet, he saw Caber close with Obal. *Too late,* he thought. *Too late.*

Caber was going to take out the rest of his anger on the Binderian. And as fragile as Obal looked, there was no guarantee he would survive the beating.

But as Caber reached for Obal's neck, something unexpected happened: the Binderian flung up one of his skinny arms and deflected the human's attempt to grab him. Then, turning sideways, he lashed out awkwardly with one of his feet and speared Caber in the knee, eliciting a deep-throated cry of pain.

As Caber leaned over to grasp his injured joint, Obal struck again. He drove the heel of his hand into the ensign's forehead, straightening him up and causing him to stagger backward a couple of steps.

Pressing his advantage, the Binderian rushed forward and, with blinding quickness, bounded feet first into Caber's chest. The impact slammed the human into the bulkhead behind him, snapping his head back and forcing a groan out of him.

It was then that Nikolas realized that the doors to the gym were open and that Pug Joseph and a couple of his security officers were already across the threshold, their mouths hanging open as they watched Obal in action.

Caber, meanwhile, was no longer a threat. He slid

down the bulkhead like a bag of assorted and unrelated bones, his eyes closed, a trickle of blood visible in the corner of his mouth.

Nikolas wondered if he had lost consciousness and dreamed it all. He was still wondering when Obal scurried to his side and put his spindly arm around him.

"Are you all right?" the Binderian wheezed.

Nikolas nodded. "Fine," he wheezed.

By that time, Joseph had joined them. The other security officers were attending to Caber.

"What just happened?" the security chief asked Obal.

Looking apologetic, the Binderian shrugged his narrow, rounded shoulders. "I regret to inform you that Mr. Caber and I have had disagreements in the past. However—"

"They weren't disagreements," Nikolas interjected. "Caber didn't like him. He bullied him."

Joseph frowned at him. "I'd appreciate it if you would let Ensign Obal speak for himself."

Nikolas controlled himself. "Aye, sir."

The security chief turned to the Binderian again. "Go ahead," he said. "I'm listening."

Obal sighed. "As I said, we have had disagreements. I ignored them for the sake of decorum." He glanced at Nikolas. "However, Ensign Nikolas chose this occasion to come to my aid, and was injured for his trouble. On Binderia, we call someone who comes to our aid a *kellis dagh*. It is the height of cowardice on my world to let an assault on a *kellis dagh* go unavenged."

Nikolas was still stunned from the beating he had taken, but he had enough of his faculties about him to understand what Obal was saying. He couldn't abandon someone who had defended him, no matter what repercussions might have followed.

Might yet follow, Nikolas amended inwardly.

After all, Caber was an admiral's son with a spotless record. If anyone was going to get the benefit of the doubt, it would be him. But Nikolas and the Binderian had the truth on their side.

Surely, the ensign thought, *that has to count for something.*

Joseph nodded. "I'll be sure to include that in my report."

Obal turned to Nikolas. "Come. I'll help you get to sickbay."

Smiling through his pain, the ensign thanked him.

"You're welcome," said Obal, smiling back.

Nikolas didn't think the little guy would be able to help him much, considering the difference in their weights. But after what Obal had done for him, the ensign certainly wasn't going to turn him down.

With the help of Joseph and his new friend, Nikolas got to his feet and began the arduous trip to sickbay.

Picard was going over repair reports in his ready room when he heard a familiar chime. "Come," he said.

It was Valderrama. As always, she looked a little tentative as she entered the room.

"Please," the captain told her. "Sit down."

The science officer took the seat opposite his and smiled warmly. "What can I do for you, sir?"

"Nothing at the moment," he said. "I just wanted to ask you a question, if that's all right."

She shrugged. "Of course, sir."

Picard leaned forward. "Tell me, Lieutenant, how did you get the idea to use radar as a replacement for our sensor devices?"

Valderrama shrugged. "I'm not sure, sir. I guess you could say it was an inspiration."

The captain wished she had given him a more concrete response. "What would you say if I told you that Ensign Jiterica claims otherwise? That she says *she* had the inspiration first?"

The science officer reddened. "I don't understand."

Picard frowned. "A little while ago, Ensign Jiterica ran into Commander Ben Zoma and asked if her radar idea had proven useful. Commander Ben Zoma told her that, to the best of his knowledge, it was *your* radar idea."

"Which it was, sir."

"Nonetheless," the captain continued, "Ensign Jiterica insisted that *she* had come up with it. She insisted that she had given it to you, trusted you with it. Nor did she understand why you were trying to take credit for it."

The science officer shook her head. "That's not the way it happened, sir. I hate to say it, but Jiterica is lying."

"Normally," Picard said, "I'd be inclined to give you the benefit of the doubt. However, Jiterica's personal logs, which are time-coded, corroborated her story. The ensign had the idea first and gave it to you, her superior. And you claimed it for yourself."

Valderrama didn't try to defend herself this time. She just stood there, looking at him.

The captain frowned. "Can you enlighten me as to why you would do something like that?"

Valderrama looked away. It took her a few seconds to

get a reply out, and when she did it was husky with remorse.

"I didn't think you would keep me on unless I did something spectacular," she said. "All I did was grasp at the first straw presented to me."

Picard took a deep breath. "I can tolerate a great many things from my crew," he told Valderrama. "However, a lack of ethics isn't one of them. I would advise you to repair to your quarters and begin packing your things."

The woman's brow creased down the middle.

"If I were you," the captain went on, "I would resign my commission rather than face charges. But either way, I can assure you that you'll be leaving the *Stargazer*."

Valderrama didn't object to his decision. She just turned and left his ready room.

As Picard watched the doors slide closed behind her, he couldn't help thinking that he had witnessed a tragedy. He couldn't absolve Valderrama of her guilt. Clearly, she had brought her troubles on herself.

But that didn't make the outcome any less tragic.

The captain had begun dictating a commendation of Jiterica into his log when he heard the sound of chimes again. *Valderrama?* he wondered.

"Come," he said.

When the doors parted, he saw that it wasn't Valderrama after all. It was Commander Wu.

"Yes?" Picard said.

The second officer stepped into the room and spoke without preamble. "Sir, it's come to my attention that you're operating as commanding officer of this vessel in clear violation of Starleet regulations."

"Indeed," the captain responded. "And if I may ask, precisely which regulations am I violating?"

She told him. As it turned out, there were a good deal more of them than he would have guessed, ranging from insufficient expertise in weapons systems to a lack of certain inoculations.

"I promised Commander Ben Zoma that I wouldn't hold any of my subordinates to regulations. But I believe that, as you're the captain, you at least should be held to a stricter standard."

Picard felt himself stiffen at the rebuke. Nonetheless, he said, "I appreciate your pointing that out, Commander. I'll take it under advisement."

Wu nodded. "Thank you, sir." And she turned to go.

"Commander?" he said, stopping her in her tracks.

She faced him again, "Captain?"

No doubt she expected him to comment on her overzealousness. He surprised her. "You handled yourself well while we were hunting the White Wolf."

Wu smiled. "It pleases me to hear that, sir."

He smiled back. "Dismissed."

Picard waited until she had left the room and the titanium doors had closed behind her. Then he contacted his first officer via the ship's intercom system.

Apparently, he still had one more problem to take care of.

Wu didn't understand. She said so, her voice echoing throughout sickbay.

Greyhorse shrugged. "There's no question about it. You're due for a physical."

She frowned. "But you already gave me a physical."

"That was when you first came onboard."

"It wasn't that long ago," she pointed out.

"Long enough," Greyhorse told her. "Lie down, please." And he indicated the nearest biobed.

Wu got up on the bed and lay down. Then she watched the doctor scan the bio monitors.

"You know," she said, "I have reports to file. I hope this won't take long."

"It shouldn't," he told her. Suddenly, his brow creased.

"Is something wrong?" she asked.

Greyhorse shrugged. "Nothing serious." But he continued to regard the monitors.

"Don't be mysterious," Wu told him. "If there's something I need to know about—"

"It's your blood pressure," he said, looking up at her. "It's a little high."

"How high?"

The doctor told her. Indeed it *was* a little high. But just a little—hardly worth discussing.

And now that Wu thought about it, she had an explanation. "I had black bean soup for lunch. It was very salty."

"That might be the culprit," Greyhorse allowed.

The second officer swung her legs around and sat up. "And everything else is in order?"

He nodded. "Very much so."

"Good," said Wu, slipping off the table. "Then, if you don't mind, I'll get back to my duties."

She was halfway to the exit when Greyhorse spoke up again. "Actually, Commander, I can't allow that."

Wu turned and looked at him. "I beg your pardon?"

"I can't allow you to return to your duties," he said. "Not with excessively high blood pressure."

"But we agreed that it's from the black bean soup."

"We agreed that it *might* be. The only way to know for certain is to test you again later this evening."

"But in the meantime, you're telling me I can't resume my duties as second officer?"

"That's what I'm telling you."

Wu scowled. "This is ridiculous. You're splitting hairs."

"It's a regulation," Greyhorse maintained.

"But you don't need to take it quite so literally, Doctor. There's no way I'm unfit for—"

She was halfway through her declaration when she realized what she was saying. And a moment later, she realized why she was saying it.

"The captain put you up to this," she said accusingly. "Didn't he? Or was it Ben Zoma?"

"Ben Zoma," Greyhorse replied.

And Wu knew why he had done it.

She had tried to hold Lieutenant Asmund, Chief Simenon, and Captain Picard to the letter of the law. This was Ben Zoma's attempt to show her how it felt to be held to that kind of standard.

The second officer regarded Greyhorse. "Thank you for your honesty," she told him. Then she left sickbay, already beginning to fashion an appropriate response.

Ulelo was on his way to the bridge when he heard someone call his name. Glancing back over his shoulder, he saw that the greeting had come from Lieutenant Vigo.

"Yes?" Ulelo said.

The weapons chief smiled at him as he caught up with his overlong strides. "Headed for the bridge?"

"That's right."

"So am I."

They walked together for a moment, Vigo reducing his strides to match his companion's. Then he spoke up again.

"So tell me, Lieutenant, do you have anything planned when your shift is over?"

Ulelo nodded. "I have some reading to catch up on."

It was his stock answer to such a question—and a valuable answer it was, enabling him to keep his options open in case the Pandrilite's suggestion didn't serve his purposes.

Vigo looked disappointed. "That's too bad."

"Why's that?" Ulelo asked.

The weapons chief shrugged. "I was hoping to engage you in a session of sharash'di. You're familiar with the game, aren't you?"

Ulelo had to admit that he wasn't.

"It's easy to learn," Vigo assured him, the twinkle returning to his eye. "If you like, I could teach you sometime."

Ulelo considered the offer. On one hand, the idea of learning sharash'di held no appeal for him. He had no patience for trivial pursuits these days.

On the other hand, it would give him a chance to spend time with the Pandrilite. And that might garner him some insights into the ship's weapons systems.

"I would like that," Ulelo said.

Vigo smiled, exposing blunt, white teeth. "Good. Maybe tomorrow, then, after our shifts are over."

"Tomorrow," Ulelo echoed, and made a mental note of it.

* * *

His shift over, Ben Zoma was plying a corridor en route to his quarters when he ran into Commander Wu.

"Sir," said Wu.

"Commander," said Ben Zoma.

"I'm glad I found you," Wu said.

"You are?" he asked, wondering why that might be.

"Yes. Apparently, Lieutenant Asmund isn't the only one overdue for a helm test. Your qualification's expired as well."

Ben Zoma hadn't been aware of that. "Are you sure?"

"Quite sure," the second officer told him. And she handed him her data padd to prove it.

He scanned it and saw that his qualification had expired, all right—at midnight the night before. He eyed Wu, hoping to find some evidence that the woman had learned her lesson.

But he couldn't see it in her expression.

"According to regulations," said Wu, "you're not permitted to take the helm until you requalify."

Ben Zoma sighed. He didn't much care whether he was permitted to take the helm or not. What he *did* care about was his second officer's attitude. Apparently, neither his advice nor her episode with the doctor had done anything to change it.

"Is that an order?" he asked halfheartedly.

As he waited for her response, something marvelous happened. Wu laughed—actually *laughed*. Then she said, "Let's call it a suggestion, Commander, and leave it at that."

Ben Zoma was only too happy to oblige.

Look for STAR TREK fiction from Pocket Books

Star Trek®: The Original Series

Star Trek: Deep Space Nine®

Enterprise™

Star Trek®: New Frontier

Star Trek®: Stargazer

Valiant • Michael Jan Friedman
The Gauntlet • Michael Jan Friedman
Progenitor • Michael Jan Friedman

Star Trek®: Starfleet Corps of Engineers (eBooks)

Have Tech, Will Travel • John J. Ordover, ed.
    #1 • *The Belly of the Beast* • Dean Wesley Smith
    #2 • *Fatal Error* • Keith R.A. DeCandido
    #3 • *Hard Crash* • Christie Golden
    #4 • *Interphase, Book One* • Dayton Ward & Kevin Dilmore
Miracle Workers • John J. Ordover, ed.
    #5 • *Interphase, Book Two* • Dayton Ward & Kevin Dilmore
    #6 • *Cold Fusion* • Keith R.A. DeCandido
    #7 • *Invincible, Book One* • Keith R.A. DeCandido and David Mack
    #8 • *Invincible, Book Two* • Keith R.A. DeCandido and David Mack
    #9 • *The Riddled Post* • Aaron Rosenberg
#10 • *Gateways Epilogue: Here There Be Monsters* • Keith R.A. DeCandido
#11 • *Ambush* • Dave Galanter & Greg Brodeur
#12 • *Some Assembly Required* • Scott Ciencin & Dan Jolley
#13 • *No Surrender* • Jeff Mariotte
#14 • *Caveat Emptor* • Ian Edginton
#15 • *Past Life* • Robert Greenberger

Star Trek®: Invasion!

#1 • *First Strike* • Diane Carey
#2 • *The Soldiers of Fear* • Dean Wesley Smith & Kristine Kathryn Rusch
#3 • *Time's Enemy* • L.A. Graf
#4 • *The Final Fury* • Dafydd ab Hugh
Invasion! Omnibus • various

Star Trek®: Day of Honor

#1 • *Ancient Blood* • Diane Carey
#2 • *Armageddon Sky* • L.A. Graf
#3 • *Her Klingon Soul* • Michael Jan Friedman
#4 • *Treaty's Law* • Dean Wesley Smith & Kristine Kathryn Rusch
The Television Episode • Michael Jan Friedman
Day of Honor Omnibus • various

Star Trek®: The Captain's Table

#1 • *War Dragons* • L.A. Graf
#2 • *Dujonian's Hoard* • Michael Jan Friedman
#3 • *The Mist* • Dean Wesley Smith & Kristine Kathryn Rusch
#4 • *Fire Ship* • Diane Carey
#5 • *Once Burned* • Peter David
#6 • *Where Sea Meets Sky* • Jerry Oltion
The Captain's Table Omnibus • various

Star Trek®: The Dominion War

#1 • *Behind Enemy Lines* • John Vornholt
#2 • *Call to Arms...* • Diane Carey
#3 • *Tunnel Through the Stars* • John Vornholt
#4 • *...Sacrifice of Angels* • Diane Carey

Star Trek®: Section 31™

Rogue • Andy Mangels & Michael A. Martin
Shadow • Dean Wesley Smith & Kristine Kathryn Rusch
Cloak • S. D. Perry
Abyss • David Weddle & Jeffrey Lang

Star Trek®: Gateways

#1 • *One Small Step* • Susan Wright
#2 • *Chainmail* • Diane Carey
#3 • *Doors into Chaos* • Robert Greenberger
#4 • *Demons of Air and Darkness* • Keith R.A. DeCandido
#5 • *No Man's Land* • Christie Golden
#6 • *Cold Wars* • Peter David
#7 • *What Lay Beyond* • various

Star Trek®: The Badlands

#1 • Susan Wright
#2 • Susan Wright

Star Trek®: Dark Passions

#1 • Susan Wright
#2 • Susan Wright

Star Trek® Omnibus Editions

Invasion! Omnibus • various
Day of Honor Omnibus • various

The Captain's Table Omnibus • various
Star Trek: Odyssey • William Shatner with Judith and Garfield Reeves-Stevens
Millennium Omnibus • Judith and Garfield Reeves-Stevens
Starfleet: Year One • Michael Jan Friedman

Other Star Trek® Fiction

Legends of the Ferengi • Ira Steven Behr & Robert Hewitt Wolfe
Strange New Worlds, vols. I, II, III, IV, and V • Dean Wesley Smith, ed.
Adventures in Time and Space • Mary P. Taylor, ed.
Captain Proton: Defender of the Earth • D.W. "Prof" Smith
New Worlds, New Civilizations • Michael Jan Friedman
The Lives of Dax • Marco Palmieri, ed.
The Klingon Hamlet • Wil'yam Shex'pir
Enterprise Logs • Carol Greenburg, ed.
Amazing Stories Anthology • various

SIX CENTURIES,
TEN CAPTAINS.
ONE PROUD TRADITION.

STAR TREK®
ENTERPRISE LOGS

INCLUDES STORIES FROM

Diane Carey
Greg Cox
A.C. Crispin
Peter David
Diane Duane
Michael Jan Friedman
Robert Greenberger
Jerry Oltion
and
John Vornholt

STAR TREK

AVAILABLE NOW FROM POCKET BOOKS

ENTL